ALWAYS LOUISA

JOANNE AUSTEN BROWN

ALWAYS LOUISA

JOANNE AUSTEN BROWN

Book One ~ Always Series

Always Louisa deals with detailed murders and sexual issues that may offend some readers. They are an intricate part of the villain's story. I do not wish to offend. If you have any issues with the details and feel the need to talk to someone, 24-hour assistance is available. You can call lifeline 13 11 14.

Title: Always Louisa

Copyright © 2019 Joanne Austen Brown

This has been a labour of love. But as my first book I wanted to dedicate this to my mother. When I was a child, she taught me to read and headed me into the direction of storytelling. She used to call me her dream princess because I was often found deep in thought. While daydreaming I came up with many stories that I often shared with my friends. She would be proud to know that this story has been published.

And to my hubby who is my own Mr Romance.

1

S ummer of 1814
    "Do you know why he wants to see me in the library?" They made their way down the hallway. It was abandoned and quiet.

"No, Miss Stapleton."

"Oh, I do wish you would call me Louisa, Chalanor. After all you are Prescott's best friend. And that means we will see a lot more of each other in the coming years. I'm sure you would not want me to call you Farraday, the Viscount Lightford?" Louisa's stomach gave a jolt. Surely, she wasn't attracted to him? He was just Chalanor. She caught her breath and tried to recapture her thoughts. After all she had just become engaged to Prescott. And she loved him. Didn't she?

They continued down the corridor in quiet, the precise tapping of his boots the only noise she could distinguish. When they reached the door Chalanor stopped and turned to look at her. His stern icy blue eyes pierced her own and she shivered.

"Prescott is a lucky man to have won your heart. I hope he realises that."

"That is very nice of you to say, Chalanor. And I'm sure he does." Her stomach gave her another kick. He was very handsome. But untouchable. She dropped her gaze, smiled and straightened her dress. His eyes would be the death of her if she continued to look into them.

Chalanor opened the door and stood aside so she could walk in. But she did not get very far. There on a rug in front of the open fire was her Prescott, almost naked making love to her best friend Bella. She didn't move. She watched with horror but also with fascination. The glow of the fire on their damp and heated bodies. She just stared at them. Then pulse speeding, heart beat pounding, heat flashed through her and she wanted to scream.

"Come away," Chalanor whispered. He took her gently by the arm.

She shook him off.

"No." Her head was buzzing. He had come to her and offered marriage after all. And she had accepted his proposal. Why was he doing this? My God, why? "Explain yourself, Prescott?" Her voice quivered as it rose. "Explain."

Prescott lifted his head and looked at her as his rush of release hit him. He began to laugh. Laugh out loud.

No. Her head was pounding. He had come to her and proposed marriage which she had accepted. Why was he doing this? Didn't he love her? My God, why?

Chalanor now had his hands on her upper arms trying to move her from the spot where she stood. But she fought him off again to no avail.

She turned her head to face him. "Leave me alone. No doubt you had a hand in this disgrace." She turned back and yelled at Prescott. "I want to know the meaning of this. Do you take me for a simpering simpleton?" She moved her hand to the right and slapped Chalanor in the chest. He did not flinch. "Get out of my way."

Chalanor dropped his arms and said nothing. But he did not leave. And he did not move. He probably wanted to enjoy her embarrassment and disgrace. Despite her churning stomach she was not only disgusted but furious. She would not swoon or cry as others might. She wanted an explanation. She would demand it.

Prescott was doing up his trousers and Bella started crying, while she looked for her clothes. She whimpered that she was sorry. "So very sorry."

"Tell me now. Why have you done this?" She was yelling but she did not care. Her pride was already wounded.

"I thought that was obvious, my dear." He continued to straighten his clothes.

"Obvious? No, it is not obvious. You could have asked her to marry you instead of me."

"Marry you? Marry her? I don't want either of you."

The sobs from Bella turned into cries of anguish. "You said you loved me, that's why I gave myself to you. You said it was me you wanted to marry. I'm ruined." She wept. Bella grabbed his arm and he pushed her to the floor. Her sobbing grew louder.

Louisa could hear voices and footsteps of others coming down the corridor. Soon everyone would know of Bella's fall and she felt sorry for her friend.

"You are nothing, either of you." Prescott continued. "I want neither of you. You are both harlots, ready to give yourself to any man. I have enjoyed both of you and now I am done."

"What nonsense is this? You're mad. I wouldn't give myself to you, ever." But her cries were useless as other people from the house party entered through the doors of the library behind her to witness the shame that lay before them. But she had not expected the performance she was now witnessing.

Prescott came to stand before her as he placed his shirt around himself.

"But I have had you. Just as you are a product of such a

dalliance. I am happy to soil your virtue, your non existing virtue."
He was not looking at her but at the gathering audience. "She," he
pointed at Bella, "was a dalliance, as are you." Now he pointed
at her.

Bella screamed she was no dalliance but that Prescott loved her.

Louisa crossed her arms and stared at him. "You are nothing but
a beast and I despise you."

"Thank you, my love." And he stormed from the room.

Louisa stood there her arms dropping to her side, unable to say
anything or move from where she stood. She began to shake. Was it
cold? She couldn't tell. He legs began to give way beneath her. This
had to be some ridiculous dream. Her father was standing before
her, looking into her eyes.

"My dear, come away."

"Father, what did he mean?"

She heard Chalanor's voice in the distance. "Take her away.
Take her home. I will deal with this." She heard the tap of his boots
as he left the room. The din around her closed in. She was so alone.
Prescott was crazy but because he was aristocracy, they would
believe him.

Her father turned her to the door and tried to get her through
the crowd that had gathered. She heard comments but could not
place from whose mouths they came. Their whispers penetrated
her thoughts.

"Did you hear what he said? That he had had both of them."

"They are fallen women."

"They must have known he was a rake?"

"She will never be accepted into polite society ever again."

"After all she is but a bastard. That is what he said."

Louisa heard them but Prescott's comment that she was but a
product of a dalliance went around and around in her head. A
bastard. She looked around her. Each word, each movement and all

the reactions she could see clearly. My God, what had he done? The things he said?

"Papa, what did he mean? I am no bastard? Am I?"

"Of course you aren't, my dear. Let us get you out of here." The noise of the crowd diminished as they made their way to her room.

2

---

1 *816—Another House Party*
  The carriage gently rocked as it continued through the gates of the great estate. She lowered her eyes to look into her lap. She was losing her courage.

"Father," Louisa whispered. "We should not have come. This is a mistake. We still have the chance to return home." Her father turned his head and looked into her pleading eyes. He picked up her hand and gave it a squeeze.

"Don't doubt yourself now, my dear. Together we can do this."

Louisa Stapleton had been sure she and her father had made the correct decision in coming to this house party but the reality of what they were about to do began to shake her resolve. She had always been determined, knowing her own mind, until that day in June two years ago. Then her courage had failed her, and she feared that it was about to fail her again.

The carriage progressed down the drive and she concluded that her pleadings were to no avail. Dappled light sprinkled through the trees lining each side of the roadway, streaming joyously over them. But it did not ease her apprehension. She had agreed to come with her father but now dreaded it would be a terrible mistake.

She turned her head to look out the window. The carriage was taking her and her father to the one place on earth she never thought she would ever be, in the family home of the man who had helped betray her. She had to be strong. She wanted more than anything to have a life she deserved, not judged and determined by others.

Sir Peter placed his daughter's hand on his lap and began to pat it, smiling. "You know why we are here, my love, you are helping a friend of mine to make up the numbers for a house party. This is the perfect opportunity to re-enter society. I know you can do this."

Louisa swallowed the bile rising from her stomach, burning the back of her throat. All she desired to do at this point, was run home or at least get far away from this place. She wiped her sweaty hands on the hanky she took from her reticule. But he was right. The two of them had agreed to take this path and it was imperative she pull her emotions into place and continue. *Continue.*

She watched the scenery change from pastures into manicured gardens. They must be getting closer to the house. She needed to distract herself from her thoughts. Thoughts of the man her father was helping. A man who was helping her. A man who had helped her fiancé betray her on that terrible day. Her stomach was doing summersaults.

At last the house came into view and her breath caught. Her mouth went dry and she continued to look at the vista. Did all visitors to the manor had the same reaction when they first saw the manor? This was no mere house, this was a mansion. The pale butter yellow of the sandstone structure held her and her father's full attention. It was massive compared to their modest home in Chertsey. Her father may be a Baronet but he was a poor one in the light of what they saw in front of them.

"Oh, how beautiful…" The words were out of her mouth before

she realized. But it was true. She could not deny it. The main building stretched out before her and a wing at either end drifted back into the trees of the park. This was grandeur beyond anything she had known during the brief time she had spent with the members of the ton. Her love of buildings in general enabled her to recognize that the stone was from Bath—the other side of the country. Getting it here would have cost a fortune in itself. And it was also obvious to her that this beautiful building could be no more than twenty to thirty years old.

The Farradays family had created something that dwarfed her and made her feel insignificant. Even more than she had felt in the last two years let alone the last two minutes. Was this the intention they had for this house? To make everyone feel that way when they viewed it for the first time? That the Faradays were the most prestigious of families? And one of the wealthiest in all England, imposing their stature and position? Grander than the other members of the ton?

The driveway came down a small decline to nestle in front of the great structure. Outer buildings lay beyond the house and in a small distance to the right, a lake stretched out to the rise of the next group of hills.

Two huge urns made from the same sandstone as the rest of the building, were on either side of the stairs. Smaller urns lined the tops of the building in each corner and across the front of the facade. This was a modern building, exuding wealth and success. The carriage came to a halt at the foot of the stairs. Half a dozen large and semi-circular steps led to the huge oak doors of this mansion.

Louisa would not allow these thoughts to go any further. She would not allow these people to belittle her anymore. She would fight to get her reputation and her life back.

Her father rose and descended from the carriage after the groom had lowered the steps. He turned to face her with a warm smile. Lifting his hand to take hers, he encouraged her with a nod to come down the steps. She was no coward, of that she had no doubt. She could do this. If her father could believe in her then she could believe in herself.

"My love, this is for you and I know we are here for all the right reasons. You will re-join the ton."

Louisa came down the steps. "We will do this, Papa." But her heart was pounding the opposite. Her feelings gave doubt to her faith.

"Most assuredly we will, my dear."

She had to believe that her father was right.

They waited by the coach as their luggage was unloaded. Her father stood tall and proud. She could see that he would not let them intimidate him either. She remained next to him, looking at the imposing house before them. Her legs were a little shaky and she placed her hand inside his. He gave it a squeeze, then took her hand, looped it into his arm and she leaned on him.

She looked at him and smiled. A smile she hoped showed him promise. Two years ago, she had turned her back on society as they had turned their collective backs on her. The ton had a great deal to answer for. Now they stood in front of Maidstone Manor, home of Earl and Countess Farraday and the Viscount Lightford. Chalanor. Her chest tightened.

The enormous doors at the top of the stairs opened, like great arms stretching out to squeeze more breath from her lungs, first revealing the butler and then Lord Farraday. The butler stepped back leaving his tall and greying master to greet his guests. Her chest loosened a little. T'was not Chalanor. She could breathe a little easier.

"I believe you are Sir Peter Stapleton?" The older man had his hand stretched out to greet him as he descended the steps. He seemed genuinely pleased to see them. He was smiling at her father.

"My son has told us so much about you, sir, that I feel I already know you. Is not the weather most delightful?"

Louisa grabbed her father's elbow and she hoped her tension flowed into his arm.

"Thank you, my lord. It most definitely is. May I introduce my daughter the Honourable Miss Louisa Stapleton?"

Louisa noted he was smiling at her father. He turned to face her and the warmth of his gaze was replaced by curiosity. He gave a shallow bow and turned back to talk to her father. Louisa's stomach began to ache, as it had over the past two years, every time she was in the presence of members of the ton. The bile was rising. She closed her eyes, forcing it back down. She could do this. She could be strong and face her fears.

It was interesting that he had come out to greet them rather than waiting for them to be announced. Did he want to see for himself the woman with the dreaded reputation? After all it was curiosity she had seen in his eyes. She gave her head a little shake to clear her thoughts and saw movement in the shadows of the foyer. She looked at her father.

Hearing the strong and sure booted footsteps of another man descend the stairs, she raised her head to look up into the most beautiful, clear, sapphire blue eyes she had ever seen. Her breathing caught at the sight of him and her gaze was fixed on those eyes. After all these years she was still attracted to him. Those eyes.

This was Chalanor, the same man she had known for some time. But he was different? Oh, she remembered those eyes and though the colour was the same she could see beyond the colour to the depths and saw or sensed something else. Something more.

What was it?

She was puzzled at what she saw.

Joy? Warmth? She was probably going mad.

She heard him greet her father with warmth. But he was now

looking at her and gave a bow. Warmth radiated through her at his smile. Her chest loosened and her breathing began again.

Could she ever remember having seen him smile?

In her mind she had only ever pictured his stern, stone-like face and his cold blue eyes and no smile.

Sir Peter had finished introducing her as Chalanor stepped forward and offered his arm to Louisa. He was tall, at least six foot perhaps more. His day clothes were of the tailored best. Blue coat and light blue vest. Neat cravat and highly polished riding boots. He wore tight beige trousers that caressed his thighs and then disappeared into his boots. Chalanor was nobility and dressed the part. She placed her hand on his arm and the flow of energy pulsed through her body.

That was not a reaction to this man, surely? Certainly not! The idea was preposterous. She had not thought of him in that way since that terrible night. Stupid girl. Stop being a stupid girl.

The warmth of that arm radiated through her hand and seeped into the rest of her body. She did not feel her usual self. He was handsome but without emotion.

She had to remember that.

She could not allow her reaction to him to take root. Heat rushed up her face again and she inwardly chastised herself.

"Please, do come in and we will have you settled before we have tea." Chalanor moved his gaze from Louisa to her father and with his other arm directed her father up the steps into the foyer. Lord Farraday followed behind.

Despite her feelings for him resurfacing she was strong enough to carry on. But she was not herself and she knew why. This man, tall and handsome beside her, was the reason. His dark brown hair curled at the back of his neck to rest on his collar.

He must be around eight and twenty years of age now, or perhaps a score and ten?

His arm lay firm beneath her hand. And those eyes. She had

remembered the blue as cold not warm and welcoming as they now were. Her breathing was tight. Her legs were working, but only just. Louisa's heart was pounding in her chest and she was sure he could hear the ragged tattoo. She was angry with herself.

How could she let this man affect her so?

Louisa knew that the next two weeks would be the longest of her life. She placed her "I'm not interested," expression on her face and looked away from Chalanor Farraday as they entered through the main doors.

---

*C*halanor gazed at Louisa. She had come. Ever since he had asked Sir Peter to attend the house party and to bring his daughter, he had hoped Louisa would come. But he had surmised that she would not. Her will was strong. He knew that. Knew that she deliberately kept herself away from society and he could appreciate and understand why. But here she was, her hand resting on his arm. His head was light and his senses heightened. The corners of his mouth lifted. His joy was palpable. When she had placed her hand on his arm, he had to restrain the pure joy pulsing through his body.

He was on tenterhooks for the past few hours, knowing that she would arrive in the afternoon. He had worn a track in the carpet in the library, walking back and forth in front of the window, until... Now she was here, more beautiful than he remembered. But that too was understandable. The last time he saw her she was suffering shock. No woman would look her best at a time like that. It was at that moment, on that day, that he knew he must meet with her again and get the opportunity to bring her back into society. A society that had treated her so badly. Whom he, amongst others, had treated her so badly. He needed to help her become part of the society that had rejected her, his part in her down fall had to be made right. It was the honourable thing to do. He would not feel content or settled until he had achieved that goal.

Her hair was more golden than he remembered, or was it the sunshine that was making it glow? She was petite. Not short but not tall. He could not discern her figure as she wore a travelling cape. But her eyes, those beautiful brown eyes, were as rich and as dark as chocolate. He could not stop staring into them. They sparkled with life unlike the last time he had seen her. They seemed to challenge him. A challenge he wished to take up.

As he continued to observe her, invisible shutters went up over her eyes and he could see nothing she did not want him to see. He understood her retreat. But his plan to make his apology, was that of a gentleman. She did not know that he had that intention. Right now, he wanted to tear away the imaginary shutters she had placed over those beautiful eyes. He was determined to remove them, imaginary or not. He remembered the shock he had first seen that evening in Prescott's house, the vision of those shocked eyes had stayed in his heart and mind's eye for the last two years.

In the entrance hall, servants came to escort the visitors to their rooms. Louisa and her father would freshen up after their journey and return to the first-floor dayroom for tea.

As his guests ascended the stairs, one thought filled his mind... she had come.

3

"I do not understand why you invited them, Chal. They are not of our ilk. That girl has been shunned by society, as she should have been and now you bring her into my hall?" Lady Myra Farraday, the Countess, was not happy. Her contempt of the new arrivals was obvious.

Unfortunately, but of little surprise to Chalanor, his father Lord Henry agreed with his wife. "You should have consulted us first Chalanor. That girl is not for polite society. You take much upon yourself." He looked at his father with dismay and noticed the strangest thing. His father was winking at him. He stared harder at his father. There was the wink again. Was he seeing things?

Chalanor returned his gaze to his mother. He paced like an animal in a cage before his parents. It seemed he was hunted by his mother and she was ready to attack. And his father was probably laughing at him.

"Miss Stapleton and her family have always been of our ilk, as you put it, until two years ago. Then they were horrendously treated by the members of the ton, you included Mother."

"And for good reason as you well know. I should insist they

leave." His mother stood before him with her arms folded and her face determined to broker no excuses.

He stopped pacing and turned to face her.

"Mother, you have always encouraged me to ask whomever I want, to these house parties. I usually do not get involved, making few suggestions, in fact I have avoided them for some time. Now that I have decided to attend and become involved you cannot really object? I have invited the Stapletons and I wish them to remain." Chalanor folded his arms and drew himself to his full height.

"I can object if you invite her sort into my house."

"And what sort is that, Mother?" He glared at her. He did not want her to answer that question. She opened her mouth ready to respond but Chalanor raised his finger to his lip. "Do not say another word Mother. I will hear no more from you." He watched as his mother changed her mind and closed her mouth. He was prepared to speak against his mother's hypocrisy and she could no doubt sense that in him. He wanted her to see his determination for her to keep quiet, not to belittle Louisa, as he expected her to do, so continued to stand his ground. He placed his hands on his hips daring her to say more. She paused for a moment, dropped her arms to her sides. She sighed, looked into his face, gave a twisted little smile. That was not a sign of resignation. Chalanor took a deep breath. He knew his mother was only temporarily silenced. He had a long way to go before she would be satisfied.

"Mother, Father, I wish for the family to be here. Sir Peter and I have known each other a long time. The rumour and innuendo plaguing the family is just that, rumour and innuendo. They will stay, so please be civil, Mother."

"You demand too much. You forget this is my house not yours, yet. I will allow them to stay but I will not be hospitable. You cannot believe she is innocent? If you do, it shows me how foolish you are. Your accepting them here in my house is a disgrace. They stay but under protest." She looked up into his eyes, "Keep her away from me and my guests. I do not wish to be put upon by her presence. And if they cause discord, they will leave. Do you understand me?"

She turned and walked out of the library before he could reply and Lord Farraday began to follow, scowling at his son. When he reached the door Chalanor saw his father look out of the library as if to make sure his wife had gone, then stepped back into the room and closed the door. His father came and stood before him.

"May I ask you son, why this is so important to you to have her here?"

Chalanor looked around the room then went over to the chairs in front of the fireplace and sat down. He wanted his father to understand but had not felt until this moment his father would take the time to listen and truly understand. "As I have stated, sir, Miss Stapleton has been badly treated. I was one of those who hurt her and I wish to make amends."

His father came across and sat in the seat opposite him.

"Why you?"

Chalanor took a deep breath and closed his eyes. Was his father interested or was he wanting the information to pass on to his mother? His father had winked at him. Perhaps his father could see the injustice and that is why he came back into the library? When his mother was not with them, they enjoyed an honest and open relationship on the most part. He let out a sigh and decided he would trust his father. He could not lie to him. "I stood by and did nothing as Prescott humiliated and destroyed her reputation, but she's innocent."

"Are you so sure she is innocent?"

"Yes, Father. I knew of all Prescott's liaisons. He had no trouble gloating of the successes he had in that area I can assure you. Miss Stapleton was not one of them. He had never mentioned her. Money was what he was interested in. I believe he accused her out of spite. I had never seen him so angry, as I did that night. He must have had a reason of his own to treat her in such a fashion. Believe me he would have relished telling me of his success with her if he had taken her to his bed."

"Does this explain why you have cut all contact with Prescott?"

"Simply, yes." He watched his father as he pondered the information he had imparted.

"Then I will do all that I can to help you." His father stood and looked down into his eyes, "I have much I wish to discuss with you, but we will do so later. I will support you if she is what you want."

"Sir? I want justice. As I said she is innocent."

"Well put my boy. Let us see what we can do. You can trust me. I will treat her well. We will protect her from your mother." He turned and left the room.

Chalanor remained in his chair, too shocked to move. His father had never gone against his mother before. Why now? He valued his father's support and hoped this was a good sign. He however, drifted back to his mother's words. She was plotting something. He knew her too well.

His plans did not involve his mother. He was sure he could keep her away from Louisa. If his mother had any idea that he planned to introduce Louisa back into society, or how Louisa made him feel so honourable, the gates of hell would not hold back his mother's fury. He was interested in what else his father wanted to discuss. But for now, he was truly excited to think his father would support him.

Chalanor stood and made his way to the sideboard and poured a small drink as he tried to gather his thoughts. There was a tap at the door.

"Come." He said as he sat down.

The butler Ramsay entered and announced, Sir Peter. Sir Peter followed the butler in and went straight over to stand before Chalanor.

"That will be all." Chalanor directed his comment toward Ramsay. As the door closed the men smiled at each other.

"Please sit down, Sir Peter." Chalanor directed his hand toward the seat in front of him.

"Well my boy, I got her here but you have no idea how hard it was. She was vexed on the way I might add. When our carriage came to a stop before the steps of the manor she was shaken. She wants to come back into society but the whole idea now terrifies her. We have our work cut out for us."

"I am pleased you were able to achieve it. We now have to help her see she is not shunned by all of society and it is time she should consider her future within it. Some of her good friends are here and were happy to attend. Though not everyone was aware she was coming or about her desire to re-enter society. But I am sure it will please them when they know she has come." Chalanor was determined for Louisa to face the truth and rid himself of the guilt of his part in the whole sordid affair. He knew that he would have to be frank with her, and make very clear to her she was not aware of all the facts in the whole event.

"I have to be truthful." Sir Peter continued. "I do not look kindly on my own actions in this affair. I only wanted Prescott to go away and leave her alone. I should not have told him she was born out of wedlock. She, of course is not a bastard. But I was desperate. I thought he would want to avoid the scandal and quietly leave. I never thought he would use the information as he did."

"You acted as any father would have when Prescott's real motives for marriage were revealed. He only wanted her money. He did not love her. I may have reacted the same way you did just to protect her."

"Thank God that she believed my intention was to save her from his lust for money. She did love him at first but she soon realised his falseness in the way he treated her. She has forgiven me and I believe her." He stood and began to pace in front of the fireplace. "She is one of the most stubborn people I know. That part of her character is from me, of course. I guess she is also strong like her mother and those aspects of her personality have come to the forefront since her mother's death. But her stubborn nature is from me. A rod for my own back you might say." He stopped in front of Chalanor, looking down at him. "The biggest concern for me is that she is not humiliated again. She has been through enough. I would like your plan to work but I must say even after two years, I am not hopeful. After all, the guest list is your mother's."

"I understand Sir Peter, but I am hopeful," he indicated with his hand for Sir Peter to sit down again. He did. "If I can win her trust by laying at her feet my actions and my part in the event, perhaps then she will forgive me. Her real friends will help her see that. I believe that."

Now Chalanor stood. He was feeling at a loss. Would his plan work? He wanted to have hope. "I have gathered enough of her previous acquaintances who were her true friends. I hope that we will have enough of them to help us." He believed what he was saying but was uncertain if Louisa would. He did not yet mention his father's offer, wanting to see first if it was true and that his father would help their cause. He dearly hoped so.

They continued to chat but Chalanor's thoughts were on how they had reached this point. Since his return from the continent and Waterloo, he knew the truth had to help him feel better in himself. He had seen enough suffering and felt strongly that he now had to right the wrong and lift the suffering he had helped lay at the feet of Louisa. Their plan—his plan had to work. He was attracted to her and needed to determine if it was just attraction or if he had deeper feelings for her. It was in part why he wanted to bring her back. His mother would not like the thoughts and feelings he had for Louisa. He needed to be sure before he declared anything to Louisa let alone anyone else.

They discussed some of the finer details and ways in which

Chalanor hoped to get to spend some time alone in her company with her father in the background so as not to add to her already damaged reputation. Sir Peter would aid him as best he could and they both believed that without even knowing some of the other guests would help them. And now even his father could join them, was beyond his greatest hope. They sat together for some time reassuring each other and also reminiscing the time they had spent at Waterloo, getting to know each other and indirectly Chalanor getting to know Louisa better than she knew.

4

C halanor strode into the morning room to await the arrival of his guests for afternoon tea. Sir Peter had excused himself from the library earlier so he could make his entrance after Chalanor. Neither wanted the guests' suspicions aroused by seeing them together. At least not yet. He was happy to see the other visitors for the house party had already assembled and had heard that more guests had arrived. They were chatting amongst themselves, as he entered. He noted several pairs of eyes settle on him.

"I say, Farraday, is it true more guests have arrived? Who are they, old man?" Lord Fredrick Ismay, known to his close friends as Freddie was a fine fellow. He was a close acquaintance of the Farradays and also Louisa's. He became Earl of Woodford when his parents were tragically killed in a carriage accident. He took on the role and managed the Estates of Broadbank and Littleton in Surrey, also looking after his sister. He had been young at three and twenty to have taken on the duty. He'd expected to have taken it on eventually but after his parents had lived a long and healthy life. But from all accounts he had risen to the challenge.

Now he enjoyed being the first to receive fresh gossip, making himself feel very important. He considered himself an authority on all the members of the ton and delighted in all the knowledge that he had gained. Freddie had been a good friend of Louisa and her family in years gone by. Chalanor was glad that he and his sister Elspeth had agreed to come. Elspeth was close to Louisa.

Chalanor was now however, reluctant to mention names dreading the same response from the assembled guests as he got from his mother. He girded himself for a negative response.

"It is Sir Peter Stapleton and Miss Louisa Stapleton."

"Oh, good show!" Chalanor could see the pleasure on Freddie's features in his announcement and felt assured that he would support Louisa.

"Is that the Miss Stapleton of a few years ago? You know the one with that rumour of a peculiar family history?" Frances Midhurst enquired. Her facial expression was not a look that gave Chalanor confidence.

"I'm sure I don't know what you mean Frances, but Miss Stapleton is a lovely young lady whom I have not seen for some years and was glad her father decided to bring her with him. When I saw Sir Peter in London last week, I invited him and his daughter to attend our little gathering."

"Not Louisa, surely?" The voice of Miss Elspeth Ismay penetrated the quiet that had permeated the room. "I will be delighted to see her again. How on earth did you manage it, Chalanor?" Elspeth's exuberance delighted Chalanor.

Chalanor had no doubt that Elspeth would welcome her old friend. Although he had not told her Louisa was coming. He had urged Freddie to bring his sister. Though he had not gone into great detail, Freddie could be such a sluggard, but he knew she and Freddie would be allies to Louisa. But before he could reply to Elspeth...

"Is that not the young lady, if you could call her that, whose family heritage is somewhat suspect?" Lady Nella Midhurst had flashed her claws with that comment. His mother's closest and dearest friend, whom she called Nell, and who always believed every bit of gossip that came from his mother's mouth, would be a force to reckon with during the coming weeks. She had a scowl on her face that Louisa would spot immediately. She also had a spiteful tongue that she would not hesitate to use. She was no ally.

Lord Sebastian Midhurst, who Chalanor had admired for many years, made him breathe a little easier.

"Oh, she was such a pretty little thing, surely she is a daughter of the ton?" he smiled.

"You have no idea what you are talking about my dear," Lady Nell snarled. "Chalanor you should be ashamed..." But Chalanor cut her off as he had his mother. He needed to make sure that everyone knew that Louisa had his full support.

"She is my guest and I would appreciate you all treating her and her father with the respect I give to each of you. Everything you have said is but rumour." Everyone was a little taken aback. The shocked looks on their faces was enough to tell him that. He had always been the quiet gentleman and rarely expressed his opinions in company. But he needed to make it clear that Louisa was under his protection. For him to speak up and put Lady Midhurst in her place was definitely out of character.

He walked over to the chaise lounge on which Elspeth sat, and placed himself next to her, hoping his actions would bring an end to their questions. It did. Quiet conversations began and the other guests chatted amongst themselves once again. But he was sure that he had laid some basic ground rules for Louisa's entry back into society. Now he had to hope that it would be enough to start with. He watched as Sir Peter entered and made his way to some of the guests. No one seemed to notice his entrance.

Elspeth let her hand rest on his arm. He looked into her smiling eyes as she addressed him. "I am delighted to know that Louisa has come. I have tried by so many means to get her to come back to

London, or even visit us at Broadbank. I can't imagine how you have achieved it but I am glad that you have." Chalanor rested his hand on hers and thanked her. He knew that Louisa had at least one person who would befriend her while she was here.

Freddie stood opposite them both and looked down. "Well, my friend, your intentions are honourable, so we will help you. What is it that you want us to do?" That was all Freddie needed to say to ease his troubled thoughts. Chalanor smiled at him and his sister and the weight lifted from his shoulders.

L ouisa stood at the window of the room to which she was taken. The maid, Alice, had shown her where the dressing room was and how she could summon her if she needed any assistance. Alice had also announced she was appointed as Louisa's maid and was at her disposal for the coming two weeks. Louisa had no personal maid but the Farradays graciously gave her one for the length of her stay. This disturbed Louisa as she could not imagine why she was singled out for such special treatment.

"I am, I believe Miss, proficient in hair design," she said. "And will arrange all of Misses belongings for her when the trunk is brought to the room." Louisa thanked her but dismissed her, promising to call her later. At this moment, all she wanted was to be alone and allow a moment of quiet. She needed to think before she went down to tea, to face the inevitable storm. She wanted to give herself strength. She was determined to get her life and position in society back. Despite any others arguing against her.

Louisa rested her forehead against the cool glass of the window. Slowly she opened her eyes to look out over the gardens. Her room was in the western wing on the first floor, overlooking the kitchen and flower gardens. There were beds and beds of flowers of all kinds. Daffodils, hyacinth, lily of the valley, daisies and marigolds, just to name a few and all laid out in neat rows. Summer vegetables were appearing. Colours penetrated her senses. Beyond the garden was a forest of oak trees stretching on for some miles.

She sighed. After two years of hiding and avoiding all the consequences of what had happened to her, she wanted her life back. Now she had to face her demons. And the biggest demon of all was Chalanor Farraday, Viscount Lightford. He had been her fiancé Edward Prescott's, dearest friend. However, that association ended on the night Louisa's life was turned upside down. She knew that Farraday had left that house party and had never renewed his acquaintance with Prescott. Her true friends had kept her informed. But that did not change the fact that Chalanor had a hand in her downfall. She closed her eyes again to block the memories pressing back into her thoughts. Why had he not protected her?

Louisa lifted her head from the window and went to sit on the bed. The moisture in her eyes started building. She took a deep breath and forced her eyes to blink. There would be no more tears this day. She had shed enough of them over the years. She had promised herself she would regain her reputation. Two years ago, the shock of the declarations gave her no opportunity to prevent Prescott's accusations from taking hold. She had run away from the problems then and had hidden away in the country. When she had the strength to fight back, she had lacked the courage. Her father was right she had the courage to face it now.

Today, her past had to die. It had too. Her father had given her a chance to redeem herself, a chance to come back into society. A chance at a future. Could she do it? This could be the moment all could be set right. She got up and went into the dressing room. She stood before the full-length mirror.

"Well, Louisa! You have a choice that may never be yours again." She looked at the strong woman she was today. She said to her reflection, "You are better than what other people think of you and you can overcome this. You have a chance to make things right. You must deal with these demons once and for all time." She was not sure that she could deal with the biggest demon of them all, Chalanor... "Well maybe one demon I can try to ignore." She straightened her dress and patted her hair and left her room to attend the afternoon tea.

5

Refreshing herself from their journey had taken longer than Louisa had expected. But she descended the stairs toward the morning room, hoping her father was already downstairs. A footman stood at the door of the morning room and opened it as she approached. The quiet murmur of voices ceased as she stepped into the room. Her gaze wandered to all the faces turned toward her. She located her father who stood next to Chalanor, the one man she did not want to be near. Lord Farraday was next to Chalanor. That did not bode well. But she had no choice. She had to go on as she had intended. She would not let these men frighten her from her objective. She was determined and strong. She headed straight for them.

"I do hope I have not kept everyone waiting for too long." She announced as she came up to stand at her father's side, not daring to look at anyone else.

"Not at all, Miss Stapleton, we have only just started to serve tea while we awaited your arrival." Lord Henry Farraday smiled at her with warmth in his expression. "Your father has been here but a few minutes. He has been enlightening us on the ease of your trip here today. The weather being so sunny. May I procure a cup of tea for you?" She had difficulty accepting his sincere gentle voice. He was all politeness.

The butler Ramsay was pouring her a cup. Chalanor indicated to him to bring it over.

"Thank you, sir. I will." As she took the cup, Elspeth appeared at her side.

"How wonderful it is to see you, Louisa. It has been so long. Though I have enjoyed your long and wonderful letters."

Louisa smiled, grateful to be greeted by a cheerful face. What a delight to have her friend standing with her. "Elspeth, how wonderful to see you again, I had no idea you would be here. But then father had told me little of the arrangements." She looked to her father who smiled and nodded toward her. She gave him a gentle smile and was surprised to see his face light up with what seemed like joy and her spirits lifted.

"May I say how grateful I am to you, Miss Stapleton, for coming and making up the numbers for this house party?" Chalanor looked at her. Louisa could hear the sincerity in his voice. She sensed it was for more than numbers that she had been drawn here. She shook her head to remove such a ridiculous thought. He did not take his gaze away from her. This was disconcerting. She knew he was one of the ton's most famous rakes. He was well-known for his rakish behaviour when she had last seen him. Though in her letters Elspeth had always spoken highly of him. Taking a deep breath, she decided it was safer to put her "not interested" shutters in place again. She wanted to be back in society and that was all. She did not need or want his attentions despite the feelings she had for him years ago. She had grown up. Crushes and alike were left behind.

"May I introduce you to the other guests?" He offered his arm. She did not want to create a scene by saying no. So, she placed her hand on his arm. That feeling of excitement went through her body again as soon as they touched. She was reluctant to be near him, but her body reacted with excitement. She just hoped he had sensed no change in her and hoped she was not blushing. Damn her blush. It would give her away if she did not control it.

---

*W*armth radiating through him and his pulses drumming, Chalanor escorted her around the room introducing her to the gathered company. The tingling shooting up his arm when she laid her hand on his sleeve was thrilling. Most of her peers greeted her with warmth and kindness. They directed friendly questions to her and seemed genuinely interested in the answers she gave. Some of them she had known from her short but memorable time in the ton. The tension was dissipating from her. Perhaps she could let her mask down? He smiled at her. She returned his smile with a nod. He took her to sit next to Elspeth. The Reverend Hutton was standing beside the chaise talking with her.

"Miss Stapleton, may I introduce you to the Reverend Hutton?"

"Ellis, is that you?" Louisa's face was animated.

"Miss Stapleton, my dear. What a delight it is to see you again." The Reverend took Louisa into his arms and gave her a gentle hug. Many of the company viewed the exchange and were whispering amongst themselves. This was not typical behaviour. This display of familiarity was rarely seen in a public place.

What? She knew him? Chalanor was a little perplexed. "You are obviously acquainted."

"Yes, my friend," the Reverend chipped in. "Louisa and I were neighbours for a short time. When you told me she was coming I was unsure as to if it was the same Miss Stapleton I once knew."

"Oh yes, we are dear friends," Louisa continued, "my grandmother lived near Lincoln and I went to stay with her for a short time before my mother grew very ill. I was but seventeen if I remember. Ellis…I mean the Reverend Hutton lived in the estate next to my grandmother's and we met on various occasions. Though he was not a reverend at the time."

"I know the Reverend Hutton from my time at Waterloo. I am delighted to know that you are acquainted." Chalanor wished to be as open and truthful with Louisa from the beginning. He watched as the two old friends chatted and he was thrilled he could add another ally to the list of people who would help and support Louisa. He had not realized the link but was glad of it. It surprised him. His friend had not mentioned the connection when he had informed him of Stapleton's coming the day before but accepted his explanation. When he had a moment, he intervened.

"I would be happy to tell you of our first meeting if you would care to…"

His mother, the great hostess, chose that moment to enter the room. With his hand he directed Louisa to the chaise where Elspeth sat and then took a position behind it. The Reverend Hutton came to stand next to him and Freddie stood to the side of the chaise. He also noted all of them seemed prepared for any danger that could come. His army of friends surrounded her. Ready and prepared for battle.

Let the battle commence. You will not win, mother.

---

*L*ouisa watched as Lady Farraday moved around the room apologizing for her delay in greeting everyone, and for her tardiness in coming for tea. Her elegance appeared to be innate, her movements refined and feminine. She was tall and slim, carrying herself with pride and authority. Her clothes were of the finest cloth and the latest fashion, far more elegant than anything she had witnessed in the past years. The rich deep red of her dress only added to her beauty. Her dark chestnut hair was most evident and enhanced the delightful colour of her dress.

It was then Louisa noticed that Lord Farraday, who had been so joyful while they were in discussion was suddenly scowling and morose as he joined his wife and followed her around the room. He looked as if he would rather be anywhere else than here in his own home. Louisa held her breath as they reached the chaise on which she was seated.

"Welcome Elspeth. So lovely to have you in my manor again! It has been such a long time since you attended one of my house parties." Lady Farraday smiled, looking directly at Elspeth.

"I believe, Lady Farraday, that it was the summer before Waterloo. So that would be two years ago. I do appreciate being asked to come again."

Her brother Freddie, standing behind her added, "I came with her but then attended the house party alone in '15 while Chalanor was...away."

"Ah yes you are right, Freddie, and you are most welcome my dears. I could not think of better company." The lady turned her head to face Louisa. "And you are?" She stated her question and her gaze at Louisa. Louisa knew full well the lady was well aware to whom she was directing her question.

"Mother, may I introduce Miss Louisa Stapleton to you. As you know she is Sir Peter's daughter." Chalanor chose to answer his mother's question before she had a chance to reply. The heat travelled up her neck as she saw the full gaze of the countess upon her. What would this lady do next?

"No, I did not know Sir Peter had a daughter."

Lady Farraday turned her back to Louisa and moved on to the next small group and Lord Farraday followed her but looked back at Louisa with concern etched on his face. Unfortunately, he did not say anything. Everyone standing around her saw Lady Farraday's torrid welcome, her slight most evident.

The heat rose from her neck to cover her face. She took in one deep breath to gain control of her emotions. Then she lowered her gaze to the cup resting on her lap. She held her breath. Hoping the eyes of all in the room would be following the lady and not looking at her, she fiddled with her cup. It was embarrassing she had not replied herself. And she was angry that Chalanor had. But more so at the blatant comment from Lady Farraday. It only confirmed she needed to be careful with how she reacted and behaved at this house party. She slowly let out her breath. She wanted to flee again but she buried the thought. Was she foolish to think she could defend herself with the likes of Lady Farraday attacking her?

Elspeth's hand appeared on her arm and she leaned toward Louisa's ear and whispered, "Do not let the dragon bring your spirits down. You are a hundred times more worthy than she ever will be. You can hold your head up high. Money does not necessarily bring good breeding."

Louisa looked into her friend's face and she could see her sincerity but also her determination.

Elspeth continued. "I came to support my friend Chalanor not knowing you would be here. But now I am happy to be here to support you. Perhaps this is what Chalanor was hoping for as well." Elspeth looked up at Chalanor and smiled and then looked back at her. Louisa rejoiced that she sat with her. She knew that the slight Lady Farraday had inflicted, was sincerely meant to hurt but her friend Elspeth would support her. She did not have to go through this experience alone. They could conquer this.

"Thank you, Elspeth. I have missed your company these past few years. Your letters have been a delight. But seeing you now in person is so much better." She placed her hand on Elspeth's. She had missed her friend. With Elspeth next to her and supporting her, maybe, just maybe, she could come through this. Looking at the other faces around her, Freddie, Ellis and her father. Even some of the other guests made it all seem possible.

Chalanor breathed an audible sigh of relief. And Louisa was surprised to hear it. "I, too, would apologize for my mother's behaviour. It was uncalled for. And thank you Elspeth for coming. I know you and Louisa have been dear friends."

She was holding her breath again, as he spoke. Gently she released it. It would appear that Chalanor Farraday was not planning to embarrass her after all. But his mother had. Chalanor had found his mother's comments distasteful enough, that he felt the need to apologize on her behalf. Perhaps the coming weeks would not be that odious.

*A*fternoon tea was soon over and the older guests retired to their rooms to rest for the remainder of the afternoon. Chalanor escorted the younger guests in an impromptu tour of the manor. Louisa agreed to walk with Elspeth. A smile came to his face.

They seemed to be listening with interest as he pointed out the paintings of his ancestors in the long gallery on the first floor. He told them of the young age of the manor, it being only completed twenty years ago. How the old manor had a long gallery but this one was twice as long. That his parents had started building the new manor as soon as they had married.

"I was born in the old manor. It was built well over two hundred years ago, during the time of Henry Tudor. In fact, the King had visited twice during his reign. Unfortunately, my mother believed the old manor was not worth restoring, so she had this building erected. I am pleased that she incorporated a long gallery similar to the old manor."

"It is truly a delightful structure Chalanor, and so stylish." Freddie was enjoying the attentions of all the young ladies as he supported Chalanor with his commentary. He trotted between them all smiles and cordiality. Everyone was relaxed and making Chalanor satisfied. He could see Louisa was dropping her façade.

"What of the old manor? Is it still standing?" Louisa asked. Her father had mentioned her love of old buildings, architecture and history in general. And he was overjoyed to hear her ask this question.

"No. I am afraid it is virtually all gone. Some brick work has been used in the ruined folly my mother has created in the woods to the east. I had some taken to build the rose rooms in the garden near the east wing. And some have gone to my personal estate, east of here. We planted new Beech and Ash woods on the old manor site." He turned to face the group. "I would be happy to escort any of you who would like to ride, to the spot. And then perhaps, over to my estate. Let us do that tomorrow morning after breakfast?" He turned to look into Louisa's face, "Miss Stapleton, will you ride with me?"

Louisa stood still. Chalanor could see her confusion. He looked at Elspeth for support.

But before Elspeth could answer, Miss Frances Midhurst intruded.

"I would love to ride there tomorrow."

"As would I," Elspeth said as she gave Louisa a little nudge.

"Yes...that would be delightful." Louisa stuttered. He could see her uneasiness returning.

"I say," piped up Freddie "I think we all should go. What do you say everyone? Shall we?"

There was a chorus of agreement from the remainder of the company.

"That settles it," said Chalanor, a smile on his face he hoped displayed his satisfaction. He glanced at Louisa to see her slight blush and then her mask was back in place again. He recognised that mask. He hoped that sometime in the coming weeks he would be able to remove that mask for good.

"I suggest ladies and gentleman that we all retire to our room to prepare for dinner. I will see you all again at eight." He bowed and turned and walked toward the stairs. Frances Midhurst, the eldest daughter of Lady Nella and Lord Sebastian called out to Chalanor and followed him along the hall. Her sister Sarah followed her sister though she seemed annoyed.

———

*W*hen Louisa reached her room, a steaming hot bath awaited her. Alice helped her undress, and then Louisa dismissed her. Louisa lay back in the water and enjoyed the warmth and the quiet, a chance to think. Her thoughts were now full of curiosity.

Louisa smiled as she brought to mind the faces of her friends who were with her this afternoon. Reverend Hutton winked at her a number of times. A smile creased her face as she remembered how he had always winked at her when she was uncomfortable. He remembered the gesture and she appreciated it. It helped keep her emotions together. Freddie's jokes were also a relief as was Elspeth's presence at her side.

Despite the events of the afternoon Louisa was more relaxed than she had since they arrived.

Why was she so comfortable if not totally relaxed around Chalanor?

She never asked questions in company but she was asking questions of him as if the conversation was between just him and her.

Why was she reacting the way she did? Could Chalanor be less the demon and more of the friend?

6

The fading sun was adding a golden glow to the afternoon sky through the window of Chalanor's bedroom. He washed, dressed and readied himself for dinner. All had gone better than he had anticipated. He loved watching her reconnect with people whom she had spent a great deal of her early life. Well almost. The Midhurst's were the exception. Louisa had known them but they had never been close, from what he could remember. He would have to remind himself that they were his mother's guests and he could not count on their support. It was obvious that they and his mother had another agenda that did not include the likes of Miss Stapleton. His mother was meddling again, of that there was no doubt and using the Midhursts to help her. He would have to be wary.

There was a light knock at the door. Chalanor went and opened it, expecting to see Sir Peter. To his surprise Freddie and Elspeth stood before him. They were already dressed for dinner.

"Now, my friend, let us enter and you can reveal all your plans. You are planning something?" Elspeth came into the room and Freddie followed.

"My sister has it aright. What are you planning, Farraday?" Freddie frowned at him.

"Freddie, please call me Chalanor." He smiled at Freddie and guided his two friends over to his fireplace and the chaise and two seats in front of it. The fire was lit as the summer was cooler than expected. Chalanor always sat before it, enjoying the homely feel it gave him. He lived at his own estate but was staying in his father's house for the house party so he could be close to Louisa and support her if she needed it. His old room always gave him comfort. It had been his fortress for many years. A place for him to escape to when his parents argued. It still felt that way.

"Yes, I have a plan but it is a simple one. It does not need a great deal of explanation. That is, I wish to help Miss Stapleton, Louisa, come back into society and be accepted by them." He smiled at Elspeth.

"I am pleased, believe me but surprised that you were able to get her here." She replied.

"That is partly due to Sir Peter. He believed from his discussions with her that she was ready to make the attempt. When I saw Sir Peter in London a few weeks ago I suggested using this house party to begin her foray back into the ton. He suggested it to Louisa and she agreed."

"You had said that you wanted help with a friend and asked me to bring Elspeth," Freddie explained. "But you didn't say that it was Louisa. I am delighted but curious why you did not mention her name. Why not tell us, old boy," added Freddie. "We certainly would help you."

"I'm sorry Freddie. I had to keep you in the dark. I was concerned that problems might arise if word spread too quickly that it was Louisa who was coming. I did not want to give anyone an advantage to create difficulties for her. I told my mother only this morning so she could not try to prevent it. And believe me she would have if she had known any sooner. The less people knew the better we were placed."

"I see." Elspeth looked into Chalanor's eyes. "Is that the only reason?" She crossed her arms in front of her. "The truth."

"I'm not sure what you mean but of course, that is the reason." Chalanor looked from one to the other. He was not sure what she was implying. He began to pace back and forth in front of the fireplace. The penetrating gazes stayed with him, drilling into him.

"It has nothing to do with the sweet Louisa herself?" added Freddie with a cheeky grin.

Chalanor stopped and looked from one to the other again. He needed to be frank. "As you are aware, I played an unwilling part in her down fall and I wish to rectify that situation. I am hoping that her time here will allow me the chance to explain my innocence to her. So yes, there is a little more going on." He began to pace again. "It is obvious to me she dislikes me. Anyone can see that. I will admit that disturbs me. If I have the opportunity to clarify my situation I would most like to do so?"

"It is putting her in an awful position. This afternoon for example. Your mother was...well...her behaviour this afternoon was appalling." Freddie looked up at Chalanor, "I beg your pardon." Chalanor noticed that Freddie was a bit taken aback, so he rectified the situation. Freddie was being honest. He needed to reciprocate.

"No need, you are right. My mother's behaviour was abhorrent. But if we three are supporting Louisa, I think we can deflect my mother's comments. Most people try to ignore my mother, knowing her gossipy nature. But she sees herself as the model of propriety. Even I am aware my mother is only listened to because she is married to my father. The exceptions are those who are intimate with her. The Midhursts for example. They believe every word my mother utters."

"Very well. We are here and aware of your plan. Other than

always being near her, how can we help?" Elspeth was the practical one. She always got straight to the heart of a matter.

"Well, for me it is making sure she is never alone. If one of us is there to support her should any comments be made by my mother, they can be contradicted or counteracted by us. Or at least deflected. That way we can diminish the damage my mother might make." His two guests nodded and he went on. "We saw that Louisa, though embarrassed, this afternoon, was able to hold her tongue and not react to my mother. She behaved impeccably. We need Louisa to feel our support so that she does not get into an argument with my mother. I know enough about Louisa's nature to know that she hates injustice and has no problem revealing that injustice. And my mother will play on that, encouraging her to react."

A knock was heard at the door and Chalanor went to open it.

"Do you often entertain guests in your bedroom?" Freddie said from behind him, then laughed out loud. Chalanor just grinned at his friend and opened the door.

He stood aside to allow Sir Peter and the Reverend Hutton to enter the room.

"Come in, my friends. I am glad that we can have a few moments to reflect on the afternoon's events. As you can see others have come to discuss similar things."

Sir Peter and the Reverend bowed to Freddie and Elspeth and came to stand at the fireplace. Chalanor sat back in his seat.

Sir Peter looked at the Ismays. "I'm so glad that you are both here. It is wonderful to know that some of Louisa's true friends will be here to support her." He turned to face the Reverend Hutton. "And you also, Sir. It is good to see you again." The Reverend smiled and nodded.

Sir Peter continued, this time addressing him. "My boy, I am concerned that there are some very hostile guests, mainly the

Midhursts. Can I at least say the Midhurst women?" Sir Peters face showed the furrows of concern.

"We had just been discussing matters along the same lines." Elspeth concluded.

"Yes, my mother is behind it, I believe. I will be truthful and it pains me to be so. My mother, has for the last two years, tried to entrap me in marriage with the eldest daughter Frances. I have resisted and done my best to discourage this but it would seem that mother has every intention of making a push again in that direction at this house party. She wants me to marry a woman of her choosing."

Freddie burst into laughter. Chalanor looked up, irritated.

"I am sorry, old man. I don't mean to laugh but I do understand. It's just that my aunt is doing the same for me. Thrusting women at me. Tall, short, fat, thin. So long as they are single and breathing. At least you only have one being paraded in front of you. Terrible bore, is it not?"

Elspeth giggled.

"It is true," added the Reverend Hutton. "Your mother has approached me to try to enlist my help in entrapping you with Frances." He looked at Chalanor. "Don't worry my friend, I have declined. I told her that you were more than capable of choosing your own wife."

"Thank heaven for that," Chalanor replied, breathing a sigh of relief. This news disturbed him. Had his mother no shame that she would approach a friend of his and a man of the cloth as well, to make the suggestion?

Elspeth asked. "So, your mother will try to encourage you to take an interest in Frances? I really thought your mother had more taste than that."

"It has nothing to do with taste but whom mother can manipulate to her own designs. She wants to control me and she means to do it via Frances."

Chalanor looked from one face to the other. Freddie was still chuckling.

"I will help you discourage the lady as much as I can." Sir Peter smiled at him. Chalanor breathed a little easier.

"That, sir, is definitely my intention so any help that you, any of you, can give would be greatly appreciated. Miss Midhurst is not my choice as a wife."

"Do you have a choice?" Sir Peter asked.

Chalanor hoped he had. But now wondered if he did have a choice? Deep down he hoped Louisa would be the right woman.

Elspeth smiled. "Who is your choice, by the way? Though I think I know the answer." Elspeth raised her hand to stop him from answering. "You do not have to answer. We will also help you," she added.

Chalanor looked at her and Freddie who now had a rather more serious look on his face. "I have no choice as yet. I just do not want to have a wife thrust upon me."

Hutton laughed out loud. Freddie and Sir Peter soon joined him. Elspeth began to chuckle.

"I really have no choice." His face had to be somewhat red. Heat rose up his neck. He really had no choice. Couldn't they see that?

"None of us do." Freddie said as he continued to laugh.

"I could always make the choice for you." Elspeth concluded. She laughed out loud and they all joined in.

It was good the five of them had reconnected. He could see Hutton listening with interest as they revealed the events of that terrible evening. Events that he had not witnessed nor had any details.

"I must say that Louisa is stronger than you give her credit," smiled Elspeth. "She did write to me during the time she hid away. Two or three letters a week. I just let her voice her thoughts. Try as I might, I could not get her to come to Broadbank. She wanted to stay in her home. It was her sanctuary. It reminded her of her mother. She needed the strength that her home was giving her. But she was wanting to come back into society already at that point. She told me she lacked the courage. But I do believe she has now found it."

Chalanor wanted to voice his part to the others so they would understand his motives. "I was honest with Sir Peter as I got to know him when we were in Brussels, as to my part in the events of that evening and he both believed me and trusted me. I had no idea what Prescott was planning to do to Louisa. If I had I would never have escorted her to the library. I was shocked at both his actions and his claims." He had developed a friendship with Sir Peter but only after being honest with him as to the part he had played had their friendship grown.

"Sir Peter and I did not know what to do to help her." Chalanor continued, "Finally that moment arrived when my mother announced she was having this house party. I then saw Sir Peter in London and well here we are."

"Then we have no time to lose. Louisa will be welcomed back into society with open arms, if we have any say in the matter." And he was sure that Elspeth was right.

---

*J*ust before eight o'clock Louisa was making her way down the western hall to the central stairs when she heard her father and Chalanor's voices travelling down the hall from the eastern wing. This was strange as that was the family's wing and her father was in the western wing along with the other guests.

What was Chalanor up to? After all he was a rake of the first order. That was his reputation, even Elspeth didn't deny it. Now however, Louisa wanted to retreat and go somewhere to think. Although he had cut all contact with Prescott after that night, he had been his best friend and they in turn had been hellions all over London before Prescott set eyes on her. Prescott had declared that his hellion days were done, when he wanted to marry her. She knew that she had been foolish to believe it. Chalanor's character may have mellowed since that day but she doubted he had changed despite his pleasantries this afternoon. He was a rake then and probably still was. Her concern was also levelled at her father. He always spoke highly of Chalanor. How he was so helpful with the work they had to do in Brussels during the war with Napoleon. It wasn't easy, her father had said, to go around and identify the officers who had died, *"He will carry the images of friends and foe with him for as long as he lives."*

Louisa ducked into an alcove so they would not see her. They came around the corner and descended the stairs. They were smiling and chatting to each other but Louisa could not make out the conversation. As far as she was concerned Chalanor Farraday may have welcomed her and was warm and concerned for her welfare when they had arrived, but she would be on her guard now. They were up to something and she knew it involved her. Her shutters would be firmly fixed in place. She was here to redeem her reputation not obtain a husband, despite being attracted to him.

7

L ouisa made her way into the dining room. Everyone was standing awaiting the arrival of Lord and Lady Farraday. All the ladies and gentlemen were dressed in their evening finery. Louisa glided over to where Elspeth was standing next to her brother Freddie. Elspeth was dressed in a beautiful dark red evening dress that matched her glorious dark hair. She looked beautiful and Louisa could not understand why she was not surrounded by admirers. She noted Chalanor Farraday was not with them and gave a sigh of relief.

Freddie was an affable young man, though it had been many years since she had been in his company. He must be at least a score and eight now. He carried himself well. His black evening dress was immaculate, the waistcoat a golden bronze. She could see why he was popular with the other young ladies. A handsome bachelor with a title and the monies to go with it. He was a man of experience and brother to Elspeth. He was safe. She didn't want to marry and from what she remembered about Freddie he didn't either. That may have changed but she would review that situation with Elspeth. She did not want to be married. She eventually would inherit what her mother had left her. She need not marry for money. She would be well looked after. As her mother was an only child, she too was an only child and her small wealth was not entailed. She would stay near her friends and hopefully that would distract Chalanor from any plans he might be cooking up with her father.

"Are you looking forward to the ride tomorrow, Miss Stapleton?" Freddie addressed her with ease.

"Please Freddie, call me Louisa. You always did when I was younger."

"Very well, Louisa. I just did not want to presume. You are not a child anymore. You are a grown woman." His smile was warm and welcoming. "Are you looking forward to the ride tomorrow?" he asked again with a hint of humour.

"I am, sir," she grinned at him. "I love to ride as you well know." Thinking about the ride and knowing he was friends with Chalanor, her curiosity got the better of her. "Do you know Chalanor's estate? I did not know he had his own estate. Is it far from here?"

"Oh yes. You young ladies are always interested in us young bucks." He laughed out loud. "I'm sorry Louisa excuse my mirth. Of course, you must be curious about the property." His smile made it clear to Louisa that she was understood. She was just curious. "It is but seven miles from here. It was his grandmother's seat. She willed it to him. It has always been an estate that had never been entailed away from any direct descendant. Similar to your position I believe. He showed more interest in it than Lady Farraday. So, the old dear bequeathed it to him."

"How interesting," Louisa responded. "I am curious about the estate. I have heard of it of course…"

"You will adore the old architecture that dates back to the arrival of the Normans. I assume you still love looking at old buildings?" asked Elspeth.

"Yes. It still is an interest of mine. Old England has so much to offer. I am looking forward to seeing the Norman influence." Louisa concluded. And she was. History was one of her passions. She was pleased they would actually see a Norman tower.

They continued to discuss the plans for the morning. She did love to ride and took every chance she could when she was at home. She was also pleased at the ease that Freddie addressed her. She smiled toward him and that reinforced her desire to stay away from Chalanor. Her friends will look after her best interests.

Chalanor came over to stand with them as Lord and Lady Farraday entered the room. Louisa was more interested in the decor of the room than the hosts' arrival. She wanted to avoid eye contact with any Farraday.

The table had been beautifully set with the finest china and crystal Louisa had ever seen. The table stretched almost the complete length of the room and was beautifully adorned with roses of every shape and colour imaginable. There were buds on the verge of opening to the world, and fully opened heads were also on display. Her eyes were fixed on the vast array. She brought back to mind the house garden that was visible from her bedroom window. She could not remember seeing roses planted there. She was wondering where they had come from. She remembered Chalanor speaking about rose rooms earlier in the afternoon. Making a mental note to find out where they were, after all it was her favourite.

As if he knew what she was thinking, Chalanor spoke.

"I would say that the rose is my favourite flower. We have a number of rose garden areas. Actually, I would call them outside rooms." He was whispering as he did not want his voice to carry across the room. "It was actually mine and my younger sister's contribution to the garden. We wanted a large room filled with roses that would last forever. So, we created one. It had to be outside of course. It is beautiful. There are now three rose rooms. I must show you, perhaps tomorrow afternoon, after we have returned from our ride?"

She frowned then looking at him, lowered her head.

"They are also my favourite flowers." She said.

She slowly looked up into those beautiful eyes and then put up her imaginary shutters. Why was he so interested in her? She was even more curious after seeing him with her father coming from the family wing. Is he just being polite? What of his sister? She had not known he had a sister. She could not remember anyone ever speaking about her. Nor her being presented at court. She glanced around the room and could not see anyone she had not already met that afternoon. He again sensed her thoughts.

"My sister Delia is no longer with us. She disappeared some years ago. But that is another story." He lowered his eyes to look at the floor.

"I am sorry sir, if your remembering her has caused you distress." What could he mean by telling her that she had disappeared? This was most unsettling.

"Please, call me Chalanor. And I am not at all disconcerted. Perhaps at another time I can tell you about her? And what may have happened to her."

"Yes, of course." What on earth was she doing? She had promised herself to stay away from him and now she had agreed to talk with him about his sister. She turned to face Elspeth and proceeded to mentally chastise herself and ensuring that her shutters were well in place. She would not allow him to get under her shutters again.

---

*W*hat had he said? That darn mask of hers up again and she had returned to the cool stubborn Louisa. What had he done wrong? What had he said? Was her lack of knowledge about his sister the problem? He had to spend some quiet time in her company. Convince her he was a friend and not the enemy. Still it was only the first day. She would warm to the situation she now found herself in.

He admired her dress. Her father had seen to it that she was dressed in the latest fashion despite her absence from the ton. Though not as elaborate as his mother's. She did not need it as she had her own beauty to lift the appearance of anything she wore. The beautiful pale golden silk enhanced the colour of her silky blond hair and her rich brown eyes. She was delightful. A true beauty. But now he was standing in front of her, admiring that beauty, with her mask firmly in place.

He escorted her to her seat and discovered that his mother had made sure he was seated as far away from Miss Stapleton as possible. Louisa seemed relieved as she seated herself next to Elspeth on one side and Freddie on her right. He went to the other end of the table where his father and the annoying Frances Midhurst were awaiting him. Dinner was going to be a long affair.

*L*ouisa was at last free of Chalanor. She breathed easier and allowed herself to look at the surroundings about her, now that he had left her side. The conversation she had with him had definitely become personal. She was now pleased to be seated next to Elspeth and Freddie and could see that Chalanor was at the other end of the table. She could open her shutters but briefly in their company. On Freddie's right however was Lady Farraday taking her position at the end of the table. Louisa felt she was too close to this imposing lady and remained quiet through most of the dinner. She answered only questions directed to her. Elspeth did what she could to keep her talking with the other guests at the table. In that way she could enjoy the dinner without worrying about who was judging her.

It was a great relief Lady Farraday spoke mainly to Freddie and Lord Midhurst who sat on the lady's right and did not direct any conversation in her direction. But she was certain the comments were being dictated by Lady Farraday so as to exclude her from the conversation. Louisa also believed despite that, Lady Farraday was watching her every move. This left her feeling both uncomfortable and vulnerable. Louisa tried desperately not to even look in the lady's direction. She did not want the attention.

"Of course, it is harder to find truly devoted staff in this day and age. However, I have some that I count on." Lady Farraday espoused.

"I agree, madam." Lord Midhurst concluded.

"Most definitely." added Freddie.

The mundane conversation went on. Freddie also avoided drawing Louisa into the conversation, obviously protecting her from any undue comments from Lady Farraday. He would often lean forward so as to block Lady Farraday even looking at her. Louisa appreciated that and would have to thank Freddie for his care tomorrow.

*C*halanor was seated on his father's left at the other end of the table. His mother of course, had placed Frances Midhurst next to him on his left. It was obvious to him that his mother was trying to do more match making. With the roses scattered in large bunches across the table he was unable to view Louisa. He should have known his mother would make sure Louisa was never seated anywhere near him. He needed to remember that so he could find other times he could devote to Louisa. He hoped the dinner would progress quickly.

"We will love the ride tomorrow, won't we Chalanor?" Frances sprouted. Chalanor looked at her and smiled briefly. He noted her comments and engaged

in polite conversation. But he did all in his power to avoid answering any direct questions. Frances was attempting to capture him in conversation centring only on her and him. Instead he tried to converse with his father, not ignoring her but limiting any discussion between them or drawing his father into conversation that would not be interesting to her, such as fly fishing. Frances soon became distracted and spent most of the dinner talking with her sister and Reverend Hutton.

---

*L*ady Farraday observed her arrangements and smiled to herself. She could play cat and mouse just as easily as her son. She would upset his plans and reveal the unsuitable nature of his schemes. She did not know what he was planning but whatever he had in mind, she was sure to upset it. She could see that it involved that slut Louisa, so keeping her away from her son was her first course of action. Her intentions were to have him married off to a woman of her choosing so that she could continue to control him, albeit from a distance. Frances would do anything she suggested. The girl was only interested in his titles and money. Perfect for her son. He had declared he would only marry for love. Any preposterous ideas he might have of a love match were not going to happen. She herself had far more experience than her son and he was going to learn that she always won every battle and eventually the war. She had just won the first battle. That of the seating arrangements.

8

Louisa watched as after the meal, the men excused themselves and retired to the library, she assumed to partake of some very old port and cigars. The ladies retreated to the evening parlour where they chatted until the men were to join them. Tea had arrived a few minutes before the men entered the room. Now she knew the entertainment would start. She just had to stay in the shadows and all would be well.

The gentleman came through the open door chatting and laughing and appearing animated. They moved to various parts of the room. She watched as Chalanor and Freddie came straight toward Elspeth and herself. It was interesting to compare the two men as they walked towards her. Both beautifully dressed, elegant and modern in their attire. One had a happy go lucky personality. Freddie. The other serious but friendly. Chalanor. Before they reached them Lady Farraday's voice rose above the murmur.

"Miss Elspeth, would you grace us with your performance on the pianoforte?" It was clear Lady Farraday was determined to make sure the rest of the evening went in the direction she wished it to go.

Louisa held her breath. Elspeth nodded and went to the piano and began playing. She played Beethoven's Moonlight Sonata. It was beautifully done. Louisa had always enjoyed her playing and could hear how much more mature and confident her playing had become. There was precision and joy as she played. She applauded her friend as Elspeth returned to her seat.

Frances was then summoned to play. She played Chopin's Nocturne in E flat major. It was not executed as naturally as Elspeth's performance had been, but it was played with skill and accuracy. To Louisa, she seemed to lack the passion she had seen in Elspeth. Frances too was warmly applauded.

It was then that Chalanor spoke up. "Sir Peter. Am I correct in saying that your daughter, Miss Stapleton, can sing like a nightingale?"

Louisa stilled at the mention of her name. Surely her father would not expose her to such an obvious display of her talent? She loved to sing but it was a singular entertainment that she rarely shared with others. She did not want the attention of others and certainly not now. Placing herself on display, opening her up to criticism both founded or imaginary was not something she expected to deal with so soon. She did not want to face further ridicule, despite promising herself to be strong, and to ignore those who would want to hurt her. She glared at Chalanor then her father. Her father was not at all put off.

"Most assuredly Chalanor my boy, a voice that any father could be proud of."

An audible "huh" was heard from one of the guests but it was difficult to determine from whom it came. Elspeth however became animated.

"Oh yes please Lady Farraday, she can sing like an angel. She plays as well. But you must hear her sing." Elspeth turned to face Louisa. "May I play for you? Then you can concentrate on your singing." Things then began to move quickly.

If she denied the ability, she would face censure from those who had already spoken in her favour. But she did not want to perform before such hostile company. Well at least the potential of being hostile. Lady Farraday looked livid. Louisa could see that her singing in front of her guests was the last thing she wanted.

That look was enough to motivate Louisa.

That woman does not know who I am. Nor does she know what I am capable of. How dare she judge me? But she soon will know that I am made of sterner stuff.

Louisa stood and walked straight and determined toward the pianoforte. Elspeth was seconds behind her. Elspeth seated herself at the pianoforte as Louisa announced she would be delighted to sing. She turned and spoke to Elspeth. They whispered as a hush fell on the rest of the company.

Elspeth began the introduction. Louisa sang as she had never sung before. Her voice was clear and gentle. She dictated her pitch with precision and solidity. She had deliberately picked a song she knew well. Mozart "Alleluia" was precisely that. She concentrated on obtaining the mood the song could conjure. Oh, how one word could entrance the listener?

As she progressed through the song, she was capturing the attention of everyone there. Every eye was locked on to her form. Even those who doubted her abilities and had even displayed animosity toward her were taken aback while listening to the notes sailing around the room. When she finished there was a hush and then a thunderous applause. She was shaking and hoped no one noticed. But she felt triumphant. Louisa had slayed a dragon and the crowd were rejoicing.

*T*hrough the whole number Chalanor was transfixed. He had no idea that anyone could sing as clearly and as beautifully as she. Her pale golden dress added to the angelic voice emanating from her. Her beauty shone from her face as she sung. As the applause echoed off the walls, he realized Louisa had been hiding away and depriving the ton of a glorious song bird. Her voice alone would make her the prize of the season. He looked at his mother and sensed her wrath. Her face was red with anger and he could see she wanted to say something derogatory about Louisa's voice or what she had sung. She wanted to hurt her.

He immediately raised his voice in Louisa's defence, "Surely no one here would deny that an angel has come from heaven itself to sing to us tonight." With that there were cries of "Encore, Encore," and he watched his mother turn her head toward him and she smiled. A smile that promised she would have her way eventually. A smile that sent a vibration down his back. He had outwitted her this time but that could not last. It was clear she would bide her time and wait.

He watched as Louisa agreed to sing again another evening but begged to be released tonight. She went back to the chaise she had been seated in and Elspeth followed her. Elspeth grabbed her hand and squeezed it. Many of the guests gathered around her to complement her on such a sparkling performance. Freddie came and sat with his sister and Louisa. He could not stop praising her.

"My dear, I have never heard such a beautiful voice. It is truly a wonder. You certainly have been practicing these years you have been away."

"Thank you, sir, I am grateful." She blushed and lowered her head.

"Grateful?" He raised his voice. "On the contrary, you have outshone every lady here." With those words he glared at Lady Farraday who was red faced despite all attempts to hide her disgust.

Lord George and Lady Ann Burgess, near neighbours to the Farradays, came and asked Chalanor to be introduced to Miss Stapleton. His father was with them. Chalanor saw his mother's face grow redder. She was angry. Burgess was once one of her lovers. His father, knowing his wife disliked their presence, took great delight in inviting them to Maidstone Manor. His father honestly enjoyed their company. Chalanor enjoyed watching his father delight in their friendship.

But now that introduction seemed to be the final indignation for Lady Farraday. His mother stood and placed her tea cup on the table and not at all gently. "If you will excuse me everyone, it has been a long and eventful day. I will retire. In fact, I suggest that we all retire." She was soon surrounded by the other matrons. They all stood there waiting for their wishes to be obeyed.

"Stay and enjoy each other's company as long as you wish," announced Lord Farraday, looking at his wife, and he shrugged his shoulders. Then his father bowed to his mother. She in turn sent daggers with the glare she levelled at him. Lord Farraday smiled at her and then turned to speak with Louisa. Lady Farraday left the room. The older ladies Beaumont and Midhurst followed the lady from the room.

He could see that his father was elated. "My dear, your voice is truly beautiful."

"I thank you, sir." But Louisa seemed confused. She was probably surprised that his father paid her such attention. But she gave him a rewarding smile.

"I do hope that I get the chance to hear that magical voice again." He bowed and turned to join the Lords Beaumont and Midhurst as they went and sat at the card table.

"Most definitely an angel. You have not changed a bit." added Reverend Hutton. He too bowed and went to join the other men at the card table.

Louisa blushed. Chalanor delighted to see her victory. Frances

and her sister Sarah came and stood with the group around Louisa.
The Burgesses also remained. Compliments flowed and Sarah was
happy to voice her delight in the performance. Something he had
not expected. Frances remained quiet, with a frown upon her lips.
Happiness was not written on her face and that did not surprise
him.

He was sure that all could see him beaming, as was Sir Peter.
Conversation was light and pleasant. Then Freddie, after showering Louisa and his sister with praise, bowed to the group and
took his leave. He reminded them of their ride after breakfast and
then retired. The Burgesses also took their leave and their carriage
was called for. They, being close neighbours planned to partake in
the house party but continued to sleep in their own home.

The evening progressed with Louisa being the centre of attention. The smile never left his face as he watched Louisa's mask
disappear. He would have sung for joy himself if he had the chance.
After an hour, Louisa made her apologies. The excitement of the
evening was probably weighing on her. The rest of the company
decided that the evening had come to a close.

Chalanor walked Louisa and the other ladies and gentlemen to
the bottom of the stairs. He bowed, smiled and said, "Don't forget
our ride in the morning after breakfast." He smiled again at Louisa.
He returned to stand with his father. The two men stayed at the
bottom of the stairs as the remainder of the company retired to
their rooms.

———

*A*s she reached the top of the stairs, she turned to notice the
Reverend Hutton had also joined the two men at the
bottom of the stairs.

Louisa floated to her room. She was excited the evening was
less of a disaster than she had expected. Her singing could have

been terrible or her voice not as sweet as it had been. But all she could remember was Chalanor's eyes, during the evening. They were delighted, thankful even joyous. Had his opinion of her changed after her performance? Tonight, she would breathe easier and sleep soundly. Demons and indeed dragons seemed to be dropping like ripe fruit from a tree.

9

"Gentlemen, I was wondering if I could have a word with you both."

"Certainly, Hutton. Come let us get a drink in my study." The men followed Lord Farraday into the room and seated themselves on the chairs near his desk.

Hutton continued. "I need nothing to drink, sir. Thank you. I just wished to tell you of my previous relationship with Louisa. She is such a delightful girl and I am so pleased you are trying to help her."

"I must say that I was taken aback somewhat that she knew you. You had never made mention of her before." Chalanor wanted to hear the connection. He knew of the relationship with the Ismays and some of the other guests but Hutton's connection was unexpected. His curiosity was peaked.

"That is simple. She is like a sister to me. I have no desires to be anything else but that to her. We knew each other...what seems like ages ago. As you are well aware, we have been through devastation since last I had the pleasure of seeing her." He stood and walked over to gaze out of the window. It was inky black outside but it seemed to help him centre his thoughts. "She was a sweet child who needed some attention. Her mother was sick and she was visiting her grandmother on her mother's insistence. Louisa had devoted all her time to her mother's care. She was soon to return to her mother who was dying. Her grandmother had told me as much. I spent time with her because I felt so very sorry for her. She was carrying a great burden at such a tender age. I wanted to add some joy and I enjoyed her company very much. We went on long walks and tours around the old town of Lincoln. Her grandmother's maid was our chaperon." He looked at Chalanor. "It was all above board, my friend." He continued. "She loved the cathedral and often sat there for hours watching the light change. The stain glass added different colours to different items in the church. Her favourite thing was to see the pillars change colour in the afternoon. At that point I don't think she truly understood how ill her mother was. If she did, she kept it to herself. The trip to her grandmother's was a distraction I believe, to give her some quiet time before the tragedy that awaited her."

"I knew she had gone through difficulties. It was good that she had you as a friend. Please sit down, my friend."

Hutton continued as he came back to sit down in the chair. "You must understand. She was delightful. And I grew very fond of her. I sought permission to write to her. We did for a few months but then her mother died. I sent my condolences but did not continue the correspondence. I lost track of her after that."

Chalanor could see the concern Hutton had for her. His genuine sadness for Louisa's predicament. Hutton continued.

"I did not keep it from you, as I was not sure that the Louisa you spoke about was whom I had known. But it is and I am pleased. Her singing tonight has changed the minds of a number of the guests. They can see she has a talent that exceeds most women in her position. I am so delighted for her. I just wanted to promise you, I will be your eyes and ears during the house party and keep you informed as to what the guests are saying about her. You have my word, I will safeguard her reputation." He stood and turned to look at Chalanor who also stood. "I am your friend and hers and I too wish to help you. Be assured, she will be well loved and accepted. I will do everything in my power to make sure that occurs. I will not hear anyone criticize her in my presence." He bowed and quietly left the room. Chalanor smiled at him as he closed the door.

"He is a good ally to have in the battle ahead. He appears to be a good friend to you as well, my boy."

"Yes father, he is. We have been through a lot together in Brussels. It was not an easy time for either of us." Chalanor stared at the door, deep in contemplation.

His father waited for a moment before he spoke again, perhaps allowing him to think through some deep thoughts.

"Chalanor, let's have a drink before you head to bed." His father went over to the sideboard, poured two drinks, handed one to his son and then returned to the chairs and sat down.

"I can tell that your mother's up to something again. I am only guessing but she seemed so angry after Miss Stapleton sang this evening. What do you think?"

"I know she is angry with her and me, sir. I am also of the opinion, that she is pushing Frances at me again. I'm just not interested in the girl. And as I asked Louisa and her father here, she thinks I have designs on Louisa. Which I do not." It hurt him to say that and he winced. In his mind she was someone to whom he could commit. "But mother is determined to make life difficult for Louisa because she imagines something between us. I have no romantic interest in Louisa but mother doesn't know that. Father, Louisa really is a lovely young lady. I have never heard a bad word said against her until that night two years ago. Can I suggest you spend some time getting to know her and Sir Peter? Then you will know why I value him as a friend and why I want to help Louisa. I believe I am honour bound to rectify this injustice."

"Very well, I will join you on the ride in the morning. Your mother is driving me to distraction anyway. I would appreciate some time out of her sight. I will discuss more about your mother another time. I have more than a few other suspicions. I am tired and wish to retire. But believe me my boy, we have much to discuss about your mother." He drained the remainder of his brandy, put down his glass, bid goodnight to his son and left the room.

Chalanor stayed seated for a few more minutes thinking on what his father had just revealed. What has his mother done now, to upset his father so? He drained his drink, placed the glass on the table next to his chair, got up and went to his room. He had much to think about this night.

"Well, you did nothing to help, my love." Lady Farraday shifted her position so that she was on top of him. She took his hand in hers, "Now you will do as I say. I want you to ravage me completely. I want no thoughts of that stupid girl in my head. I want to feel all of you, overpowering me completely, my wonderful lover. Do you understand?"

His movement was quick and she found herself under his wonderfully sculptured body. She could never get enough of him on or in her.

"I want all of you, my lady, my beautiful, wonderful lady." His mouth descended on her lips and he kissed her as if he could not get enough of them. Not just her lips but every part of her body. He suckled at her breasts till she cried for him to fill her. But he did not. He would not. Not yet. For a long time, he found many ways to distract his lady but all he could think of was the girl, Louisa. He imagined very easily that the actions Lady Farraday thought were for her alone were in truth what he wanted to do to Louisa. His mind was filled with thoughts only of her making him more aroused than anything his lady might do to him. Her beautiful face, her glorious singing. She was going to be his. He would see to that.

After he had sated Lady Farraday, leaving her asleep, boneless in her bed, he went back to his own room. But he was not satisfied. How could he be? He wanted to feel his member inside Louisa and he was becoming impatient. She had only been here a day and she was already falling for that cock-sure Chalanor and that disturbed him, greatly. Because he wanted her. No one else was allowed to have her. He paced the floor till near dawn. He would have her. Then he undressed and lay in bed waiting.

Perhaps he would rest now and wait for the moment when he had his sexual satisfaction with Louisa and then the satisfaction of killing her. Either or both would give him the peace he craved. His desire for her had not waned. Maybe he would have her before and after he killed her? That would be very satisfying. He had done that before. Warm flesh or cold flesh, both were satisfying. Bringing those memories of other murders and rapes he had performed, made him hard again. Those experiences had thrilled him and he wanted to feel that again. But this time with someone he knew, not just a stranger. Yes, he wanted more. He took his member in his hands and satisfied himself.

10

The summer was promising to be both warm and dry. This morning was no exception and Louisa's heart expanded with delight. Breakfast was eaten and all the other younger members of the party were now gathered at the stables awaiting the arrival of their host.

Sarah had come to stand next to her and Elspeth. This made her feel uneasy. She knew the sisters disliked her.

"This will be a great treat. Chalanor's estate is so much more pleasant than his family seat."

"What do you mean?" Louisa asked, not sure she would even get a response or even if she wanted to hear one.

"He has invested more into his estate to make it produce more foods for his retainers, for sale and for himself. Unlike his mother who spends money on follies, parties and alike. That is how his grandmother wanted it and why he inherited it directly from her. It vexed his mother to be overlooked by the Dowager Kentworth but the old girl was determined Chalanor would get it." She turned and looked at Louisa. "You do know that Lady Farraday is only the dowager's adopted daughter?"

Gossip of any sort usually disturbed Louisa but these snips of information surprised and intrigued her. She wondered why Sarah was so forthcoming.

"She was legally adopted though, so what is the problem?" Elspeth turned to face Sarah. Louisa listened intently.

"No problem of course but it has taken many years for her to be respected. She had to marry money and power to get that respect. That is why she is determined that Chalanor marries a titled lady."

Louisa was perplexed. Was the information so easily given, meant to vex her? The only thing bothering her at the moment was if Lady Farraday was adopted, and life had been hard, why was the lady so determined to make her life so difficult? She would have helped someone in her position before she would have hindered them. Why would the lady not help her? It was confusing. Louisa had no designs on Chalanor or his estate, the man had played too big a part in her downfall. Besides she had her own wealth. Not great but substantial for her needs. Lady Farraday must know that? But what if the lady believed the lies of her downfall? After all she was there when the declarations were made against her.

"Of course, my sister is titled and our mother such a dear friend of Lady Farraday. I am sure that she will win Chalanor's hand."

And there it was. Louisa got her clearest message that Chalanor was for Frances Midhurst. It didn't bother her but did someone let Chalanor know? He gave every indication of disliking the girl. Even having been here but a day it was obvious Chalanor had no time for Frances and seemed bored in her company. Louisa smiled at Sarah but did not respond. What could she say? Elspeth saved her from any further embarrassment.

"I believe," Elspeth remarked, "that you might like to confirm that information with Chalanor. He has no intention to marry. I do believe he is quite happy to remain an unattached gentleman for a while yet."

Louisa did her best not to smirk, lifting her gloved hand to cover her mouth as she gave a little cough. Sarah sent her a disparaging look.

"Oh, I am sure once he has spent time with my sister," Sarah continued "He will see what true breeding is worth." On that note Sarah turned and walked over to her sister and the other group of riders.

"Spend time with her? He's known the girl all her life and knows exactly what she is like." Elspeth turned to face Louisa and laughed. "Sarah really has not got any idea how men think. Chalanor despises Frances. Just ignore her. Sarah has no idea what she is saying." Elspeth smiled at her.

"I have no interest in the man so I have nothing to ignore. I have no concern as to who Chalanor intends to marry. I just wish they could see how foolish they are to think that I would even be interested or he interested in me. My reputation for one, and his mother would never allow it. Or the man himself may very well have someone else in mind. I am sure that I am the last person Chalanor would see as bride potential. It's ridiculous."

"Oh really," Elspeth raised her brow.

"Yes really. I have been here but a day. What on earth are you suggesting?" But she did not allow Elspeth the chance to answer. "Don't even think to answer that question." Louisa stared back at her friend, wishing for her to say no more. "But answer this for me. Is it true that Lady Farraday is adopted?"

Elspeth smiled at her. "My parents had mentioned it every now and then over the years. But there is more to her story than we have been told or that we are ever likely to find out. It would be interesting to discover what Sarah knows. For one so young she has a wealth of information, even, more than my brother." Elspeth laughed.

Louisa gazed at her friend but her mind tried to grasp what

Elspeth had just revealed. Could scandal hide behind the experienced and regal Lady Myra Farraday? Surely not, the woman is far too controlling and elegant to have scandal dwell in her midst. After all she despises it in anyone else.

Other riders gathered around them waiting for their horses to be brought from the stables. A young gentleman came over with Freddie to be formally introduced.

"May I present the Honourable Vincent Bartlett?"

"So, delighted to meet you. I arrived late last evening, coming in just as you started your beautiful performance. But I did not wish to disturb you last evening and have asked Freddie to formally introduce us now." Bartlett smiled at Louisa and gave a little bow.

Heat rising in her cheeks, Louisa lowered her head and curtsied. "Thank you, sir." She didn't know why she was being bashful but she assumed it was due to the sudden interest from the new arrival. The accolades she had received last evening were more than she had ever hoped for. Something flickered down her back that made her uneasy. An air of concern perhaps but brushed it away.

"Do you not remember me, Miss Stapleton? We met some years ago."

"I am very sorry, sir, I do not remember." Louisa searched her memory but could not place him in any other circumstance. The chill she had felt down her back heighted her awareness. She could not recall where she may have met him. Who was he?

"It was at the Prescott house party." His smiled. This piece of information disturbed her greatly and she tried to remember who he was. But she could not.

"I'm sorry sir, I do not remember." She was worried that this gentleman may have witnessed her downfall and would not look kindly on her. Or worse still saw her as prey. He could be yet another rake trying to seduce her. He could give her comeback into society obvious difficulties. She now wished to get away from him as soon as possible to avoid any further complications. "Would you excuse me? It would appear that my horse is waiting."

"Please excuse us." Both ladies curtsied then turned to hurry over to their waiting horses.

As they walked Elspeth added, "That young man is a known rake. We will need to be careful around him."

"More so," Louisa continued, "because he was at the Prescott house party. He will know of my so-called reputation. I just don't remember him or anything about him. Do you?" Louisa stopped and looked at her friend. "He also made me feel uncomfortable. I have no idea why. I cannot say what it is about him but he made me feel strange."

"I don't know him other than by his reputation. So, we will have to avoid him." Elspeth took her hand and they went to their horses.

---

*T*he party planned to head south through the village of Loose and then veer to the east. The day was warm but Louisa enjoyed the gentle breeze. Chalanor rode between the small groups giving information of the area and what was growing in certain fields. And so did his father. They both seemed in good spirits sharing their love of the land. Lord Farraday, again away from his wife, was both pleasant and a delightful wealth of information.

The life of the house party.

Frances, on the other hand appeared to be bored. There was a constant sneer on her face. And from all the looks that people were giving her, the sneer was obvious to all.

First, they stopped at the new wood, planted over the remains of the old house. Very little of the old mansion could be seen. There were but a few small ruined walls looking like some ancient monument. It was almost totally obliterated. Originally, the drive to this house would have been a short one. But the new house was placed further back in the park. It was obvious to Louisa that Chalanor looked unhappy. He walked through the small woodland stopping every now and then to pick up a small part of a brick or tile. He distanced himself from the rest of the group and everyone allowed him his privacy.

Lord Farraday enlightened Louisa. "He was still only a child about ten years of age, when we moved to the new manor. It was just before Delia was born. He had loved his old home and I believe still does. His grandmother, whom he adored, died the same year we moved into the new manor and his heart was broken. When Lady Farraday had the old house pulled down about two years later, he was devastated." He paused and looked into her eyes and continued. "I was also heartbroken. It was the house I had grown up in. It only needed to be repaired and refurbished and it would have returned to its grandeur."

Louisa stared perplexed at Lord Farraday. A flash of longing went through her. Why was he telling her such personal details? He did not approve of her, or did he? Well he had not approved of her when she had first arrived. But his dealings with her since then had been cordial and open. It was confusing at best. At that moment Chalanor came towards them. He had in his hand a large piece of a wall tile.

"This was the beautiful delft blue tiles that adorned the walls in part of the kitchen block. They had come from the Netherlands." He placed the tile in Louisa's hand. The distinctive blue on white, although smeared with dirt, was still obvious. It seemed to be a sailing ship. She had no trouble picturing him as a young boy running in and out of the kitchen block. "I was able to save some of the tiles and have used them in the kitchen on my own estate. I was only a boy but my father allowed me to take what I wanted. I saved them. And when I had inherited my hall..." He smiled at his father and took the tile from Louisa's hand and placed it in his father's.

Lord Farraday gazed at the piece of tile as if it were a gem stone of wondrous value.

"Would you mind if I kept the tile?" Louisa asked in a quiet voice. Chalanor smiled at her as his father gave the tile back to her. She adored the tile and the history it gave her. She held it with reverence imagining all the faces the tile would have experienced from the staff working in the kitchen to the various housekeepers, cooks and owners of the house.

Louisa was perplexed. Why was this happening? She had made a vow to stay away from Chalanor but here she stood, having deep conversations with both him and his father. Why could she not stay away from them? Why was she continually found in Chalanor's company? A question she could not answer.

Chalanor shook his head, "Such a shame. I would have loved to have shown you this beautiful old building." His perfect blue eyes matched the blue of the delft tile. And now those eyes were gazing into hers. There was longing in them but before Louisa could determine what that meant, Frances, who had come to stand next to Chalanor, disturbed their peace.

"It was a terrible old wreck that should have been pulled down. How could anyone have had any people of distinction in a rotten building like that?"

"And when did you ever step foot in it, Frances? You were a babe in arms when the building was pulled down. You would not even remember it?" Frances turned a bright shade of red. Louisa wished she had the determination to be able to say something to this bitter spoilt girl. But she didn't have too.

"I suggest you keep your thoughts to yourself. T'was my home and I liked it." Turning, Chalanor strode to his horse, mounted and trotted south east towards Loose.

"You'll not win him with sour words, Frances," piped in Lord Farraday as he turned to walk to where his horse was tethered. Frances turned a darker shade of red which seemed impossible. She then turned and fled to her horse. The rest of the gentlemen helped the ladies to mount their horses, then they in turn mounted, and all rode after Chalanor. He had not gone far and they soon caught up with him.

Sucking in a quick breath, Louisa's eyes widened. What had just happened? Frances had been rude and that was not unusual from what she knew of the Midhurst sisters. She had known the Midhurst's from a distance all her life. They did what they wished and thought out loud without thinking of other's feelings. She could not blame Chalanor for putting her in her place. But the fact that Chalanor wanted to share his feelings about his old home with her seemed bizarre. She had also known him from a distance. At least till she became engaged to Prescott. He'd always been so aloof, so distant. As she rode on, she contemplated the look on his face while he handed her the tile. Loving, longing and yet remote. She was glad that she now had the tile in her reticule hanging from her saddle.

*H*e stood in the shadows. This was going to be harder than he had thought. The main reason was that he could not get a moment alone with her. They had been standing in the woods but too many of the company were too close. So, he needed to change tactics. Their next stop meant he had to sabotage her horse. It was the only thing close to her that could damage her and he could make it look like an accident. He could not think of another thing. He could not wait. He wanted her. His lady would be grateful and reward him for his effort. A reward that he would be happy to extract from her if she was not prepared to give it to him. But his lady will. She despised Louisa. And that boded well for him.

He would not be able to take the girl then and there. Which was a problem. Well maybe later, back at the house in private as the body was laid out, that is if she died. But if she did not die, he would find a way to take her as she recovered from her injuries. He preferred that idea. Either way he would have her. Oh yes, he would have her. He smiled and followed the rest of the guests watching carefully every move that trollop Louisa made.

11

Chalanor rode the party into the bailey in front of his old Norman tower. Louisa immediately understood his desire to have wanted to save his old Elizabethan home at Maidstone. This old rocky but well-kept keep tower was where his grandmother had lived and died. They had been some distance off when the old Norman Tower had come into view. But her love of old buildings held her captive immediately. Kentworth Tower was magnificent.

Louisa had known of its existence but had no idea it was Chalanor's home. She had always assumed he lived at Maidstone Manor. But the beauty of the tower was now in front of her. The bailey contained all the usual keep buildings, stable, old kitchen and many fine stone huts. They were all well-kept. Some were made of the native stone and others had been whitewashed. But what was most impressive was the old tower connected to a very recent Georgian addition, also made in local stone. All the buildings were surrounded by beautiful gardens and lawns. This place was a moment in time, captured for history but transplanted into the eighteen hundreds.

Chalanor, with his guests gathered around him, went on to

explain its lineage. Louisa stood spellbound. "The keep was built in the early 1100's after the arrival of the Normans in 1066. Over the years it has been strengthened and repaired many times as it changed hands. When my grandfather inherited, he started extensions to make the tower an integral part of a much larger building, as you can see. That stopped unfortunately a few years later when he died rather suddenly. My grandmother had inherited the estate from my grandfather. Eventually my grandmother completed the most recent building works."

"That seems somewhat strange as most properties usually go to the nearest male heir and not the spouse." Vincent Bartlett declared.

"Not really. The estate was not entailed and had been successfully handed down the family to either male or female, husband or wife. There are many noted women in our family line that have owned and run this estate, my grandmother being one of them." Chalanor looked toward her, she assumed to gauge her reaction. She looked at him and smiled. What she was hearing was interesting to her. And she wanted him to see that. She knew some families excelled on keeping their powerful women involved in the running of families and dynasties. Now all she could concentrate on was Lady Farraday and her formidable position in this family. Lady Farraday would not allow even a friendship with Chalanor to exist.

"My grandmother wanted to extend the property to allow for her growing family but when my grandfather died, she had to change her plans."

"Had your mother been born?" Frances asked.

"Yes, but she was a babe. Mother grew up here and she had said when she would inherit it, she would have the monstrosity pulled down. Grandmother had finished the extension but it was not good enough for my mother."

Louisa looked at Sarah and saw her smile at Frances. She

wondered if Sarah was going to say anything about Lady Farraday's lineage but she remained quiet. Obviously, she was not yet prepared to announce Lady Farraday's so called secret.

"Perhaps that is why your grandmother passed the estate on to you, knowing your love of the history and the area," commented Elspeth to Chalanor.

"That you, in turn, would keep it safe," Louisa contributed.

Chalanor smiled warmly at her. His gaze lingered on her face. She could not resist returning her own gaze.

"I would like to think so. It is our history, my family's and that of England. I want to preserve it. I continued where my grand-mother left off and have renovated all the other buildings on the estate. Yes, I want to keep it safe." Chalanor looked around at the guests but his eyes came back to her. Chalanor had kept the estate safe. This made her smile.

"How magnificent," Louisa stared at the tower as she stood in the courtyard, unsure she herself had not stepped back in time to Medieval Kent. Chalanor and Elspeth stood beside her. The other guests gathered around them. All looked up at the tower.

"Oh Chalanor, it is truly beautiful. I did not know that you had done such beautiful renovation work on it. Your grandmother would be so proud of you."

"Thank you, Elspeth. I do believe Grand'Mere would approve."

"Grand'Mere?" Louisa repeated. "That is French for grandmother?"

"Yes, she liked me calling her that, when we were alone together. My mother didn't approve of the title. But I think my Grand'Mere felt she had gone back in time to when the Normans had built the keep. She loved me calling her Grand'Mere." She watched as the years since her death disappeared and he seemed to be standing in front of her and not just the tower.

"The work that has been done is astounding. So many of the old castles and keeps are but ruins! I admire what you and your

'Grand'Mere' have tried to do. The new additions add to the history not distract from it. It truly is beautiful." Louisa's comment was honestly meant and she hoped that Chalanor could sense that. She noted the changes and the preservation work, admiring what his family had achieved with this historical building.

"We all think it is wonderful but can we please enter the building now so that we can refresh ourselves?" demanded Frances, sarcasm most evident. Everyone looked at Frances as she broke the spell which had taken hold of the small group. Frances could curdle cream with her moods.

Chalanor offered his arm to Louisa but before she could take hold Frances had grabbed his arm, "For pity's sake..." and dragged Chalanor into the tower.

"I would move a little more quickly if I were you," Elspeth suggested to Louisa.

"I agree." replied Lord Farraday offering his arm to Louisa and his other arm to Elspeth. A warmth travelled from the top of her head to the tips of her toes.

12

Luncheon was held at the large dining hall in the new part of the building adjoining the tower. Warmth filled Chalanor and his chest expanded with happiness to have Elspeth and Louisa sitting with him. His mother could not dictate the seating arrangements in his home. Frances, much to her disgust, had been placed at the other end of the table with Lord Farraday and the other guests were seated in between. His father had shown delight to escort the Misses Midhurst's to that end of the table. Except now he didn't look so delighted. Chalanor could not imagine what his mother saw in Frances as a potential bride.

Louisa was beginning to relax while in his company and her mask had dropped again. The conversation around the table was enjoyable. She listened intently as he told the guests more of the running of the estate. His estate workers were made up of families who had been part of the fabric of Kentworth Tower for centuries. He was thrilled to see her so contented.

*T*he midday meal completed, Chalanor escorted everyone on a short, guided tour around the new building and the tower. After they had refreshed themselves it was time to head back to Maidstone Manor. The guests gathered near the tower as the horses were brought to them from the stables. Louisa could not stop smiling. This had been an exciting day full of new information and knowledge that she had not anticipated. From the ride and the tour of the wonderful historical tower. Nothing could distract her from the day they had. She and Elspeth stood waiting for the servants to help them onto the horses.

"Louisa, would you mind terribly if we changed mounts? Mine is a little too spirited for my liking and I know how much you like a spirited animal."

"Of course not, Elspeth, my horse is very docile. I take it you still do not ride very often?"

Her friend smiled at her. "You know me well. No, I do not ride often. It is one of my least liked activities. Give me a chaise and a good book." She chuckled.

"Chalanor told me over luncheon that your horse and mine are brother and sister. See how much alike they are?"

"They do look alike. I was never much of a horsewoman. One horse looks much the same as another horse in my eyes. This ride has been delightful though but I am tired and want a horse that will take me home even if I fall asleep on top of it."

Louisa laughed along with Elspeth as they exchanged mounts. She had to agree it was such a wonderful day.

---

*T*he ride back to the manor was blissful. His dreams seemed to become reality. Chalanor knew that she was beginning to see the real him. Not the old rake. He watched all his friends and could see all enjoying themselves. Even the joking Freddie was enjoying all the day had provided.

"What a perfect day. Wouldn't you agree, sister?" Freddie rode close to both his sister and Louisa keeping an eye on them both and joking around. Bartlett also rode near Louisa and continued to involve her in conversation. Chalanor did not know him well but he seemed pleasant enough. He involved her in conversation and was jovial with all the people around him.

Hutton rode just behind Louisa. Knowing his friend was also keeping an eye on Louisa pleased him. Watching everyone relaxed, especially Louisa was what he had hoped the ride would provide. The mood was even lighter than the ride had been in the morning. The weather had remained sunny and mild with just a hint of breeze. Everyone was in high spirits. As they entered the final field before arriving at the manor, Frances called out.

"Last person to the stables has to help clean them out!"

"I know nothing of horse flesh nor anything pertaining to the beasts," Freddie cried out to Frances as she began to gallop toward the stables. "Does this nag even run?" He and the other riders began to gallop after Frances. Everyone was laughing when suddenly a scream filled the air. Chalanor immediately drew to a halt and turned his horse back to the direction they had just come from.

It was Elspeth. She was on the ground crying in pain. Chalanor galloped back to her. Elspeth's horse stood quietly a few feet away.

"What happened, Elspeth?" Freddie called to her.

"I don't know," she cried "One minute I was happily galloping with you all and oh…" She cried out in pain again.

Chalanor had reached her first. He got off his horse, took his coat off and laid it under Elspeth's head. "Keep still Elspeth," he pleaded with her.

"Don't talk my dear," Freddie jumped off his horse and was by her side, gently checking her left leg. "I am afraid it looks broken."

Elspeth was in a great deal of pain. He could see the pain in her expression. She tried to push herself up but collapsed. Her left arm also seemed to give her difficulty. Tears began to roll down her face and she was finding it hard to breathe. Freddie checked the arm. He looked at him and mouthed 'broken'.

"Chalanor, call for the doctor," Frances cried out still atop her horse. Chalanor had walked over and stood beside Elspeth's horse once Freddie began to check his sister's leg. Chalanor stood looking at the horse rather than at poor Elspeth. He did not move or react to Frances' demand.

"Frances, please ride to the manor and ask my mother to have the doctor fetched." His eyes were now glued to the saddle lying on the ground next to the horse.

"Surely we should both go?"

"Please do not argue with me," his anger taking the place of his previous politeness.

"But…"

"Now," his voice was almost a shout. He never once took his eyes from the saddle. He looked up and saw Frances turn and gallop toward the house.

"Father, please come and assist me?" He called out.

Lord Farraday walked over to the saddle and knelt down next to Chalanor who was now bent down holding the girth strap.

"This has been cut!" Lord Farraday whispered to his son.

"Yes, but not all the way, and why? Who would deliberately want to cut the girth strap? They must have known that she would fall off her horse if the strap gave way. Who would want to hurt Elspeth?"

"My boy, that horse was the horse Louisa was riding this morning! She had the mare. Elspeth had the stallion."

He wanted to sit down. The reality of the connection his father had made hit him square in his stomach and he was sick. He looked at his father and nodded. He looked at the two horses in question. He was right. He had himself picked a docile animal for her not knowing how well she rode. Louisa must have swapped with Elspeth at some point. But then who wanted to hurt Louisa? This disturbed him even more. He stood up as did his father.

Chalanor could make out the cart from the manor, steadily making its way over the field.

Louisa was sitting in the grass with Elspeth's head in her lap. She was lightly patting her head with her hand and whispering to Elspeth, attempting to keep her calm. He could still see tears flowing down her face. He came over and picked up his coat and gave it a shake. He watched the ladies on the ground in front of him for a few minutes trying to work out the meaning of these current events.

"Chalanor?" Louisa suddenly called out in distress. He was by her side immediately. "She has fainted. What are we to do?"

"The cart is on its way. We will carefully take her back to the house and see," he pointed to the rider making his way at speed down the driveway. "The doctor has been fetched. She will be well as soon as we have her in the house. I'm sure."

Louisa had tears making their way down her cheeks. Chalanor knelt down next to her, "Our friend is a strong girl but she has fainted due to the pain. I am sure she will be fine." He hoped his words would give her comfort.

Louisa lifted her head as she reached out and grabbed his arm.

"The horse was mine. She was such a docile animal. I can't believe she would throw her or anyone for that matter. Elspeth is hurt because of me. This should have happened to me."

He picked his words carefully as he answered her, "Do not fret, my love. We will find out who caused this horrid accident to occur."

Louisa stared at him shocked, as if she had been hit a painful blow. He only hoped she could gauge what he meant. That she had been the intended victim. He hoped that she had recognized his meaning and that is why she appeared in so much distress. He put his arm around Louisa and with his other hand checked the fore-head of Elspeth, who was becoming paler by the minute. Lord Farraday reached down and patted both Chalanor and Louisa on the back. Freddie was walking back and forth in front of them. He was wringing his hands and mumbling as tears flowed down his face. He called out to the cart driver,

"Come quicker, man."

Bartlett came over to stand with him and tried to keep him calm by putting his arm around his shoulders and whispering what he hoped were soothing words.

The remainder of the riders gathered the horses, leaving Louisa, Chalanor and Freddie to ride in the cart back to the manor. Chalanor was quiet and disturbed on the drive back. Who was trying to hurt Louisa? More disturbing still, when had Louisa become "his love"?

13

Louisa remained at Elspeth's side and Freddie allowed it. He had been distressed and seemed glad for the company. But she was worried about him. He paced up and down the room like a wounded animal, unable to settle. All she wanted to do was wake her friend and be assured she was alive and well, knowing that would ease Freddie's mind. After all she knew that Freddie was responsible for his sister regardless of any accident. He was in pain and she understood that.

"I can't believe this has happened. The saddle, why did it come off her horse, it makes no sense?" Freddie was questioning everything. He stopped, looked at his sister. His eyes glistened and one single tear slid down his face. He then turned and continued to pace the floor.

Louisa kept quiet, not wanting to distress him with the news that the horse had been hers not Elspeth's. She had difficulty enough thinking about the accident and the possible implications of what had happened. The concern was for her friend but also that it was her horse Elspeth had been riding. All she could see in her mind was Chalanor's eyes looking, no, begging her to see that there was more to this affair than a mere accident.

Finally, the doctor arrived, much to everyone's relief. She and Freddie stayed with Elspeth as the doctor examined her. Louisa was only interested in what he had to say. Was her friend safe? Was she badly hurt and would she recover?

---

*C*halanor had retired with his father to the library to have tea in quiet, while they discussed the implications of what had occurred. Someone had made an attempt on Louisa's life and he and his father were determined to find out who. It had to be one of the members of the house party as she had only been at Maidstone for one day. Besides none of his staff even knew the lady. News of her being at Maidstone Manor and back in society could not have travelled to London in such a short period of time, let alone anywhere else.

The remainder of the guests had been served tea in the morning room on the first floor, hosted by Lady Farraday.

---

*T*he doctor walked into the library with Freddie following on his heels. The doctor bowed at Lord Farraday and Chalanor and then asked if he could use the desk for a moment. Lord Farraday escorted him to it. The doctor sat down and began to make notes.

Chalanor got Freddie a brandy and directed him to a chair hoping to get him to sit down. His distress still obvious.

"Listen Freddie, let us hear what the doctor has to say. I know you're worried about Elspeth but I am sure she will be fine. Please be patient." He was concerned for his friend.

Freddie fidgeted and muttered to himself under his breath. He kept pushing his hands through his hair. Everyone turned to the doctor as he stood and came to stand before the seated gentlemen.

Freddie jumped up. "What is your opinion? Will she live?" The doctor did not seem worried by the question.

With an encouraging smile, he responded to the distressed Freddie. "She was in a great deal of pain but I gave her a draught to help her sleep. The left leg and left arm are both broken. I have put the leg in a splint. It was not comfortable for her. She fainted I'm afraid. So, we need to watch her carefully." He looked at Freddie. "Yes, she will live. Unless she develops some unseen complications. Having said that I believe she will be fine. There is no need for you to worry."

The gentlemen all looked from one to another, gauging each man's mood. "Luckily it was a clean break," the doctor continued. "She must remain in bed for some weeks until the swelling has gone down and I am satisfied it is healing. Her arm is a clean break also and it too is in a splint. She will have to have assistance to bath, dress and eat. May I add, she should not be moved under any circumstances? She should not yet be sent home. It will take her some time to recover."

No one could say a word. Everyone kept quiet. The reality of what she would have to deal with in the coming months began to penetrate Chalanor's consciousness. The house party for her would last months, not weeks.

"I will come and check on her tomorrow and I will give your staff clear instructions at that time, on how she is to be looked after. If the staff can be gathered together tomorrow afternoon, after luncheon, I would appreciate that. Miss Stapleton is sitting with her now. But Miss Ismay should sleep till late tomorrow morning. The draught should see to that. I suggest that Miss Stapleton be encouraged to get some sleep also. It has been a terrible shock to her as well. May I add, sir," he looked at Freddie,

"Sleep might also do you some good. Would you like me to prepare a small draught for you?"

"Thank you, sir, but no. I want to be able to help my sister should she wake during the night." With that the doctor bowed to the gentlemen and left.

The three men sat together sipping their brandy. It was only then that Chalanor and his father expressed their concerns to Freddie as to the so-called accident. They did not want the doctor to hear of their suspicions. They also wanted Freddie to recognize their concern without the influence of another person.

"Freddie, we believe that Elspeth's accident was not an accident at all. We discovered that the saddle had been deliberately cut. You do know what that means?"

"Who on earth would want to hurt my sister?" Freddie lamented. "She is the sweetest of women and a great catch for any man. I cannot, no will not believe it." Chalanor could see that Freddie could not come to terms with what he had just revealed. Chalanor rose from his seat to stand behind Freddie and placed his hand on his shoulder.

"Freddie, I know this is hard for you to accept but the accident was not meant for Elspeth. She was riding Louisa's horse." Freddie turned to stare up at Chalanor as if he were mad.

"What are you saying...my sister got in the way of some mad man trying to do damage to Louisa? But who in their right mind would want to hurt her or Elspeth? This has to be some crazy accident. Not everything is about Louisa. Surely it was a freakish accident."

"The girth on the saddle was cut." He came around to the front of Freddie, bent down and grabbed his shoulders. "This is no accident and I believe Louisa was the intended victim." He paused for a moment while allowing that information to sink into Freddie's mind. Freddie looked at Chalanor. He saw that Freddie understood what he had said. "And my father and I have been trying to determine since the accident, who would want to do this. But there is no denying the saddle was deliberately cut. I will show the evidence to you in the morning."

"I do not understand it. It just makes no sense. But I will take your word on the matter, Chal. I just can't fathom the meaning behind it. Who could hurt her, who? My poor sister, why did she change horses? I hope you are wrong."

Chalanor reached for the bell pull. Moments later the butler entered.

"Ramsay, will you please go and ask Miss Stapleton if she would join us here in the library as soon as possible. It will be in relation to the accident, should she ask."

"I am going back to stay with Elspeth. I will come down for dinner but spend the evening and the night in her room, if that is acceptable? I want to be there when she wakes."

"Of course, Freddie, I will have a cot set up in her room, so that you can be near her."

"Thank you. I will think on what you have said and see what comes to mind." His mood seemed to soften. "When Elspeth is better, I will discuss this with her. But I still can't imagine who would want to hurt either lady. I will talk with you both tomorrow." With that, a confused Freddie left Chalanor and Lord Farraday.

"I know that your mother is hardly pleasant to Louisa but even this is beyond what she is capable of doing. Beside she did not accompany us on the ride." They remained quiet for a few minutes.

"Someone could have done it on her behalf?" Chalanor suggested.

His father shook his head. "No, I doubt it. It has to be someone else. Her current lover is not the kind of man who would ever do such a thing."

"You are aware of mother's current lover?" Chalanor stood before his father somewhat taken aback with the ease in which his father spoke of his mother's lovers. He had wondered for years why his father allowed his mother to continue to behave in such a scandalous manner.

"Yes, but he was not on the ride this morning either."

Chalanor wanted to ask more questions but could see that his father was also distracted with the events of the day. He decided not to press him for further information. They could discuss his mother at another time. Lord Farraday continued.

"We galloped in a number of areas this morning and Louisa was fine. The cut would have given way then. The fact that it didn't would indicate that the saddle was tampered with while we had stopped at your manor."

Chalanor sensed an accusation in his words. "Well, it would not have been any of my people. What knowledge would they have of Louisa? I don't believe that any of them would act against another person like that." He paused to contemplate his servants being involved but ruled them out. He began to pace.

"It had to be one of the riders but I will send word to the tower to see if anyone had a recollection of people or persons around the horses while we were at luncheon."

Chalanor's worry made him feel sick to his stomach. He had no idea who could be behind this. More concerning now was if this villain intended to have another attempt to hurt Louisa. Or was this accident against the wrong victim, enough to put the villain off? He also would talk with Sir Peter to determine if Louisa had any more obvious enemies. People who may have made threats to her over the past few years. Prescott was the only person who came to mind and there was no way that man would even be aware she was here. He would still be in London. So, he could not be behind it. Could he have arranged something? But how would he know?

It was now obvious to Chalanor, that he had feelings for Louisa which went beyond wanting to help her back into society. He had always assumed that his longing to bring her back into the ton had been for her benefit and to relieve himself of his own guilt. Could he be in love with her? He knew her real nature and had for years, innocent, sweet and cultured. He had wanted to keep her away from Prescott but she seemed so in love that he could not raise the question of his rakish tendencies. After all he had been on a similar road.

But he had changed and was now considered an eligible match. It certainly would explain his wanting to bring her back into the fold. His own confusion in regard to his feelings only added to his concerns. She had been here but a day and his world had been turned upside down.

He went to the sideboard and poured another drink for his father and himself and then returned to sit with his father. He had no desire to pace anymore. Not only was he baffled but he was tired.

Louisa entered the library still dressed in her riding outfit. Even with dirt and stains on her outfit and her dishevelled hair and dislodged cap, she looked beautiful. Chalanor got quickly to his feet and went to Louisa's side. He took her by the elbow and escorted her to the big leather chair near where his father was now standing and waiting. Touching her like this, he could sense the energy between them. Could she also feel it? Lord Farraday walked to the sideboard and poured her a small sherry, returned and handed it to her.

"Please Miss Stapleton—can I call you Louisa? Take small sips. It will help to calm your nerves."

"Thank you, Lord Farraday and yes please call me Louisa." She leant back in the chair and released a deep sigh.

"I am sorry to have to request your presence after the events of the afternoon, but I must discuss the accident with you, while things are fresh in your mind. We also must reveal the possible consequences of what occurred today." Chalanor hated the thought of putting her through this. But he knew they had no choice.

"What on earth happened? Do you know? This is such a ridiculous scenario. I can't imagine what has happened."

He could see the shock of the events which had her speaking so quickly. She searched his eyes as she spoke, longing for confirmation that he knew it was not her fault.

"Do you know? I know that I can't explain it. But I sense you have a suggestion, don't you?" Her hands were ever so lightly shaking. And her voice quivered as she continued. "I am truly shocked that this could happen. The horse was mine. I should have been on her. She was a placid animal and Elspeth is not a great rider. So, we changed horses after luncheon. Elspeth's horse had much more spirit and I was enjoying the ride on him. I can't understand how she fell off the mare. She was so docile. But you said the saddle, what was it…how could the girth on the saddle break?" She looked questioningly at Chalanor.

He watched as tears filled her eyes and his heart tightened as a pitiful sob escaped her mouth. This brought Chalanor to his knees in front of her. He took the glass from her hand and placed it on the side table. He then took her hand, drawing her watery eyes to look into his.

"Please don't cry, Louisa. This is not your fault. Elspeth didn't fall off by accident."

"What do you mean?" The shocked look on her face had him reaching out to her. He gently rubbed her fingers, to help keep her calm.

"We believe the saddle was cut and it gave way when we started to gallop. Elspeth then came off the horse."

"Then someone deliberately was trying to hurt her? That was what you were suggesting after the accident?" Louisa's tear-stained face was turned to him waiting for some kind of response.

Lord Farraday then knelt in front of Louisa. He too took her hand in his. "No, my dear, it was your horse. Whoever did this was trying to hurt you."

Louisa's mouth dropped open and she gaped at them kneeling in front of her.

He could see the confused look on her face. Did she understand the enormity of the statement?

"You, you...can't be serious." She questioned. "Surely no one hates me that much that they would try and hurt me? And they didn't. Poor Elspeth got in their way. This can't be right. There has to be a mistake. Besides, who would want to hurt Elspeth even by accident?" She seemed panicked at what he had suggested.

Chalanor let out a heavy sigh. "I am so sorry, Louisa. I had no idea that you coming here would produce this kind of situation. All I wanted was for you to come back..."

Louisa lifted her tear streaked face and looked into his beautiful blue eyes. "There is no need for you to be sorry. You have been nothing but kind to my father and me. I didn't want to come here at first but I am glad I have. I am bewildered as to why I have stirred the anger of someone to want to do this to me, let alone Elspeth. I want to clear my name but someone doesn't want that to happen, I fear. I have been here but a day. Perhaps I should go home and forget about re-entering society."

As if hearing her thoughts, her father entered the room, announced by Ramsay. Her father came to kneel in front of her as well. Chalanor could see the concern on his father's face. And he too was weakening seeing her tear stained face.

"Father, I think I should go home..."

"But why, Louisa," he looked at Chalanor. "Can you please explain, sir?"

Chalanor with the help of his father explained their concerns and the manner of the accident. He watched as Louisa sat quietly absorbing the information as she heard it again. Finally, her father intervened.

"I know it was a terrible accident and how scared and confused you must be but Elspeth will recover. Thank God, it was not as bad as we first imagined. She will survive and perhaps she could use your company over the next few weeks as she recovers?"

Chalanor seized on the chance Louisa's father had provided. "Louisa, it would give me the greatest pleasure if you would stay and help Elspeth. She cannot be moved for some time. And I need to find out who did this to you and her. They must not be allowed to try again."

"But if I leave…"

Her father shook his head. "You cannot leave. If someone is trying to hurt you, I want to know who. Chalanor and his father and I will not allow anyone to get near you again. You cannot allow what they did to Elspeth to occur to anyone else let alone yourself. I want you to stay. I want you to stop hiding."

"Father, I am not hiding." She paused and picked up the sherry and took a sip. "I understand why you think that I have been. I want to stay and be with Elspeth but you have already seen there are those who find my being here distasteful. Is it safe for Elspeth if I stay to keep her company? She might again get in the way of whoever is doing this. I could never forgive myself if anything else should happen." She looked at each of the faces of the men before her and Chalanor hoped she could see how determined they all were.

"I promise you that you will never again be placed in a situation where anyone can hurt you. One of us will always be with you. I will have one of my footmen outside Elspeth's door from this moment on, and another not far away from you as well." He turned to his father. "I will have some of my staff sent from my estate. I know they can be trusted." He turned to look at Louisa. "I had no idea this would happen but I really do believe you need to come back into the society you were taken from. We must stop whoever it is who is doing this. Please allow me to protect you and help you to achieve that goal."

14

The room was beginning to lighten. Louisa drew in another deep breath and turned on to her back. She was surprised that she had slept at all but she had, deeply and was glad of it. The shock of hearing Chalanor, her father and Lord Faradays' words and of witnessing Elspeth's accident, had made her believe that she would be deprived of much needed sleep. She lay in bed believing that the previous day was already part of some dream she had not woken from. Last night when she had gone to bed, she had almost immediately fallen into a deep dream filled sleep. Now she lay in her bed still dreaming, but this time of possibilities she had not given thought to for some years.

Chalanor was concerned for her. Even his father was concerned. Did he have feelings that went beyond mere friendship? It seemed so. He called her "my dear" several times and she had not heard him use those endearments on any other lady.

What to do? She was changing her mind about him. He was different. He was not the same man she knew a few years ago. Could he have changed so much? Perhaps he was not the demon she had envisaged him to be when she first arrived. A knock at her door disturbed her contemplation. Her maid Alice came in and went to the window to open the curtains.

"Are you awake, Miss?" she asked quietly.

"Yes Alice. I have been for a few minutes."

"Your father, Miss, has asked if you would come to speak with him after you have breakfast. I have taken the liberty Miss, to have your breakfast brought here to your room."

"That would be wonderful, Alice. I'm not ready to face the crowd downstairs. Can you prepare my yellow muslin for this morning?"

"Yes, Miss."

"And I will also wear my mother's pearls." Alice went over to the drawers to get them out.

"They are so lovely," rattled off Alice. "Your mother must have lovely taste."

"Actually, my father gave them to my mother on the day they were married. I wear them as often as I can. My mother passed away some time ago. The pearls remind me of happier days and of her."

Alice handed her the box with the pearls in them.

"Oh, Miss. I am sorry about your mother but wearing them for her? That is a lovely thing. They must be expensive."

"No, actually they are not. My father could not afford the perfect ones. These have imperfections but they are beautiful none the less. They might not be extravagant but they mean everything to me."

At that moment another staff member brought in her breakfast and laid it on the table near the window. Alice helped her into her dressing gown and promised to return to help her dress after she finished her breakfast. Louisa promised to ring for her. Holding the pearls in her hand she gazed at them thinking of her mother and then placed them around her neck.

Louisa was content. Her mother's pearls helped her maintain

what strength she had and for what she might need in the coming days. Her fingers ran over them. Her mother loved her and her father also did. Getting her life back might bring love but on that she placed no hope. She had to get through the difficulties of what was to come.

---

*L*ouisa entered the library. Her father was standing at the window, his hands cupped behind his back. She remembered her mother saying *he was the most handsome of men* and she could see that he still was a tall and solid man, healthy and strong. His hair was greying a little, from his usual light brown. He turned to see her enter and then looked back out of the window. Handsome, yes, he was still a handsome man, and she could at that moment understand how her mother had fallen in love with him. His brown eyes were his main attraction and she had inherited his eyes. Something else her mother always said popped into her mind. That he was *more handsome every time she looked at him especially when she looked into his eyes*. Oh, and how mother would stare into his eyes. She went and stood beside him waiting patiently for him to begin.

"After our concern for you last night I wanted to tell you why I trust Chalanor and why I want you to stay. Not just for your sake and Elspeth's but for what could be. As you know we were in Brussels together, Chalanor and I." Louisa went over to the chaise, and sat down. She looked up into her father's concerned face.

"You know that I was heartbroken when your mother died and although you suffered from what Prescott had done to you, I wanted and needed to help the Prince. My only fear was leaving you alone." He came and sat next to her and leant back into the chaise. "Chalanor was appointed to me directly by the Prince and we spent a great deal of time together. Together, we ended up sharing our concerns with each other. His was for the way he treated you and me for being away from you." Louisa was listening intently. "For us the main reason we wanted you here at this house party, was to right a wrong, hence, my insistence that you attend. And I could see that you were scared but you also wanted to come back into society. It would be easy to leave right now. Some would even think it sensible. But Elspeth will need you. And there may not be another opportunity for you to come back into society, if Lady Farraday has anything to do with it. And I believe Chalanor has a deep affection for you which will help you regain your position. I don't want you to leave."

She wrapped her arms around her papa.

"Yes Papa. I feel the same now. I have slept well and know that I cannot leave Elspeth nor allow myself to be haunted by the events. I also know that you, Chalanor and his father will do all in your power to protect me."

For the next few hours they stayed together in the library talking. It allowed her to share some inner thoughts. No guests disturbed them. She assumed that Chalanor had made sure of that. Louisa was impressed at the lengths he went to, not only to give her father and her time to talk but also, she believed, to impress her. A footman was placed outside the library door and another on the door that led into the garden. No one disturbed them.

Later in the morning, Louisa left her father so she could spend some time with Elspeth. Elspeth was tired but they spoke briefly, going over the events of the afternoon before. Neither of them could work out any reason for such an attack on either of them. Louisa continued to wonder if Chalanor might be mistaken in his theory.

Poor Elspeth was still in a great deal of pain and slept most of the time Louisa stayed with her. That time enabled Louisa the opportunity to think of the many things that she and her father had talked about. She now had a chance to regain some of what she had lost. Her father's being away in Brussel's, though it caused them both pain, had helped her to become the independent lady she was today. She had developed her skills in running the household and not needing to make decisions with her father. She had managed to come out of the pain she had been in without the help of others on the most part. Elspeth had helped as they wrote to each other and maintained the friendship they had both needed. Now her confidence was high. Could she gain her place back in society? It was at her fingertips.

Her friends, Elspeth and Freddie had remained loyal to her and she had won over some of the other guests. Chalanor had opened his home and even his father had made her welcome. Her only concern now was the attitude of some of the other guests and Lady Farraday. She would also talk it through with Elspeth when she was feeling better. She knew she could trust her opinion.

As for the attempt on her life, she was sure it was just an accident, despite the cut girth strap. Perhaps one of the stable boys had damaged the strap by accident? Surely there was no reason for anyone to hurt her? She was a threat to no one. Her wealth was insignificant to most of the other people at the house party. So, she tried to convince herself there was nothing else to worry about. Deep down her concern was for her friends and mainly Elspeth. She did not want them in the way of a possible enemy if there was one.

15

At afternoon tea many of the guests talked with Louisa to see how Elspeth was doing. She was glad. To Louisa, it appeared no one guessed the accident was anything but an accident. It was also obvious that Chalanor was not allowing anyone to see Elspeth except her and Freddie. Chalanor was true to his word in regard to protecting Elspeth. A footman was stationed outside Elspeth's room at all times of the day and night. This eased her thinking and convinced her to remain at the manor to help Elspeth as best as she could.

After tea, Louisa chose to flee the confines of the house for a few hours and headed towards the garden paths. Fresh air and sunshine would make her less tired and more rested. She smiled to herself as she saw a footman following her into the garden, keeping a discreet distance. A further example, that Chalanor would protect her. She made a mental note to thank him for his kindness next time they saw each other.

It was there in the garden that Chalanor caught up with her. "Miss Stapleton, Louisa, may I walk with you?" He gave her a small bow.

"Certainly," Louisa replied, surprised to see him. She curtseyed. He had kept his distance at luncheon and she assumed he was giving her time to digest the myriad of revelations she experienced in the last twenty-four hours.

"How is Elspeth, to your eyes?"

"She is still in much pain and I do hope that she will be over the worst after the doctor comes again this afternoon." They slowly moved toward the lake. Louisa lifted her face to the sky and for a moment, stopped walking and closed her eyes. The warmth penetrating her bones was blissful. She opened her eyes and admired the beautiful blue sky. Summer was warm in Kent and she was thrilled to be here enjoying it. The blue reminded her of the eyes of the man standing silently beside her. She looked at him and he turned and smiled at her. They continued to walk in silence for a while before Chalanor chose to speak.

"Is it too soon for me to share with you my part in the Prescott matter?"

Louisa stopped walking and dared not look at him. A thousand insects suddenly inhabited her stomach. She did want to listen to his explanation but also feared his role in the matter. She so wanted to believe he was the exceptional man her father believed him to be and she hoped he would be.

"My apologies, Miss Stapleton, it is obviously too soon." He bowed to her again and turned to walk away.

"No sir, I mean no Chalanor, it is not too soon." She chose her words carefully. "You took me by surprise, tis all." She looked at him, willing him to turn around and see she was sincere. She was twisting her hands. "I do not want to hold on to my own thoughts because I can see now how wrong I have been. I misjudged you. I would like to know your thoughts."

He turned to face her, his features giving her no indication how he felt. "May I escort you to the rose rooms? It is a beautiful day and the rooms are quite private for our discussions."

She nodded.

He came and took her hand placing it on his arm so as to guide her to the eastern end of the house where the rose rooms lay. They did not speak. The footman she noticed, came with them but continued to keep a discreet distance. As they came to the eastern side of the house, she could see the beautiful red Elizabethan bricks from the original manor. They had been reused to build the walls around these impressive gardens she had heard him speak of. But until now she had not visited them.

Turning into the outside room, she discovered the most glorious place she had even seen. To walk into a bricked garden filled with rose bushes was like walking into a room full of cut flowers. The scents were at first overpowering. But it drew her into the enclosed space. Sweet, subtle hints of cinnamon and mint. She stood for a moment breathing it in. Chalanor had paused too, she assumed, to allow her to take in the wonder she saw and could smell. But now he gently escorted her down the path. Passing different bushes her senses were overwhelmed by new aromas. Tea roses, strong lavender and subtle sandalwood. She loved her garden at home and especially her roses. She had all but ten rose bushes and she spent as much time as she could, pruning, weeding and cutting the beauties for the house. Now she stood in a garden almost entirely dedicated to the flower she loved. The experience was intoxicating.

They moved to a seat up against the rear wall and sat down. The footman stayed at the entrance to the garden, his back toward them, preventing anyone else from entering the area. She noted Chalanor was again immaculately dressed. The green of his jacket was perfectly in tune with the outdoor room in which they sat. The silence had gone on long enough and she decided she must speak first.

"Please tell me what happened that night. Did you know?" She looked up at him.

He turned his head to look into her eyes. "On my life, Louisa, I had no idea what Prescott had planned. If I had known I would never have escorted you to that room. I felt he did not love you but I had hoped your kindness and your gentle nature would tame him. I honestly believed that. I was very much mistaken in that hope."

Louisa closed her eyes to help her absorb the words he was saying. He had not known.

Thank God.

It meant more to her than she had imagined. He had not been part of the planning. She let out a deep sign not realising she had been holding her breath as she waited for the words he had said.

He continued. "I unfortunately was so disgusted with what he had done that I only wished for your father to take you away. I wish I had escorted you elsewhere. It was all I could do from stopping myself from wanting to beat him to a pulp. I was very angry. And if I had stayed, I would have. In fact, I still want to."

Louisa looked at him. She was not sure what to feel as she absorbed the information. "I am relieved to hear that. I understand your anger as much as I understand my humiliation. It is not right, a woman wanting to hurt anyone but I certainly would have liked to have beaten him up myself." He smiled, recognizing her attempt at lightening his mood.

He gazed over the bushes that spread out in the garden in front of him. She could sense that he was struggling with the events of that evening and how it all came about.

"You must believe me, I truly had no idea what to do for you. I placed you in the hands of your father as I believed you needed your family, at that point in time. I swore I would never step a foot near Prescott again and I never have." He took her hand into his and she allowed it.

"I want you to both believe and understand that."

"I do believe you. It would seem I have misjudged you. My

thoughts that you had helped him were unfair. I apologise." She listened to him breath out a sigh. He seemed relieved.

"As time passed, I realized the devastation you must have experienced that night. Your father later confirmed to me the doubts you held of me, believing me to be as cruel as Prescott. I would ask that you forgive my lack of feelings for you at that moment. Although I called him out as a liar that evening, his accusations took hold." He turned to face her again and Louisa quickly turned her head away.

"My sincerest apologies, Louisa, I did not want to add to the pain you have gone through. I had no intention to hurt you. Could I change time, I would have swept you up in my arms and carried you to safety. After your father took you away, I tried to explain. I declared him a brute, and a villain and revealed his foul nature to all who would listen. But I, too, was known as a rake and no one would believe what I said." He wiped away her tears as he looked deeply into her eyes. He waited for her to respond.

And she carefully considered her reply.

"I did hate you. Because I thought you were a part of what he had planned. I recognized almost immediately he had crafted the meeting to deliberately hurt me. I just could not understand why until much later. I am happy now to know that you were not a part of his scheming."

"Can we both from this moment on, go forward as if this event never occurred in our lives? That this is the first house party to which we have been invited and that we had never heard of Prescott? Truly Louisa, I would like that more than anything else, to put it all behind us."

He picked up her hand and kissed her fingers. The thousand insects in her stomach went on the rampage. She had always been attracted to him but had never allowed her crush on him to take hold. She now ached to touch her lips to his. Where that thought had come from escaped her. All she wanted at this moment was to spend the rest of the afternoon with Chalanor and longed for his kiss. Her life had taken a complete turn and at this moment she desired to be in the presence of a man, who she knew was socially beyond her reach. But still that is what she wanted.

"I would like to forget all but I am concerned, I have a reputation that might follow me regardless of the truths I now know." Louisa lowered her head again.

Chalanor lifted her chin gently, looking into her eyes. "Then we will rectify it together, if you will allow me?"

"I would like that but how? Too many do not know the truth. And how will they discover it? It may be more damaging if I declare it as untrue. It will become a woman's word against that of a powerful man." She wanted more than anything at this point in time to believe that he wanted to help her.

"I believe we can try. They can then see the real person and ignore the gossip. And may I add you have already won over several guests. They have already seen that you are both gifted and intelligent and perhaps not what they had imagined before. Talk with Elspeth when she is feeling better. She also may have some ideas. We all want what is best for you. We can do this. People will believe you."

He leaned toward her and repeated, "We can do this." He stood and took her by the hand and they walked the rest of the path through the garden. She clung to his hand, excited that her life was beginning to turn around.

---

*H*is lady love would not be at all happy about this change in feelings in Chalanor. What he heard from the other side of the brick wall was very disturbing. He had to make some plans so his love would not be angry when he told her. He would seek his lady love out tonight, slip into her bed and love her as passionately as he had the night before. Then he would tell her of his next plan to deal with Louisa and what he had just overheard. His true plan his lady would never know. That was for him alone.

Louisa had to be removed from every future picture with Chalanor. She belonged to him. How dare Chalanor take interest in the woman he wanted to devour? What he wanted was to hurt her, after slowly peaking his lust for her. Not that his lust for her wasn't already aroused, if he could only get her alone. No, that was too dangerous at the moment. Give it some time. When Chalanor was not on the alert? Then perhaps, it might happen? He would keep watching.

What he had just heard concerned him more. His lady would not want Chalanor anywhere near Louisa. That worked in his favour. Chalanor was obviously interested in the little chit despite his saying otherwise. She escaped his foolishness last time but his new plan, would see her crushed completely. Yes, kill her outright. That was the answer. If he could not have her no one else would. He turned to return to the house. No one must see him nearby.

16

"I am so glad you suggested we go for a ride," Freddie took in a deep breath. "Indoors was starting to get somewhat stifling."

"I agree Freddie, the weather is delightful. I feel like I could ride all day." Louisa also took in a deep breath of fresh air.

"You were not that excited about going for a ride an hour ago." Chalanor turned and grinned at her. She was looking beautiful. Her riding outfit had been cleaned after the other day and she almost sparkled. It was deep dark blue and her blond hair glistened under the matching hat. To say he was one of the happiest men alive was not a mere cliché. Only a week had passed since their time in the rose garden. If someone had told him he was in love with Louisa, but a week ago, he would have scoffed at them. But now he had to admit his feelings for Louisa were akin to love. He had never been so energised, so happy. Nor so thrilled to be in any lady's company as he did with Louisa.

"Thank you for the suggestion, Chalanor." She was grinning back at him. "I know I was reluctant but I am glad you convinced me." The spark between them was getting stronger the more time

they spent together. He was sure they were growing their friendship as well. She trusted him. He could feel that above all else.

"Let's gallop," intruded Frances. "Everyone can trot later. Let's
feel the wind in our hair."

"Thank you, Frances, but I am quite happy trotting. Galloping
can wait as far as I am concerned." Louisa smiled and hoped Frances
could sense she was not quite ready to go that far. The memory of
only a week ago was fresh in all their minds. Louisa hoped Frances
would reconsider. But Frances did not want to listen.

"Come on Chalanor, gallop to the next hedge with me."

"I am also quite happy to trot, Fran, perhaps another day."

She scowled, turned her horse in the direction of a faraway
hedge and began to gallop towards it.

"I will follow her Chalanor." Freddie added. "Watch over Louisa.
I will talk some sense into her and bring her back." He took off
after her.

In the quiet moment alone Louisa took the opportunity to
speak with Chal. "Both Elspeth and I appreciate the care you have
taken to watch over us. I can see my footman is not with us at the
moment. Why is that?" Her smile took his breath away. Seeing her
this relaxed and content gave him more joy than any thanks that
she could verbally give him.

"I am with you and the poor man needed a rest." She laughed
out loud and he joined in the mirth.

"I really am very grateful." She continued. "More than I can say."

"I know but I am pleased to do what I can for you. And Elspeth."

He hoped that the desire to help her was obvious to her. At all
times she had been kept in view by someone he trusted. Her morn-
ings were spent with Elspeth, reading to her and keeping her
company. He had sent for some of his footmen from his own estate
to help keep an eye on the ladies. Two footmen were outside
Elspeth's door while both ladies were together. One remained

outside the door permanently, the other followed Louisa wherever she went even if she was walking with her father or himself.

The other two joined them and they continued the ride. As they went on, their conversation was full of their childhood experiences and adventures. They talked about everything, of farming, the old tower, even the political state of the nation. Chalanor did all he could to draw her into conversation so they could get to know more about each other. Their likes, dislikes, loves and hates. All that could bring them closer together. Though Frances was still trying to get his attention, he devoted as much attention as he could to Louisa.

Someone other than just himself was always nearby both to protect her physically but also her reputation. Those who bothered to observe his attentions could see that he was totally absorbed by Louisa. That included his mother and he knew she was not happy about it. He only included Frances in their rides to pacify his mother. Too soon they were heading back to the manor and luncheon.

*M*any of the guests took the time to talk to Louisa and for some getting reacquainted with her. Louisa was changing many preconceived opinions of her character. This she did by just being herself. That was what he had wanted her to do. Be herself. The evenings had been spent singing, playing games and cards, or listening to general conversation. They even had tried some country dancing. He had arranged with his father to have a small band of musician to come and play some of the popular dances. Most of all the guests loved to hear her sing and most evenings she obliged. His mother still avoided her but his father, out of the sight of his wife, spent time also getting to know the real Louisa. All the time Louisa was winning over many of the guests.

Her voice alone had charmed the majority of them. Reverend Hutton was totally smitten by her voice often commenting on how much better it had developed and that it was angelic when he had known her years ago. He often called her angel and would sit with his eyes closed soaking up the heavenly sounds as she sang.

After luncheon Chalanor was seated in the library talking with his father. They had retired there to await the arrival of Louisa. They planned to walk in the garden together, his father chaperoning them.

"Well father, I won't deny it, I have feelings for Louisa that I am still trying to fathom for myself. So, I ask you please not to mention this to mother. I want to be sure before I make any declaration."

"I understand completely, my boy. Your mother is determined for you to marry someone whom she would choose. And Miss Stapleton would not be her choice. I, however would have you marry for love. I will admit to you now, my boy, that which I believe you have already determined. I married your mother for her beauty. She truly was the most beautiful girl that season. She had everyone eating out of her hand. I was convinced she loved me as much as I loved her."

Chalanor did not make a sound. He waited patiently for his father to continue. They had been close over the years, spending as much time together as they could. They had also talked about many and varied topics. But he had never heard his father speak in such an open manner before about his mother. He was opening his heart, something he had rarely seen or heard. His father walked over to the glass panelled door that led to the garden.

"We married quickly and it was not until you were born that I saw your mother was not the same sweet girl I had married. She was angry all the time and kept me at a distance. As you grew, I spent more time with you than I did your mother. She despised me and I could never determine what I had done."

He was looking through the glass of the door but he believed his father had travelled back in time to those early days. He was distant and absorbed in his thoughts. After a moment he continued,

"I would want for you, a truly wonderful love match. So, take your time and get to know her. Get her to talk about her interests and desires if you can. It is not hard to cover those real emotions if you are both interested in each other. Right now, I see sweetness and light in her but make sure it is true and not a display to trap you. For you I would want a partner that you could not only love but respect. Someone, who will partner you in the desires of your own heart as well as her own."

Chalanor had long known there was no love between his parents. He had been an only child in truth. His mother had given his father an heir. She had openly said he had his heir but she had no intention of giving him a litter. But she had a sexual appetite that did not include his father. Her reputation with other men was known to most of the ton but politely ignored in respect of his father. His sister, he was certain, had come from one of these liaisons. His father had loved the girl anyway and had doted on her. When his sister had found out the truth at sixteen years of age, from a well-meaning relation, she had run away from home. Despite his own and his father's efforts to find her they never did. She had vanished literally from the face of the earth. That had been four years ago. Chalanor felt it strange that even he had been born from the union.

"I promise you, Father, that I will be very sure. Thank you for your honesty. I do appreciate your wisdom in this matter." Chalanor came to stand next to his father.

"Well my boy we all have to learn from our experiences." He lifted his hand and placed it on his son's shoulder. "I will leave as you contemplate what I have said. I will be awaiting you both at the front of the manor."

Lord Farraday slowly turned from the glass and glanced at his son and then left the library. Chalanor appreciated that his father allowed him a moment to think about Louisa. Could they end up being truly in love with each other? Chalanor hoped so.

Louisa would be arriving at the library any moment. Chalanor spent the next ten minutes gazing out of the window and wondering what his future would hold. The library door suddenly opened and his father re-entered.

"Your mother's on the war path, son. You need to be concerned. The ball she had planned for this evening is not going well. Two more of the guests and their daughters are leaving this afternoon. Your constant attention to Louisa is driving them away, so says your mother."

Chalanor sighed. "Father, she has to stop meddling."

"That's fine by me Chal, but your mother wants you to pay these other girls some attention. I wanted to come and tell you immediately because she is on her way here. She was ranting and raving in the morning room and I walked straight into it. So, after our earlier conversation, I rushed back to let you know. Can I suggest that you spend some time with your mother this afternoon? Calm her, tell her you will spend some time with her examples of womanhood." He gave himself a little shake. "I will take your Louisa for a walk around the gardens. It will allow me the opportunity to get to know her better. I will bring her father with us. He is in fact waiting at the front of the building for you anyway. I was about to join him when I came across your mother. Do not be concerned. I am sure we will have a jolly time."

"Very well, Father. But I will join you after I have talked with mother for a while."

His father turned to exit the room but he hesitated. He turned back to face him. "Tomorrow my solicitor is coming from London and we are going over some paper work. I will keep your mother busy with me so that you can have some more quiet time with Louisa." He looked out the window toward the garden. "You know my boy, you could say, that I backed the wrong horse."

Again, his father voiced his sorrow in his loveless marriage. It was a revelation he had never expected to hear from his father and now he had heard it twice in an hour. But it made him content to know the truth, yet sad a marriage that promised greatness had left nothing in its wake. He smiled at his father. "I think you might be correct, Father."

Lord Farraday nodded and continued toward the door, just as Ramsay the butler opened the door to announce his mother. Her pompous display made both men cringe. His father bowed toward her and left the room. Chalanor put on a pleasant smile and greeted her with a kiss on her cheek.

"Chal, we need to talk."

"Of course, Mother. Would now be convenient?" She looked at him with surprise then looked at the door his father had just gone through. She returned her gaze to him.

"I thought you had little time for me. I have seen little of you this last week. Why the sudden change of heart?" she asked.

"Now Mother, I have had to keep my eye on many of the guests and I am also making sure that Elspeth is being looked after."

Before she could respond Ramsay opened the door again and announced Louisa. His father came in right behind her.

"Ah Louisa, would you do me the honour of accompanying me around the rose garden? I understand you have a great fondness for the flower?" His father declared before Chalanor could welcome her. "It seems these two have some words to share."

"Of course, Lord Farraday, I would be delighted." Louisa's smile was soft and there was a definite hint of curiosity gleaming from her eyes. She curtsied at Lady Farraday and Chalanor. She took his father's offered arm and they left.

Chalanor turned to his mother ready to face the onslaught. She did not disappoint.

"How can you do this to me?" She hollered. "Disgrace me in front of all my friends with that trollop."

Chalanor took a deep breath and held it for a moment. He looked at his mother. "You have not taken five minutes Mother, to get to know Louisa. If you had you would see that..."

She did not allow him to finish.

"I know all I need to know about that sort of girl. She is not for the company of good society."

"Mother, this is old ground. You know full well that Prescott fabricated the slurs on Louisa's character."

"That girl has no character. Now Frances, there is a woman with character."

Chalanor was unable to hold his tongue as his mother raved. He did not want to argue but also did not want Frances thrust at him again. He had had enough of her meddling.

"Mother, Frances is not a woman but a sulky girl who whines when she does not get her way. I do not want to speak ill of any woman but let me make it perfectly clear to you Mother, I will not be marrying Frances or any other woman you put in front of me. When I marry it will be for love. Do you understand me?"

"You cannot be serious. You have no idea what love is. It is over-rated, I can tell you. You need breeding, good conduct and a woman who will care for you as I have cared for you all your life." She fixed her gaze on him. "If you marry that dirt, I will have you disinherited. Do you understand me?"

Chalanor took a step toward her. He was not going to be intimidated by her any longer. "Madam, let me make it perfectly clear. I have at this moment no intention to marry. Do you understand me? As for inheritance, you do not have that power nor will my father allow it." Chalanor paused at that thought remembering the words his father had said about the lawyer coming. He decided to argue down a different path as he did not want to pursue that revelation.

"I do not need this estate as I have my own, as you well know. Thanks to your mother who did not trust you with it." He knew he was being spiteful but could not let his mother continue. He would fight her if she intended to present her ideas of womanhood in front of him.

"Be careful my boy, do not argue with me. I have more power than you give me credit. You will do my bidding or you will regret it."

"No madam. I will not do your bidding and if you threaten me, beware." Chalanor was appalled at the level to which his mother now sank. She set her cold stare on him and fear ran down his back that chilled him.

"She will never marry you. I will see to that." Her words held a cold threat. There was no denying it. There was an almighty crash. Then a woman's scream penetrated the room.

"Louisa."

His mother stood before him, her arms crossed and a smile on her knowing face. No shock, no surprise. My God, what had she done? Chalanor turned and fled the room.

---

*L*ouisa was a little disconcerted at the sudden change of plans but happily walked out the front door of the manor with Lord Farraday. At the bottom of the steps her father was waiting for her.

"Louisa, is not the weather delightful? We have had so much sun. It truly is another beautiful day."

"Yes, Papa, the weather is truly wonderful." She smiled at her father as she made the final steps toward him.

"I say Farraday, shall we walk together? I assume that Chalanor has been delayed?"

"Sir Peter," he gave a gentle bow, "my thoughts exactly! Chalanor will join us later. He is having a discussion with his mother."

Sir Peter gave a knowing smile and nodded to Lord Farraday.

"Then we had best be on our way and leave them to their discussions. I can imagine how interesting they will be."

Both men offered their arms to Louisa and she grinned at them both. It was a delight to be among relaxed and happy spirits. Taking hold of both offered arms, they slowly walked to the corner of the mansion chatting about the birds, the sunshine and the beauty of the estate. As they reached the corner, they all turned to the direction of the drive to see a curricle coming toward the house.

"Are you expecting more guests, Farraday?" her father asked.

"Not that I am aware of. We have had departures but I know of no arrivals."

They stood patiently waiting for the curricle to arrive.

"Do you hear that grinding sound?" Louisa asked looking around her trying to determine where the sound was coming from.

"'Tis but the crunch of the wheels on the drive," replied her father.

But Lord Farraday was looking around. He seemed confused. He looked up and shouted out "move" and pulled Louisa and her father away from the house. One of the ornamental urns that were positioned on the top corners of the mansion crashed at their feet spraying stone and debris in all directions.

Louisa screamed as she landed atop her father. Lord Farraday landed on the ground next to them. She turned and tried to get up. She looked at the gentleman descending the curricle but a few feet away. He was rushing toward them.

"What the hell are you doing here?" her father demanded. It was Prescott.

She fainted into her father's arms.

17

C halanor came charging down the front steps looking right and left. He ran to the corner of the mansion where the dust was still settling around the still form of Louisa's body lying in her father's arms. He ran and pushed a man out of the way to get to her.

"Steady on." Prescott said.

He knelt next to her and ran the back of his hand over her pale forehead. He had already failed her. He could not believe he had failed her. He wouldn't believe it. Chalanor looked at his father.

"What happened?" he demanded.

"She has fainted, that is all, calm yourself. She screamed, after I pulled her out of the way, and then fainted when she saw him." Lord Farraday glared at Prescott.

Louisa had small scratches on her face he assumed from the debris of the urn smashing to bits. He couldn't see any major blood flow.

Without taking his eyes off Louisa he asked, "What the hell are you doing here, Prescott?"

"I'm here by invitation of your mother. She thought it was high time we mended our friendship. I was inclined to agree."

"Get out of here." It was not a request.

Other guests were arriving to see what the commotion was about. Two of his footmen came running from the side of the mansion.

"Prescott, my dear boy how wonderful to see you." It was his mother greeting his and Louisa's enemy as if he was a long-lost friend. She had positioned herself on the top step as if she was on a dais, holding court. Chalanor wanted to grab him and drag him away and beat him to a pulp. Instead he gently lifted Louisa up into his arms and carried her toward the house.

"Is that Louisa Stapleton?" Prescott asked as he followed Chalanor to the steps.

"Yes, it is." replied Lord Farraday.

"As you are very well aware," added Sir Peter. Both men followed Chalanor into the house leaving an array of confused guests and servants.

Lady Farraday swanned over to Prescott placing her arm through his and turned him toward the manor. "Come and make yourself at home, Prescott. We have a lot to talk about."

Many of the guests were left standing, whispering among themselves, wondering what in the world they had just witnessed.

---

*H*e couldn't believe that he had missed the blasted girl again. It would have been wonderful to have taken all three of them out of his life. He had expected Louisa out for her usual walk with Chalanor. But to have Sir Peter and the Lord Farraday there was even better. It was not what he planned but if fate gave him that body count, who was he to question it? But he didn't even get what he wanted. He must have victory and he was determined to get it. Tonight, he would slip into his lady love's bed again and see what she had to say. She could not be angry because he knew what to do to turn her into his compliant lover. She would melt in his arms.

He was only concerned as to who the man in the curricle was. He didn't get a chance to see who it was. His lady love will know. He was sure she had something to do with it. He headed down the stairs, off the roof. He closed the door that led to the stairwell. Looking from side to side, he then turned around and walked toward the only person he could see, Louisa's maid Alice. She would keep her mouth shut. He would make sure of that. No one must know that he was on the roof.

He greeted her. "I have so enjoyed looking around the manor. I am glad you are here though, Alice, isn't it?"

"Yes, sir. What can I do to help you, sir?"

"This door was locked." He reached over to the door next to her and sure enough it was locked. "Can you show me what is inside?"

"Yes, sir. It is the old nursery and nanny's room." She took the keys from her pocket and unlocked the door. Opening it she stepped inside and stood to the left to allow him to come in.

He stepped into the room and closed the door, stretching his arm out to Alice. She seemed puzzled.

"Give me the keys."

For the first time a look of concern crossed Alice's face. His heart began to race. He was sensing the beginning of fear in this chase. He loved this and what it did to him.

"Is there a problem, sir? Have I done something amiss?" She handed the keys to him gingerly. He took them, turned around and locked the door. He swiftly turned back to Alice and grabbed her by her wrist.

"No, you have done nothing wrong." He lifted her hand and kissed the inside of her palm. "I want you tis all."

He held her firmly by the wrist and with his other arm pulled her closer into his aroused body.

"I beg your pardon, sir. You're hurting me sir." She began to struggle to get him to release his hold.

His grip on her waist became tighter and he smiled as the fear showed on her face. Closing his eyes, he breathed her in. She was clean and fresh despite having spent the morning cleaning. This was going to be grand.

"I want you." He reached up and ran his fingers down her cheek. He smiled at her. The smile sent fear through her body that he could feel. He felt every muscle in her body tighten. Small tears leaked from her eyes and he licked them away. Her fear was multiplying as he licked her. He could feel it all. He reached up took off her cap and watched as her hair fell to her shoulders. "What beautiful blond hair you have. I love blond hair. Now, you will do as I say or I will have you dismissed from this house, do you understand me?"

She nodded but continued to weep. He placed kisses on her neck and nibbled at her ears.

"Please don't hurt me sir." She pleaded but he did not listen. He continued with his instructions.

"You will not make a sound. Do you understand me? I am not going to hurt you but love you. Everything I will do to you will show you how much I love you." His left hand squeezed her breast as his right hand held her tightly around the waist.

He picked her up and took her to the bed in the corner. He knew he was safe here. They would not come looking for a culprit, believing that he was long gone. They would be fussing over that beautiful trollop Louisa. They would search eventually but he was safe behind this locked door. He laid her on the bed as she shook with fear. He took his kerchief from his pocket and put it in her mouth.

"You must be quiet. Do you understand?" She nodded again. He reached down and lifted her skirts. He ran his hand up her leg and she cried out but it was muffled by the kerchief in her mouth. She tried to push him away. He batted her hand aside. He took off her apron and tied it around her hands and then to the bed post. Tears were streaming down her face.

"You will do all that I say. I will have you for me and me alone. If you scream or resist me, I will kill you. Believe me." He ripped the front of her dress and he devoured her breasts first with his eyes and then with his mouth. She was crying harder. He slapped her face a number of times to quieten her. Surely, she had to see how wonderful it was that he had chosen her? He continued to devour her nipples with his mouth. Then he bit her hard on her right breast leaving his glorious mark. He was even more aroused by that action. He did that to all his victims, mark them as his. Her fear was all consuming and he loved to feel it vibrating through her body and into his. He could see that she felt the pain of his bite. She still sobbed, the stupid girl. She was lucky to have him. He got up and undid his trousers letting them drop below his knees. He knelt on the bed and looked at her. Fear was all he sensed. He had a powerful erection. She was so lucky.

"You will love me. Do you understand? I am wonderful, a man worthy of your affections. I will have you, my Louisa." He saw Alice's eyes widened in fear. She screamed, her cry muffled as he came down and thrust himself hard inside her. He continued to thrust becoming more elated as he took her. This was ecstasy. He called her Louisa over and over again and closed his eyes believing her to be beneath him. He ran his fingers through her blond hair and pictured Louisa's brown eyes in place of Alice's blue. He was so full of Louisa he wanted to scream. But he did not.

As his pleasure was sought, he took Alice's neck in his hands and wrung the life out of her. Harder and harder he pushed. Harder and harder he squeezed. Finally, he climaxed as she breathed her last. He lay on top of her breathless body for but a moment and then with relish, he suckled her breasts and took her again.

Before he left the room, he took his kerchief from her mouth and placed it back into his pocket. He straightened his clothes and smiled. That was glorious. He had outdone his love making this time. She was now one of his. He had been her first and rejoiced at what he had taken from her. Not just her maidenhead but her life. He looked back at Alice's body and smiled. "You are so lucky."

---

*I*t was almost quiet, but Louisa did not want to open her eyes. Because she knew she was not alone. Whispering voices travelled in the air. Someone was sitting beside her on the chaise. The heat from their body penetrated the coldness of her hips. Actually, her whole body was cold. Someone was holding her hand and gently rubbing it, trying hard she thought to make it warm. If she opened her eyes, she was afraid of just what or who would be in front of her. Would it be the disgusting face of Prescott, whom she had once adored? Would he be scowling down at her, belittling her and making her want to promptly close her eyes and run screaming from the room? She didn't know what to expect. So, she decided just to keep her eyes closed.

"Are you sure she was not hit by any large pieces of the urn?"

That was Chalanor. It was he who held her hand and sat with her. That calmed her somewhat. He was there to protect her from Prescott, wasn't he? He would this time surely? She mentally gave her head a shake. Where was Prescott? What on earth was he doing here? She had to get away from him as soon as she could.

Louisa slowly opened her eyes. She looked up into Chalanor's face and noted his eyes. Those beautiful blue pools filled with concern. He rubbed his thumb over the back of her hand.

"What happened?" she asked.

"That was what I was going to ask you. Are you hurt? Is there any specific pain that you can detect?" She could see that he was eager for her to respond.

Louisa let go of his hand and pulled herself up into a sitting position. Chalanor got up and placed a cushion behind her back and went back to sit beside her on the chaise. She was surrounded by concerned pairs of eyes, her father's, Lord Farraday's and Chalanor's. Prescott was not there. A deep sigh of relief left her lips.

Ramsay entered the room with a bowl of warm water and a cloth and came to stand near the chaise on which Louisa sat. Louisa suddenly remembered the urn and how close they had come to being crushed.

"I am sorry. Father, are you alright and Lord Farraday? That urn..."

"That urn my dear, came crashing down from the roof but I pulled you out of the way. I too heard the grinding noise and knew the sound was not coming from the driveway." Louisa breathed a little easier. "I am sorry if I hurt you but I did not want to see you or your father crushed." His voice was timid as if the shock of what could have happened was only now penetrating his thoughts. "Here my dear." He rinsed the cloth in the bowl that Ramsay held. He handed her the cloth. "Wipe your face. It will refresh you and make you feel better." She did so but Chalanor took it from her hand and began to clean her face for her. She gazed at him and then looked back to Lord Farraday.

"Lord Farraday. Thank you for saving my life." She was truly amazed that a man she thought despised her but a week ago actually saved her from the crashing urn.

"It is definitely a life I am glad has been saved, my dear."

Louisa stared up at him in total disbelief. She never expected to hear those words from his mouth. But she rejoiced that he had. She shook her head to clear it. Ramsay placed the bowl on the table next to her and left. She took the cloth from Chalanor and used it to wipe her hands. She noted the fine cuts and scrapes on her palms.

"Thank you." She turned to face Lord Faraday again. "Thank you also sir, for your kind words. However, it would seem that someone has not given up the chance to rid the world of me," she declared, trying to make light of the situation. She was terrified that someone had again tried to remove or hurt her. And this time they did not even care that it included her father and one of the highest Lords of the land. Any thoughts that the previous attempt was not levelled at her, fled.

Chalanor stood and began to pace the floor. It was clear to Louisa that he was holding on to his emotions, but only just.

"Rest assured it will not happen again. I have failed you twice but I will not let it happen again. I have no idea who could have done this. But I will find out. Believe me. But you will not leave my sight from this moment on. I will always be nearby to save you. Do you hear me?" He was angry but she could see that it was at the situation, not her. She wanted to reason with him to make him see sense. She smiled at him in an attempt to calm him.

"You did not fail me Chalanor. None of you have. You have saved me, all three of you. Please keep that in your thoughts. I am saved." She looked at each of them in turn. She paused to contemplate the enormity of the most recent events and Prescott came back to mind. And a tingle of fear raised its head. She needed to know why he was here.

"Prescott is here. This nightmare will never be over. He must have an ally here who is helping him. I know he has only just arrived so could not be involved in the accident that hurt Elspeth. But he could have had help, don't you think?" She was concerned. "There is no other explanation. He came as that urn crashed. He came to see me crushed surely. I have no choice. I must leave. I cannot allow him or anyone else to hurt me or any other innocent. You must see that?" She was desperate and hurt. Things were going so well and now all was dashed. Prescott would see that she was sent from the manor with her bags thrown out after her. "I am not a weak woman but I will not risk others." She placed her face in her hands and began to weep.

$\mathcal{T}$his would not do. He did not want Louisa losing heart. She was safe here despite the arrival of Prescott. He had to convince her.

"Prescott is here by my mother's invitation, and I am sure that my mother is up to something. But I don't believe she would stoop to hurting you so openly. I am not happy about her asking him here but she was with me when the urn fell. So, it could not have been her. I just can't imagine who could be plotting with her, nor if she is involved with Prescott and doing his bidding. Someone else had to have pushed that urn from the roof." Chalanor spoke softly. His anger had mellowed. He wanted her to see she was his responsibility now. He was desperately trying to keep his anger reined in. He came back to sit with her, taking her hand in his.

"Prescott will be kept away from you until we can rid ourselves of him." He sighed and then kneeling in front of Louisa, he declared, "I want you to stay. Will you?"

He watched her as she contemplated his words. He only hoped his face displayed the love he knew he had for her. He had to keep her by his side.

"My head hurts and not from any damage done to me by the urn but why Prescott would be here in the first place. Whoever wants to get rid of me is determined to place all the things that I dread most, in front of me. Why else would he be here? I am not sure how much more I can take."

"You are not leaving." Chalanor stood and stared down at her. "That is a declaration by the way. I will not let whoever it is beat you. You are too good to be banished from society again. We will show them. You and I."

"Chalanor, please see reason." It was Lord Farraday who spoke. "This person, whoever they are, is determined to do what it takes to hurt or kill her, even if it means that others might get in the way. The fact he has now tried on two separate occasions must convince you?" His father again was the voice of reason. But Chalanor did not want to listen to reason. He did not want Louisa always looking over her shoulder wondering when this madman would strike again. Whoever it was he was certain that the attacks would not stop and would follow her to wherever she was. She will never be free of this threat.

He bent down on his knee in front of Louisa again. He needed to convince her.

"I know this is terrifying. I have no knowledge of why someone would want to do this to you. All I do know is if you flee now, you will be running for the rest of your life. Never again will you be able to go where you will. Society will be closed to you. You will always be looking over your shoulder, waiting, wondering if they are still determined to hurt you or even kill you."

She sighed. He hoped his words had made a difference.

"You are right. I know we need to find whoever is doing this. But I am scared and I don't want anyone else to suffer as Elspeth has. Or what could have happened to my father and yours, all because they want to hurt me."

Her father also knelt in front of her and said, "I agree with Chalanor you must stay but we need a plan."

Chalanor turned his head to face him and said. "And so, we shall."

18

Louisa's world had become surreal. Nightmare, reality and daydream penetrated her thoughts. She was finding it hard to distinguish what was real, imaginary or only talked about. After discussions with the gentlemen in her life, and the plans on how to deal with her possible attacker she had retired to her room to rest. Her world had been turned upside down. She needed time to digest all that had happened and all they talked about. She rung for Alice but she had not come. She pushed that fact away and rested on the bed. When she was ready to dress for dinner and the ball, she called Alice again.

While she awaited Alice's arrival, she went to her drawer to get out her mother's pearls, ready to wear for the evening's event. She wanted her mother close to her tonight. They were not there. The box was but not the pearls. She searched all the draws and could not find them in any of them. Panic hit her. Where was it? And why was Alice taking so long? There was a knock at her door and although she expected Alice, she was surprised to see another one of the maids.

"I am sorry, miss. But we are not sure where Alice is."

Louisa went cold. Fear sped through her body. No not Alice. She ran from her room and demanded the footman, who was diligently waiting outside her door, to escort her to Chalanor immediately. Her anxiety must have been evident as he did not hesitate to take her to him. She needed to tell Chalanor what she feared. She started shivering.

---

*T*here was a tap at the door and then the footman, who was watching over Louisa, opened the door and announced Miss Stapleton wished to speak to him. Chalanor was dressing for dinner and he grabbed his coat and put it on as he came to the door. He greeted Louisa with a small bow.

"I am so sorry to disturb you but I need to speak to you about my maid."

"Alice? What is wrong?" He could see the fear on Louisa's face.

"She has disappeared."

Chalanor could see that Louisa was not only certain about her declaration but very upset. He took Louisa by her arm and guided her to a chair in front of the fireplace. He turned to the footman and told him to have the butler and the other servants meet him in the servant's dining room immediately. He did not need to question Louisa, he knew she was certain. It was as if he was in tune with her every thought.

"I want to go with you," she whispered.

"I will get the servants to check around the house for her. Don't fret Louisa. I am sure she will be fine."

"You don't understand. My pearls are missing also. But I don't think Alice could have taken them. This has something to do with the person who wants to hurt me. I just know it. I think Alice disturbed the person while they were trying to take my pearls.

They have hurt her. I know it." She was convinced that her instincts were correct.

"I am sure Alice could not do such a thing either. There must be an explanation. Now come with me and we will try and work this out." Louisa stood. He wanted so much to take her into his arms, but he resisted the urge.

He closed his bedroom door and escorted her toward Elspeth's room. She went inside and Chalanor followed her in.

"I will return shortly. Elspeth's footman will remain outside the room should you need him." With those words, Chalanor left the room. Louisa hated to be left out of the events happening around her, but the fear running through her at this moment encouraged her to listen to Chalanor. She was no coward but she wasn't foolish either.

"What on earth is the matter?" asked Elspeth. She was still in her bed and awake.

"I believe something terrible has happened to my maid." Louisa went over to the bed and sat down beside Elspeth.

"Don't be silly, Louisa. She probably is helping the other staff get ready for the ball tonight. Do you wish me to call my maid?"

"No. Thank you. No one has seen Alice. I just know something is wrong." She paused and looked into Elspeth's concerned face. "My pearls are missing also."

"Oh Louisa, I am sorry." Elspeth picked up her hand and held it. "It would seem your maid may have been a dishonest girl. She has probably stolen the pearls and fled. I am sorry."

"No, it can't be." Louisa pleaded. "Just think about it. She knew the pearls were not of any great value. I told her myself. It has to be something else. Alice is a good girl. It has to be some kind of trick or distraction. Perhaps from the very villain who tried to hurt me this afternoon?"

"Are you sure the pearls are not of value?"

"Of course, I am. My mother and father have told me the story of how he gave them to her. I have known it all my life. But that does not matter. Something has happened I just know it." Louisa turned her whole body to face Elspeth. "Truly, I can feel it."

"I believe you. I do understand. I am sure that Chalanor will find out what has happened. Maybe the maid thought you were lying about the pearls?" Elspeth suggested. Louisa let out a frustrated sigh. What could she say to get her friend to see what she truly meant?

"There are so many wealthy guests in the house. I am sure she could have found greater wealth in other rooms if she wanted to steal something. I just can't believe it. It feels wrong. It just goes against what I have seen of her. She does not appear to be a dishonest person. Besides, she has worked in the house since she was twelve years old. Other members of her family work here. Why would she choose to steal and run now?"

Elspeth shook her head. "I don't know. But don't let yourself get all undone. We'll just wait to see what Chalanor can find out."

Louisa breathed a little easier. Chalanor had immediately listened and acted on her concerns. He didn't doubt or question her. He just acted. That piece of information certainly made her feel better. But sitting here was not helping her at all. She wanted to know what had happened and where Alice was. She wanted to go and find Alice for herself. Louisa stood and began to pace the room.

*C*halanor could not believe Alice would have stolen from anyone in this house. She had grown up on the Estate and trained in the house and was always happy and helpful. But the evidence would indicate that is exactly what she had done. But he could not believe it. He would not. No one had seen her since the early afternoon. He had all the staff search all areas of the house and the outer buildings to see if they could find her. He was now standing in the upstairs corridor where she was last seen by the housekeeper, Mrs. Jennings, who was standing next to him. He did not want to believe Alice had gone and he did not want to believe she could have been hurt by the villain who was after Louisa. But his fear for her was growing as the minutes passed and she still had not been located.

"I sent her up here after luncheon, sir. Miss Louisa was going for a walk so I had sent her up here to clean the floors. It should have taken her only a few hours. She should have finished before afternoon tea. I gave her the keys so that she could do the floors in each room. The hall appears to have been done." Mrs. Jenkins was looking up and down the hall.

Chalanor glanced up and down the hall as well. Then, a cold shiver travelled down his back. At the far end of the hall was the door, the only door that led to the roof. Could Alice have seen the person who had pushed the urn off the roof? She would not have seen or heard the commotion from up here. But if asked, she would have known who had also been up on this floor. The villain would have known that, if he knew the house. And all indications were that he did know this house. There was no question. They would have to search each room on this floor. He dreaded what they would find. He walked to the end of the hall.

He opened the door to the roof but nothing seemed out of place at first glance. However, the floor was a little dusty and footsteps could be seen both going up the stairs and down again. The foot print looked like that made by a gentleman's boot. So, it had to be a man. Being the only entrance to the roof space he already deducted the urn was pushed off by someone who had come this way. He closed the door and then began to check each of the rooms one by one.

Mrs. Jenkins used the spare keys to open each room in turn. All were locked except the last one. The key was still inside the door.

He opened it slowly. The housekeeper who was standing next to him screamed. His eyes rested on the disfigured face of the maid Alice. She lay dishevelled on the bed in the far corner. In the fading late afternoon light, she looked like a broken doll.

He had seen too many dead bodies before. He lowered his eyes. Never had he expected to see death in his family home. Not like this. He placed his arms around the shoulders of the housekeeper and turned her away from the sight before them. They left the room and he closed the door. He hugged Mrs. Jennings. The poor woman was both weeping and shaking. The butler Ramsay, in response to the scream, was now coming up the corridor to him at a pace. Chalanor gave over the care of the housekeeper to the butler and asked that his father and Sir Peter be notified and sent to him.

He stood for a few minutes just staring at the door in front of him. He had no concept of time. All he thought about was death and dead bodies. Then his father and Sir Peter were standing by his side. Chalanor leaned over and opened the door.

"Alice has been murdered," and both men looked toward her body with disbelief etched on their faces. "We need to determine what happened." he continued. They walked over to where Alice's body was on the bed.

Chalanor saw the dead body *but his vision transported him back to fields covered in dead bodies. Men and horses. The stench of death and carnage. The confusion of coloured uniforms, and people wandering through the mess trying to bring order to a definite chaos or steal from the bodies of honourable men.*

"Dear God. How could anyone do this to another person? This villain is an animal." His father's voice seemed to be travelling from a great distance. Chalanor took a deep breath to bring his thoughts back to the room he was standing in.

He stared at the small area of chaos that lay in front of him and tried to make order from it. It looked like she had been hit about

the face several times and strangled. Her clothing was out of place
and screwed up. The front of her dress had been ripped revealing
her naked chest. Her right breast had a terrible bite mark, all
bruised and red. It looked as if blood had been drawn from the bite.
He was sure she had been taken advantage of, but by whom? He
went to the other bed in the corner of the room and took off the
cover. He brought it over and covered poor Alice's body. He had to
give her some dignity. A family on their estate would be broken-
hearted and devastated to know what had happened. The murderer
had made no attempt to hide what he had done. Now he needed
not only to protect Louisa but avenge the death of an innocent.

"*L*ouisa, I am sorry but you were right. We have just found
Alice and I am afraid she is dead." He allowed a few
moments for that information to penetrate her mind. She
looked at him in total disbelief. "It would appear that she has been
murdered." Chalanor did not know what else to say. There was no
way he could break this news to her in any other way. He stared at
her. Helpless. Wondering what it was he could say or do, to bring
her comfort. There was nothing. He knew she had imagined the
worst, and was now having to face the truth.

Louisa sat back onto Elspeth's bed. Elspeth began to cry. He had
only been gone for about an hour. He had known Louisa was right,
Alice would never have stolen her pearls. Alice's family had been
part of the estate for generations. She loved her work and was
overjoyed when he had asked her to be Louisa's personal maid.
Louisa's instincts and his own had been correct. But right now, he
would do anything to be wrong. Alice was dead, her family
distraught and Louisa in total shock. She sat on the bed in front of
him, pale as a ghost, unable to voice the pain she now felt.

"We don't know by whom. But I would say that she disturbed

the man or men who had pushed the urn off the roof this afternoon. She was in the wrong place at the wrong time."

"She was my maid. Is that a coincidence?" Louisa pleaded.

"Yes, to me it feels she was just in the wrong place. That is all. I wish that it were not true. The villain I believe, after disposing of her chose to confuse things by going to your room and taking your pearls. He knew Alice would not be there. Perhaps he wanted to delay the finding of her body and to put the scent of other persons into the picture. It probably thrilled him to implicate you, even if you are not involved." He was again kneeling in front of her.

"He probably thought you were dead. I doubt he would have looked to see that the urn had crushed you or not, in case someone may have seen him in return." He took her cold hands and rubbed them. "Louisa, my dear, please believe me. She would have recognized who had come down from the roof. She was working near the only door that led there. She could have identified who had tried to kill you. He had to silence her."

"You seem sure it is a man? What makes you so certain?" He knew she was thinking of his mother. They would have been his first thoughts too.

"I saw footprints in the dust on the stairs from the roof. They were from a gentleman's boot." He did not want to tell her he also believed Alice was raped by the villain. He wanted to give her enough information to help her feel she was being kept abreast of the whole situation. But he still wanted to protect her.

"This is my fault." Louisa looked at him with empty eyes. Then she fell into his waiting arms and wept. He picked her up, then turned and sat on the bed himself still holding her tightly, allowing her to weep. Elspeth also wept and he looked at Elspeth. There was nothing he could say or do. He closed his eyes. He had just given the woman he loved the worst possible news. He only hoped she would forgive him.

19

"You cannot be serious. Cancel the ball, at such short notice? Are you mad? I will be disgraced, made a laughing stock." Lady Farraday stood there with her arms crossed and made it clear to Chalanor that she would broker no excuse.

"Mother, for once in your life, can you think of someone other than yourself? Our staff are distressed. One of their own has been murdered and in this house and most probably by one of our guests or one of their servants."

"Don't be ridiculous, she was only a servant. She probably had a lover, a villain who got her to steal that girl's pearls and then he killed her and ran off with them." He watched as she paced back and forth, like a caged animal.

"Mother, I will say it again. Two attempts have been made on Louisa's life and now her maid is killed and Louisa's pearls stolen. Someone was trying to discredit, even kill Louisa. It isn't you, is it?" She stopped and stared at him as if he were mad.

"Now, I know you have lost your mind. I do not like her. In fact, I will go as far as to say I hate her. But I have not made my opinions a secret. I have ridiculed her to her face. She knows what I think of her and so do you. I do not need to resort to the dramatics nor dare I say murder. I would not dirty my hands on her. She is not worth the energy. And good servants are hard to find."

She walked over to Chalanor and put her finger to his head. "I think, young man that you have let her get into your head and it has spoilt your intelligence." She lowered her hand and turned away from him. "Do what you have to do for this evening. I wash my hands of it." She looked at her husband. "You can deal with the complaints. This is your responsibility not mine. I will be in my room for the rest of the evening and I do not want to be disturbed. Do you understand?"

With that his mother left the library not waiting for any reply or response. She slammed the door.

"I believe it is safe to say my boy, that your mother is not very happy." Under normal circumstances he would have been laughing with his father at the irony.

"Yes sir, I believe that is obvious but it needed to be said. If she is involved in some way, even helping Prescott, she needs to know I plan to find out who has been doing this. If she is involved, trust me I will find out."

"I agree. She needed to be placed on notice. At least we can cancel the ball. I will deal with that. Do you think Prescott is involved?" He came over to stand next to his son.

"I just don't know. Prescott arrived as the urn fell so he didn't do it but I don't know if he has a friend here helping him. I can't work out who could be involved." He looked at his father unsure of what else he could say. His father chose to change the topic.

"Son, I want to speak with you. Now seems the best time. Tomorrow my lawyer arrives and I really believe your mother is more interested in his coming than anything else."

"Why is that, Father?" Chalanor looked at his father not sure what information he could get from him if any. A cold dread settled in his guts despite the distractions of the day.

"I will tell you after he has come, if you don't mind. I don't want to put your mother off and I don't believe she wants you to be aware of his coming or why." He put his hand on Chalanor's shoulder. "Don't be concerned. I will keep her busy for some time. Then later you and I will talk and I will tell you all. Believe me, I will tell you all."

Chalanor watched as his father turned and left the room. Normally, words like that would have raised concern for him but he was sure his father would make him aware of whatever it was his mother was up to, in due course. His strength of character, often displayed away from his mother, convinced him he would tell all. He was not the only person who had changed in the last week. His father had also.

What concerned him now was his mother and what she might do. Chalanor could not believe his mother, though ruthless in all she did, could be part of this. It was beyond imagining. He began to pace backward and forward before the fire place.

Besides she was in the library with him when the urn fell.

So, she could not have done it. She would have had to have a man with strength to move that urn. And poor Alice was taken advantage of so it has to be a male. But who could it be? If mother was involved, was it her current lover? He had to find out who he was. Perhaps his father was aware who she was with? His mother was many things but an accomplice to murder?

"*I* am glad that the evening's plans were cancelled." Lady Farraday fondled the pearls around her neck. "I love your gift. I know where you got them and it does give me a wonderful degree of pleasure to know they are now in my possession and not in hers." She cuddled closer to him.

"I thought you would enjoy that." He said as he nuzzled her bare breasts. "And I am glad you enjoyed what I just did to you." He nibbled at her nipples and then kissed his way to her neck and his pearls.

"Oh yes," she moaned. "And I am so very ready for you to do it all over again. But I want you to promise me something?"

"What is it, my love?" he purred as he continued to lavish his mouth around her neck.

"No more killing. I know she was just a servant but they can be so hard to find."

"She saw me come from the roof. I had no other choice."

She moaned again. "I am sure Chal thinks I am involved. If anyone finds out what you do to me here... Well, they might make a connection. No one knows what we do here together at the moment. Of that I am certain. So, whatever you're planning for Louisa...just keep away from her for a time. Do not try to do anything to her for a while. That way Chalanor won't suspect anything or any connection. He will see them as just accidents."

She moaned even more loudly as he made his way down her stomach and to the private oasis of their love. She had told him she never allowed any man but him to be as intimate as this. He relished that news because it confirmed she was a liar. Her exploits were well known in the society of men like him.

She was soon back on topic. "I hope to use Prescott to put the slut back in her place and that might rid us of her for good. Will you do that my darling, for me? Leave her alone? Let me try my plan."

He was so sexually alive he would have agreed to anything. So, he did. But he had no intention of doing as she wanted.

"I will, my love. I only wanted to rid her from your presence. You know that I would do anything for you but now I must have you."

"You will?" she moaned yet again. "Wonderful. Then fill me my darling, over and over again, hard, the way we both like it."

He took her hard but thought only about Louisa and dreamed of the day he would do it to her. He remembered the pure bliss he felt when he took Alice. God, he was so excited. They both cried out in the ecstasy of the moment but for totally different reasons. The lady had no idea he used her for his own means and pleasure. She cared for no one just like he cared for no one. But he did care. He did not care for her. He cared only for Louisa.

After they had finished, they laid in each other's arms, and he contemplated what he promised. He had no intention of doing what the lady begged of him. He had his own agenda. He would watch and wait for his lady's sake. That would allow her time to fail in her own plans and perhaps even get caught. That would distract everyone and then he could finally have Louisa to himself. But when he got the opportunity, he was going to physically take Louisa and enjoy every moment. He had worked out another plan. He would keep her alive, after all. The fates had protected her so he could get what he wanted. He wanted to see her reactions and fear as he took her. Every detail of her face as he filled her. Taking that stupid maid had convinced him of that. Louisa would die and by his hand, but not until he was satisfied the only way he knew and had taken all of her for himself.

20

The ball was cancelled and the guests were either turned away when they arrived or fed and housed till the next day. The local magistrate was sent for but whoever killed Alice was a total mystery. Servants and guests where questioned but no one saw or heard anything other than the commotion of the falling urn. Many of the guests chose to escape this particular house party and ball, the first chance they got. They were not convinced Louisa was the target and they believed any of them could be attacked at any moment by some mad man.

The next day Louisa spent the morning with Elspeth. Chalanor had waited in the hall while they talked. He was determined to stay close and this indeed made Louisa feel safer.

The two young ladies spent hours talking and continuing to renew the friendship they had once had. Elspeth did her best to comfort Louisa over the stress of Alice's death, and expressed her remorse at accusing Alice of theft. Alice's death was something Louisa could not come to terms with. She knew whoever had killed Alice did it because of her. Her pearls were still missing and this was distressing. Lord Farraday had conducted a search of the whole estate, much to Lady Farraday's disgust, but to no avail. But even the guests didn't mind under the circumstances.

"I had no idea all this was going on while I'm laid up here. Of course, I was concerned about the accident but could not imagine murder was a possible result."

"Do not distress yourself, Elspeth. I am sure Chalanor and the others will find out who is doing this. You have a footman for protection and I am sure the pearls will show up." She tried to sound convincing but, in her heart, she knew Elspeth could see through her bravado. "I am more concerned for the safety of the remainder of the staff and the other guests. This person doesn't care for anyone or anything. He's hurt you and killed Alice and nearly killed my father and Lord Farraday. He will stop at nothing." Louisa breathed a sigh of pent up emotion.

"Don't fret Louisa, please." Elspeth begged. "I am sure you are right that Chalanor will find out who he or they are. I know you are concerned and I really wish you would not take that concern on, but your beautiful nature..." Louisa smiled at her and then lowered her eyes. Elspeth continued, "You are in love with him, are you not?"

Louisa looked at her not with shock but resignation. This was Elspeth. She never did keep her comments, thoughts or concerns to herself. She never had. She was always one to state what she thought was obvious to all around her. She loved that characteristic in her friend. And wished she could be as honest and open. Elspeth was usually right but Louisa had no intention of admitting that.

"I don't think love has anything to do with it. Chalanor is trying to protect me as any true friend would. And yes, I believe we have become friends." She looked at Elspeth and smiled. "You know he feels the need to make amends for the dreadful time I have had over the past years." Louisa leant back in the chair beside Elspeth's bed and turned her head to look out of the window.

"You really think he is only a friend? My brother is your friend,

I am your friend even Lord Farraday is your friend. But believe me when I tell you, Chalanor is so very much in love with you. He is so much more than a friend and my dear, I envy you."

"How can you envy what does not exist?" She gazed long and hard at Elspeth and then closed her eyes. She asked herself what she really felt when it came to Chalanor. She opened her eyes and with determination changed the subject. "And besides you're a wonderful woman. Look how he has protected you. It could be you he loves."

Elspeth chuckled at this.

"Except that it is not. It is you. I think it always has been you. Freddie and I have both seen it. Chalanor wants to protect you when it would be easier to send you away. Your father and he planned for a long time to arrange this get together. You told me that yourself. Chal follows you everywhere. He wants to hold your hand when he thinks no one is looking. He wants to give you the time to come to terms with all the revelations you have discovered over the last week. But at the same time not let you out of his sight. Say what you will but I believe he loves you. And despite your denials you love him."

In an effort to try and change Elspeth's thoughts once and for all, from her possible love interest Louisa interrupted, "What is it that you envy in me, Elspeth? You have been the belle of the balls for many years. I have not."

"And that is just it. No one wants a woman who has her own opinions, not for a wife. Men have a tendency to ignore those kinds of ladies."

"But you are not ignored. Men are always near you. Even in your sick bed they have sought to visit you here." She leant forward curious at what her answer would be.

"I know but not one of them will have me for a wife. They want a lover, a plaything, a mistress but never a wife. They do not value me as a potential bride."

Louisa was shocked to hear this comment from her friend. "You are telling me that none have proposed to you?"

"Oh, I have had offers but from men who want my money more than me. But no one has given me the excitement that only love can create. That deep longing of being carried away from everything painful in one's life. To immerse oneself totally and wholly in the arms of another person, to share the loads together, no I am still waiting for that to occur. And I doubt it will ever happen." She looked out of the window, lost in her own thoughts. "Louisa, this is about you. Not me." She turned her head to look at Louisa. "Please tell me as your friend, what you truly feel?"

Louisa contemplated for a moment. Looking at Elspeth she could see her true friend. She did not keep her thoughts to herself. She was open and truthful at all times. Not like her friend, Belle, who destroyed both their lives by keeping her true feelings from her. She was feeling flushed but knew Elspeth would come to her own conclusion if she did not talk about it with her.

"In truth...I think...I don't know. Strange, I have hated Chalanor for so long. What I had imagined he had done to me, was incorrect. Now, I am enjoying getting to know the real man and forgetting the man I had imagined. But truly Elspeth, I do not yet know how or what I should feel for him."

"That is an honest answer. Thank you. Can I make one request?"

"Certainly."

"Keep thinking of him and continue to get to know him. I believe the reward will be love."

Heat suffused Louisa. Then she lifted her eyes to her friend's and said, "I think whoever eventually finds you will see the treasure in you, not your money." Elspeth in turn blushed.

"I say, why has the wonderful Miss Stapleton and my sister, both gone a lovely shade of red?" Freddie came waltzing up to the bed and sat on the end. He looked from one to the other, smiling.

"I do believe sister, you are sharing secrets and it is not fair. You need to keep me informed of your entire collection of trysts."

"Oh Freddie, you're a wonderful and silly brother and I love you."

"And so, you should my dear, for what are brothers for? But to tease and torment their little sisters and their friends." The three of them laughed.

"$\mathcal{I}$t is difficult to believe we are not all under attack here." Prescott had the attention of some of the luncheon guests. "After all Lord Farraday was nearly killed."

"Thank you for the concern Prescott but you don't seem to understand. I was in the wrong place. If anything, my son should have been walking with Miss Stapleton, which would indicate he was the intended victim."

"That is certainly true, sir." Prescott acknowledged. He smiled at Chalanor, a cold fake smile and Louisa shivered at the sight of it. If he had not arrived at the same time as the urn fell, she would have guessed him to be the villain. But in her mind that did not leave out the possibility he was behind the attack. Perhaps he wanted to get back at Chalanor for ignoring him for the past two years. As much as she tried to sort out conclusions, her mind continued to lead her back to the fact that she was central to the attacks.

"It amazes me that all the other guests are running for the hills. Surely it was a terrible accident? Who could even think of doing such a thing to Lord Farraday?" said Frances Midhurst.

"You seem to be avoiding the truth here, Frances. The attempt was not directed toward me." Lord Farraday was looking at her and frowning.

"Can I suggest that we change the topic of conversation to the weather? It would seem to be a far more joyful experience as the day is so beautifully warm." Lady Farraday brooked no excuse and continued to discuss the weather to all who would listen.

Looking at the Reverend who was sitting on her right, Louisa asked, "Have many left this morning?"

"Yes. It would seem that nothing could keep them here. Apart from yourself and your father, only those here at the luncheon table remain for the rest of the house party. Unless something else should happen."

Louisa looked at those sitting around the table. The Reverend Hutton was to her left and the Edward sisters to her right. Chalanor sat across from her with Freddie and Vincent Bartley on either side of him. Elspeth was still in her room upstairs. That left the Beaumont's and the Burgess' at the end of the table with Lord Farraday. Lord and Lady Midhurst sat at the other end of the table with Lady Farraday. Prescott was seated at that end of the table. Since his arrival he had been showering praise and attention on the Midhurst sisters who also sat at that end of the table. That made her more comfortable as his attention was concentrated on them.

But she still hated that he was here.

The only face that was different was that of the lawyer Peterson. Lord Farraday had introduced him at the beginning of luncheon announcing that he and Lady Farraday would be indisposed for the rest of the afternoon, as they had some pressing details to work through with the lawyer. It was strange that he would appear in the middle of a house party but then this house party had to be one of the most unusual she had ever heard of let alone participated in.

---

*A*fter luncheon, as his father and mother sat in the study with Mr. Peterson, Chalanor, Louisa and her father were on their daily stroll of the estate. They had walked in various directions on other days. Today they strolled toward the old woods at the western side of the estate, well behind the house. Her father was riding but was never too far away. He asked to forgo the use of the shanks pony as he was not as young as he used to be.

"Elspeth is mending well, I believe?" Chalanor was keen to hear her thoughts on how their friend was doing.

"Most definitely, however I believe being confined to her bed is beginning to play havoc with her mental state of wellbeing. She is bored."

He was surprised he had not noticed this himself. "Then we should give her time out in the garden perhaps? The summer weather is delightful. We can have her carried down and the maids can make her comfortably dressed so as to be modest for her. What do you think?"

"Chalanor, I think that would be wonderful. You have been a good friend to her."

"That is true but then I have known her and Freddie, a great deal of my life. Elspeth is Elspeth. I can trust her to always tell me the truth and always put me in my place if I do the wrong thing. You should have heard the roasting I got from her after that...after Prescott."

Louisa blushed.

"Please forgive me." Chalanor looked crestfallen.

Louisa smiled at him. "No need Chalanor, all is forgotten. Do not fret." She paused, smiled and continued, "She, no doubt was right." and she laughed. Soon Chalanor joined her in the laughter. After a few minutes they continued with their conversation.

"I know that your friendship with Elspeth has been deep. What about Freddie?" he asked.

"Freddie, well, he makes me laugh. He always sees the good in everyone until they are revealed to be not so good."

Chalanor jumped in. "And then he will declare them the worst sort of person and that he knew all along they wore the boot on the wrong foot." They both laughed. "But I would say I have talked more with Elspeth over the years. We are good friends." He smiled.

"I have known them as long as I can remember. My mother was friends with their mother. We often met and stayed with each other's families. Elspeth and I were always close but I guess for a time I was closer to Belle."

They were silent for a while.

---

*T*hey continued to walk and entered the woods by a rarely used path. Her father followed on his horse. The path meandered through the trees and it was there that Louisa spotted a structure. Her father called out to them.

"Why don't we stop for a moment? I wish to water the horse in that stream," trotting past them to the stream flowing at the rear of the cottage.

"Very well, Sir Peter," replied Chalanor

"Chalanor, what is that building?"

"That is an old crofter's cottage. It has not been used in years and I believe the gardeners use it for storage of old implements. I had forgotten it was even here. As children, my sister and I used to play here. I was fifteen and she five. She loved to go exploring through the woods. She would pretend to be a great explorer and the cottage was a new country." He looked around. "I honestly thought it would have fallen down by now. Would you like to see inside?" Louisa nodded.

They walked to the door and opened it. To her surprise, Louisa found the one room cottage was neat and tidy and looked like it had been lived in. A few pieces of furniture were scattered around the room. There was a bed in the corner, but there was no linen on it. A linen cupboard was on the left side and two chairs and a small table on the right. At the back was a bench with various jars and bottles on it, all empty. There were no personal items or signs that someone had been staying there. But that was all she could see. No old farm implements in sight.

"This is not what I expected. I thought the place would be more run down. The garden staff have really looked after it. Perhaps these accommodations are for extra gardeners we hire in the summer? I must ask the staff about it." Chalanor stated. They left the cottage and walked over to her father. Once he had mounted, they continued on their way.

Louisa admired Chalanor's ability to entertain her with stories of his childhood but she was also admiring his openness. He was again well dressed. He was wearing a blue jacket today. She loved that colour, probably because his blue eyes seemed bluer every time he wore it. But she wanted to know specifics about him and today she was determined to ask him more personal questions that might reveal more about his character.

"Can I ask you a few questions?" Louisa asked. "I know how you know the Ismays and I know how you met the Reverend Hutton. I know that you met while you were in Brussels, but how?"

"That's easy enough. I met him in Brussels after Waterloo. He had been wounded. We spoke a lot about his regiment and he helped me identify some of the fallen. He healed quickly of his physical injuries but no one would appoint him a parish when he returned to England. He was war weary. He contacted me and I spoke to my father and we agreed that as the parish at Loose was vacant we would offer it to him. He's not married and has a sister, I think? Is that sufficient?"

"Yes, thank you. He and I have known each other but he is much changed since his return from abroad. He is still Ennis but gentler and quieter. He's still a gentleman."

"Are you suggesting that I am not?"

"No," she laughed with him. "But he is not of the *ton*. I was curious as to your thoughts of him."

"Yes, I believe he is a good man. That is why he is my friend. Being part of the ton does not make you a good man. The war was hard for him but he has come through as we all must. He has a heart that is considerate to all mankind, I do believe. I would imagine that would help him greatly in his work."

"Chalanor please do not misunderstand my meaning. I think that it is a good thing that we are friends with all sorts of people. Having been shunned by the ton, I am sure you understand that being part of the ton is not important to me. However, being shunned by them can mean you will be shunned by those who should know better. I knew you would be one who would not be biased against those who are not necessarily of the same class."

She looked up and smiled at him and went on. "And yes, Ennis has a sister. Now what of Bartley. Do you know him?"

"I have met him a few times in town but I do not really know him. He seems a gentleman and comes from a good family. I have heard that he is a bit of a rake. He is more a friend of Freddie's. I believe Freddie suggested him to my mother when she was making up the list." He smiled at her.

"Can I ask you some more questions?"

"Certainly, I want you to see that I am not your enemy. What is it you would like to know?" Chalanor did not seem surprised by this question perhaps anticipating she wanted to ask more. She was happy he seemed to be enjoying their tête à tête.

"You are not my enemy, not now. A week ago, I would have declared differently." They both smiled at each other. "I would like to know the things you are interested in, music, reading?"

"Ah." was his knowing response.

Was she overstepping the mark? She wanted to get him to talk about himself so that she could get to know him better. She knew a lot about him but she wished to know more, more intimate things. So much had happened in his own life since that fateful evening. His character meant more to her now than ever before. She waited for him to respond and after a few moments he did. She could see that he was deep in thought.

"I love to ride. It is one of my favourite past times. I, of course am very much a farmer at heart. I try to develop my land holdings so they benefit me and the people who work them for me. I once enjoyed the city life but I do not believe that is part of my demeanour anymore. I still occasionally visit London but my estate is where I enjoy spending the majority of my time." He paused and stood still for a moment. He turned, looked at her and continued the discussion. "Here in the country, well on my own estate, I have concentrated on the renovations on the tower and other buildings. Father and I do a lot of work together on both estates. Let me think…" He paused again. She looked across at him and her lips tilted in a slight smile. He smiled back. He seemed to be enjoying her line of questioning. "I am an avid reader and I could listen to you sing for the rest of my life."

"Thank you, you are very kind." was all she could muster. She could feel the heat in her body rise to her face.

"Ah, but I have not finished yet. I like to travel, every now and then. It is good to see other beautiful parts of this wonderful country. I am a royalist and I believe I have been a good magistrate to my people. I enjoy the company of friends. And I could listen to you sing forever. Oh, I said that already, didn't I? How does that all sound?" She laughed with him.

"Wonderful." She knew he had seen the real reason she was asking the questions. She was taking his measure. But now Louisa felt exposed and wished to distract him as soon as she could.

They continued to stroll.

*H*e could not stop thinking about her questions. She really did want to know about him and how he thought and felt. She continued.

"You have promised to tell me about your sister. Delia was her name, was it not? Would now be a suitable time? But only if that will not make you feel troubled."

"My sister Delia," he paused to stop and picture her face. "Where to begin?" He did want her to know. About Delia. He rarely got to talk about her. "Well the beginning is probably the best place, but be warned I expect you to give me your complete family history when I am through."

"You have already obtained most of that information by your own efforts." She replied. She looked ahead to where her father trotted on his horse and then looked back at Chalanor.

"Ah yes, I take your point." He chuckled.

They had come almost full circle around the western edge of the inner estate boundary and were now near the lake. Chalanor called to Sir Peter suggesting a rest for them and the horse. Chalanor went over to the horse and took off the blanket that was tied onto the saddle. He laid it on the grass near the edge of the lake. Sir Peter dismounted and wandered some yards away and sat on a well-positioned rock leaving the horse to drink at the edge of the lake. They sat on the blanket.

"No doubt, yes, no doubt at all you have heard of my mother's love affairs?" Louisa nodded but said nothing. "My father is a good man but he did not choose wisely when it came to picking a wife. Terrible thing to say about one's mother but unfortunately it is true. I am the son of my father of that I have no doubt but there is ten years difference in age between me and my sister. She is not like me or my father. In fact, she does not look like any member of our family. Her personality and looks were not like my mother all that much either. When she was sixteen, she heard from a well-meaning relative, of our mother's affairs and dalliances. It was obvious to her that she was a product of one of them. Delia was heartbroken and would not speak to our mother for a full week."

Chalanor got up and paced back and forth in front of the rug for a moment. He continued. "It was not long after that, she disappeared. That was just on two years ago but we have not found her. I was away at Waterloo at the time she disappeared. My father searched and when I returned to England, I continued the search. My mother has not even asked about my sister. She either does not care or her grief is so great she cannot express it. Unfortunately, I believe the former to be the reason."

"I am sorry. You need not say any more. I do not wish to cause any further distress." She lowered her head.

Chalanor sat down again next to her. He lifted her face so she could see his eyes. "This was an area of my life I have not discussed openly before. Even while discussing many things with Elspeth, this I have kept to myself. But I want you to know. I would like you to know. I miss my sister. My mother is a difficult woman but she must suffer something at the loss of her child. Well, at least I hope so. Unfortunately, my sister's departure has only driven my mother to bed with whatever man she can lay her hands on. She has had a string of men both here and in London. She does not care that it upsets my father. I am sorry to be so frank but that is the way it is."

She looked at him and asked; "Are you sure she has a lover now?"

"Yes, I have no doubts. The staff are certain someone is sharing her bed. They have yet to determine who. I can only assume we will find out eventually. They usually do. They are devoted to my father."

She was shocked and he seemed to detect that.

"Yes, the staff are watching her. Mother believes she is being discreet and to the majority of the household she is. None of the guests would know. Men will do foolish things for a woman. I want to know if he is behind the attacks against you." He looked at her and her smile took his breath away.

"I am surprised at your frank confessions to me. I am but a friend, yet you are prepared to share some innermost thoughts with me."

"Louisa, let me make it perfectly clear to you. I want to find the truth behind the attacks against you. I will not keep you in the dark with regard to this information. You are becoming more than just a friend to me. And I do want to protect you from what has happened and what might still occur. If I share what is in my heart it is because I trust that information to you."

---

*L*ouisa was transfixed by his eyes and then knew he spoke the truth. Many times, she had heard that the eyes were a mirror to the soul, and looking into his blue depths she could easily believe it. At this moment she truly could accept he loved her and she might just be in love with this wonderful caring man. But she knew he had to marry a woman of rank and importance despite his not caring about such things. That had been made very clear by guests and his mother. The reality of the world they lived in told her that what she was thinking was but a dream. A dream she had to forget. So, he would have to forget about her too, despite what he might desire.

"I have said it to you before Chalanor. You take too much on yourself. I am concerned that my reputation although unfounded may damage yours and that of your family. We really can't imagine…" But Chalanor did not allow her to complete her sentence. He lifted his hand and placed his finger on her lips to stop her from saying any more.

"Louisa, your reputation is not deserved and it is changing. You have won over many of the guests. Those who have left the house party have not left because of you but because they believe that my eyes are only for you."

He lifted her hand and kissed her fingers. He looked into her eyes.. Did she dare to believe what he had said? He seemed to be telling her there was more to what they were feeling.

"You can't be sure of that?"

"Ah, but I can. That is what I was arguing with my mother about the morning the urn fell. Louisa, I will not put pressure on you but please be assured they left for that reason and that reason alone."

They sat there in quiet contemplation. She believed him as she had also seen he was always attentive to her. But to hear him speak it openly was not what she had ever expected. Men did not share their feelings with women. That was what she was led to believe. That was not the case with her mother and father but from what she had observed they were the exception to the rule. Her parents had loved each other. They spoke together about everything. However, the usual rule to relationships was what she witnessed between Lord and Lady Farraday. Tolerance, silence and occasionally outright hostility.

"I have liked this time we have had together." She finally replied. "It is what we need—if well should we believe—that we should see more of each other."

"Ah Louisa, you are both wise and beautiful." She looked into his smiling face and was ready to believe anything he said from that moment on. She wanted to reach over and kiss him. Such a silly thought. She had never been kissed by anyone other than Prescott and that was but a peck on the cheek as their engagement was announced. So, she looked for a subject that would distract both of them and found it. He reached over and took her hand and lifting it to his lips he kissed her fingers again. If she did not distract him, she would be kissing his beautiful smiling lips.

"Can I ask you to tell me more of Belle, my friend who was ruined by Prescott?" He continued to hold her hand.

"What do you already know?"

"I am aware that she was turned out by her family when her reputation was revealed. I had a letter from her mother who told me she had disgraced her family and had fled to the country. They gave me no forwarding address and demanded I never contact them again."

Chalanor looked at her and she could see he was calculating what more he should say.

"I know there is more, I have heard the rumours," she stated "and believe me, I want to know so I can lay that whole event into history. Are the rumours true?"

"It will not be easy for you to hear." He looked at her carefully. He was trying to determine her current state. He was looking after her again. But she knew she could take it. She slowly nodded.

"Very well. She did go to the country because she was with child."

"I had heard as much." She looked out over the lake.

"I have friends in the village to which she had fled to some distant relations. They kept me informed as to her condition. Unfortunately, Prescott ignored all requests from her and her family to make amends. When the time came for her to deliver the child, she had lost all hope. It was bad for her I understand. She did not survive the birth by more than a few days, nor, did the child, a girl."

Louisa turned her head to look into Chalanor's eyes. He told the truth and it pained him.

"That is what I had heard. Thank you for telling me." She lowered her head and a tear came down her cheek. Chalanor squeezed her hand, lifted it to his lips and kissed her fingers again. With his other hand he rubbed his fingers on her neck. From a distance she saw Sir Peter smile and then turned his head to look back over the lake.

21

W hen they arrived back at the house all was quiet. Many of the remaining guests were seated on the terrace at the rear of the manor enjoying the summer sun. Louisa and Chalanor went to sit with them as Sir Peter handed the horse over to the stable boy.

"I say you two," called Freddie. "Shall we play a game of croquet?"

"That would be delightful, Freddie." Louisa replied, and then took a sip of the cool lemonade that was handed to her by Lord Farraday. She went to sit at the table where Freddie was seated.

"Are you exceptional in that too, Miss Stapleton? You sing, you dance and ride. Now croquet?" remarked Lady Farraday.

"Madam." Chalanor jumped in before Louisa had a chance to respond.

All eyes were fixed on Louisa. She wished to ignore the comment but she could see that everyone was waiting to see how she would react. She took a deep breath. She needed to be very careful with what she said.

"Lady Farraday. I know you have a certain opinion of me and

the only reason I remain a guest in your home is due to the insistence of your son and husband. I do appreciate your forbearance. Please excuse me." She stood and curtseyed. She then turned to Freddie, "If you will excuse me Freddie, I will go and visit with Elspeth and play croquet with you another time."

"Certainly Louisa." He stood and bowed at her, she curtsied and then turned and went into the house.

---

*L*ouisa went into the manor and straight to Elspeth's room where she threw herself on the bed and sobbed.

"I love him, Elspeth. You were right and he does love me. I do not doubt it. Now I have to decide what to do. We may both desire to be together but his mother will never allow it. She just belittled me in front of everyone."

"My dearest friend, do not cry. This is wonderful news. You love him, that's delightful."

"You do not understand." she pleaded with her friend. "His mother will do all in her power to prevent us ever being together."

"Louisa, Chalanor will never allow her to do that. She is a dragon I know. She thinks she can control him but she cannot. Surely, you can see that Chalanor is his own man. And you are so much better than this. I know you. You are strong and determined. Do not let the dragon get under your skin. You came here to enter back into society. Other women would never have dared. But you wanted a future and so here it is, being handed to you on a silver platter. Louisa, look at me."

Louisa sat up, composed herself then looked at her friend.

"You will shine. Do not let her think she has won. She cannot and will not. I will not allow it for one. And just watch Chalanor. He will never let his mother win."

"Can you tell me why you see things more clearly than I do?" Elspeth reached out and took her friend's hand.

"That my dear one, is easy, I am not in love. You and dear Chalanor are and I am delighted for you both. Now go and freshen your face my dear and come back and sit with me. I wish to have tea with you and we can determine how we will deal with the dragon."

Louisa left the room with her head held high. Her spirits had lifted. The tears had been shed but had given her strength along with the wisdom of her friend. She was going to win over her ladyship and have the heart of Chalanor.

---

*L*ouisa came back later and stayed with Elspeth for the remainder of the afternoon, talking about her feelings for Chalanor and what she was going to do about them. They also discussed ways in which she could counteract the vile words directed at her by Lady Farraday. Elspeth laughed when Louisa repeated what she had said to the lady that afternoon.

Having been out of the ton's limelight for so many years, Louisa dreaded making any sort of declaration or commitment to Chalanor. If her reputation could not be regained, it could destroy him. She knew that those who had changed their minds about her would eventually tell others about the deception that had been put in place by Prescott. But it would take time. She also had to wait and discern what Chalanor's real feelings were for her before she allowed events to go any further. He felt strongly for her, no doubt, and he called it love but was it really love or compassion?

Louisa also wanted to gauge more about the people in the house party. She still thought Prescott was behind the attacks but he had someone helping him. She knew Elspeth could fill in the gaps of her knowledge about the guests she knew little about.

"Tell me of some of the others in the party. What do you know about Bartley?"

"He's a friend of Freddie's but I know little of him. He seems friendly enough. He came the same day you arrived but later in the evening. He brought his own valet. In fact, all the gentleman brought their own valet. Even Reverend Hutton."

"I didn't know Ennis had a valet?"

"He's more like a butler. He didn't want a housekeeper so Chalanor helped him find a man who could be a valet cum butler. The only other staff he has is a cook." Louisa was amazed at the depth of knowledge Elspeth had.

"The Midhurst's are an interesting blend. Frances, I have a fairly good idea about. She hates everyone around her. She also has her eyes on Chalanor. Sarah seems to be supporting her sister but reluctantly."

"That sounds about right."

"Lord Midhurst is seen as a man downtrodden by his powerful wife. But her power seems to be connected only to Lady Farraday. It is power of gossip and innuendo. Very few of the real members of the ton will have anything to do with them. Having said that, they still carry some weight. That can be seen in how they contributed to your downfall. They helped the gossip spread unabated."

"I understand and that is why I want to be careful before committing to Chalanor. They can attempt to destroy him and succeed. The rest of the guests seem to be moving in my direction to which I am grateful. But to me there is no clear indication as to who could want me to suffer, other than Lady Farraday and Prescott. I can understand why Chalanor wants to be careful with me. He does not know who to trust. This is truly a difficult position to be in."

"Trust Chalanor. If he knows anything, he knows how to discover the truth. Trust him."

"Elspeth, are you sure it is not you, that Chalanor loves? You both know so much about each other. I might be nothing more than a distraction."

"Truly, we are friends. To me he is like my brother Freddie. I love him but only in that way. And friends know things about each other. Trust Chalanor that is all I can say."

"I will my friend, thank you."

---

*I*n the evening Louisa asked to have her meal in her room and then had an early night. She had spent the time thinking and sorting out her own feelings and emotions. After her meal she received a note from Chalanor.

"My dearest Louisa,

I apologise again for the rudeness of my mother. And I will do so until the day I die. Remember our conversations. Remember the openness we have given to each other. Remember our walks and the time we spent with each other.

Remember also that I love you. My dearest, dearest Louisa. Sleep well. I look forward to our time together at breakfast. Please sit with me.

Your Chalanor

She had to stop thinking of how Lady Farraday could interfere. She knew she had to trust Chalanor, if he really loved her, he would find a way. In the morning she would feel more refreshed and relaxed. One thing that Elspeth had said resonated through her. She was stronger and more determined than she had ever been to regain her life. She was going to follow this path regardless of the great Lady Farraday. Trust Chalanor.

22

The next morning Louisa came down to breakfast determined to spend as much time with Chalanor as possible. After reviewing the events of the night before, the conversation with Elspeth and her own desire to re-enter society she had determined that wanting to know Chalanor at a deeper level was essential. His note had made it clear, he loved her. She walked to the table and Chalanor stood and pulled out the chair next to him. She went straight over and sat down.

The small group of guests remaining at the house enjoyed the breakfast and the light conversation. The weather continued to be warm, though occasionally cloudy. It was soon agreed that the morning was fine enough that they should enjoy riding. Louisa could feel the change and revealed in it.

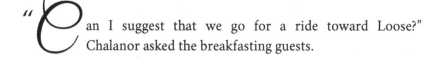

"Can I suggest that we go for a ride toward Loose?" Chalanor asked the breakfasting guests.

"I will give this ride a miss, old man," Prescott replied "as I have some pressing correspondence."

Chalanor dismissed him with a glance. He noticed his mother send him a disapproving look. But he didn't care. He did not want Prescott on the ride.

"We'll come." The Midhurst sisters chorused. "We can visit the church at Loose," added Frances. Others were nodding in agreement. "It is such a quaint little church."

"On second thoughts, I would love to accompany you lovely ladies," continued Prescott. Chalanor was now thinking of how he could rearrange the ride to exclude the Midhurst's and Prescott.

"Why don't we all ride?" intruded Freddie. Chalanor smiled at Freddie but could see no way out of the situation. Being near Prescott was not what he wanted for either himself or Louisa. There seemed no alternative. He would have to put up with Prescott.

"I say Chalanor, would you mind if Miss Stapleton and I stay behind in the library? I can give you the key to get into the church." Reverend Hutton had been speaking to Chalanor about some books he thought Louisa would enjoy. He looked at Louisa and she gently nodded. Well, that got Louisa away from Prescott at least.

"I will happily keep them company," Sir Peter interjected. Chalanor again smiled knowing Sir Peter would keep a close eye on his daughter.

"And son, I would value time with you in the study, if you can spare some?" Chalanor breathed a sigh of relief as he looked at his father with a knowing smile. He could now safely escape time being spent with both Frances and Prescott.

"Well, that would appear to settle matters. Prescott if you would be so kind as to accompany Frances and Sarah on their ride, I would be grateful." Chalanor stood gave a little bow and began to head toward the door of the foyer. It was now up to them to change the arrangements made.

Frances was not to be put off so easily. "But Chal we have not had your company on a ride in the last two days. Surely, you can see your father later?"

Chalanor turned to face Frances. Lord Farraday answered before his son had a chance.

"I'm sorry Frances, but my lawyer needs to return to London this afternoon and I have some issues that need to be discussed with my son. Please excuse us."

He stood and Mr. Peterson also did. They headed for the door.

"Is there anything that I should be aware of, my dear?" Lady Farraday was staring at her husband's back.

"No, my dear, this is in relation to Chal's estate. We thought we would use Mr. Peterson while he was here." Chalanor said nothing but knew his father was lying. He had no business with Peterson. Perhaps his father wanted to reveal to him the information that he and his mother had been working on yesterday.

"Will it take long?" she persisted.

"I doubt it. However, I have some farming matters to discuss with him as well. We should surface in time for luncheon."

"Very well," she continued, though she was not happy with the arrangement. "I will bring morning tea in for you..."

"No need." He interrupted. "I have arranged with Ramsay to have it brought in."

It was obvious to Chalanor that his mother was angry. She sat there red faced and unable to say another word. He feared she would completely lose her temper. Lady Midhurst was next to her with her hand on his mother's arm, endeavouring to persuade her to keep quiet. Her face also indicated she was not at all happy by these unexpected changes to the day. No doubt she wanted him with Frances and Prescott.

His father never stood up to his mother or arranged things without discussing it with her in detail. It was clear this arrangement was not discussed previously with her and was very unwelcomed. But it was done and he felt the day would be better for it.

---

*C*halanor, his father and Mr. Peterson headed to his father's study near the library. As he reached the door, he saw Louisa, Reverend Hutton and Sir Peter heading toward the library door. It would appear the morning would go more smoothly than he had hoped. It was not the way he had planned but still appropriate.

"Well, my boy," his father began, "I have a great deal of information to pass on to you. Mr. Peterson, would you mind getting the paperwork ready as we discussed yesterday?"

Chalanor and his father went and sat at the chairs near the fireplace while Mr. Peterson went to the desk and began to prepare some documents.

"I have discovered much in the past few days. Ramsay has been working hard with some of my trusted staff and I now know who your mother is currently bedding."

"Who is it?" He clenched his teeth and fisted his hands. He was angry but the anger was being held on to and not levelled at his father.

"Unfortunately, I am somewhat disappointed with her current interest and I feel that you will be too."

"Father, who is it?" Chalanor leant forward in his chair. His temper was rising and his anxiety, even more so. He did not want to be demanding toward his father but saving Louisa from the villain was overpowering all his thoughts and patience.

"I would rather not say just yet, my lad. I am hoping that he will see the error of his ways and stop this affair. But I am convinced that he is not the villain who is chasing Louisa."

"That may be the case Father, but I would like to make up my own mind. Please tell me." He did not care anymore who his mother bedded. He'd given up long ago. But he needed to protect Louisa and had every intention of doing so.

"My boy, please let me reveal my other bits of information before I reveal anything as to his identity. If you still don't trust me, I will tell you."

"Father, it is not about not trusting you. I do." Chalanor sighed and leaned back into his chair. Resigned, he said, "Please tell me more of your other discoveries then."

"Your mother arranged for Mr. Peterson to come and had it all organised before I knew about it. Your mother wanted to change my will. She wished to have you disinherited if you married anyone other than Frances Midhurst."

Chalanor sat there staring at his father as if he had just been told that the world was coming to an end at sunset today. Finally, he gathered his courage to say to his father, "Surely you did not agree to such a request? Is that even possible?"

"Of course, I didn't. But she would not let up. She was demanding I take action."

"Father?" Chalanor's concern went up another notch.

"On an occasion when she was not in the room with us, I endeavoured to ask Peterson what we could do to stop this lunacy. So, we came up with a counter plan, knowing that nothing would put the lady off. We prepared the documents she wanted and had them duly signed and witnessed etc. to her satisfaction. Those documents were placed in our secure room with all the other important documents. But Peterson and I removed them this morning and have placed them in my locked draw. I will destroy them."

"Father, I have no intention of marrying Frances. I despise the chit." His temper was now at boiling point. His mother's meddling had to stop.

"I am well aware of that, son. But we needed to keep your

mother happy as she would brook no refusal on my pleadings. Trust me once those documents were signed, I have been locking my bedroom doors. I do not trust her."

"If you do not trust her...then what is your counter measure?" Chalanor responded with desperation.

"Quite simple, Peterson is now drawing up the correct documents that he and I discussed in more detail on yesterday evening's walk through the garden away from your mother. Your mother wanted everything to be entailed to her, should you fail to marry whom she wanted—Frances—of course. However, I will be leaving everything to you as is the custom. The important thing was to have a will dated later than the one your mother wanted as it will make 'her' will null and void. And just to be sure I plan to destroy the others before your mother has a chance to take them out of our secure room. That is why they are in my drawer now."

Chalanor was dumbfounded. His mother was a manipulator but even these measures were beyond belief.

"Well Father, I believe now that I am totally aghast. I had no idea that mother would stoop so low. I can't believe she honestly felt she could get away with disinheriting me? But you have these new documents that will make mother's documents null and void?" He looked toward Peterson busily writing at his father's desk.

"Yes, son. There is no need for concern. She believes her plans will eventuate but they will not. Ramsay will bring in the tea later this morning and he will open the doors of the study that lead into the garden, allowing my two witnesses to come in and sign the documents without your mother knowing what is afoot."

"Who on earth will you get as witnesses that will outweigh the ones who signed your other documents yesterday?"

"Ah, that is part of our cunning arrangement. We used two servants for your mother's documents, Ramsay and the housekeeper, Mrs. Jenkins. Ramsay had known of our plan almost immediately and had told Mrs. Jenkins just to do what was asked and say nothing. This made your mother pleased as she felt she now had even greater power over the staff. However, Sir Peter and Lord Midhurst will be our witnesses later this morning. Ramsay on my instructions has arranged privately with the two men to come in from the garden."

"Well Father, I admire your ingenuity. But why not tell her to mind her own business? Surely that would be easier? You seem to spending more time arranging events than putting her in her place."

"The problem, my boy, is that she believes it is her business. And when have I ever had control over that woman? I endeavour to do this now to gain the control of her I lost many years ago. But there is more. She has also tried to convince me you are not my son."

Chalanor stared open-mouthed at his father. He could not believe what he had just heard. The world began to spin and he was glad he was sitting down.

Surely that was not the case?

But his sister was definitely of another father. Perhaps she had deceived everyone.

"Do not fear, you are my son no matter what she says. Just look at you. The same eyes, the same hair colour and you're almost the spitting image of my father. You are a great deal taller but look at your mother. She is very tall for a woman. But to be sure we are also preparing a document to make you my heir regardless of what she says. It becomes a battle of your and my word against your mother's. Her word will not be believed over yours nor mine. I am determined to protect you and the estate. Your mother has manipulated me for the last time. It will stop here and now."

"I am totally bewildered by this turn of events." Chalanor sat slumped in his chair. Placing his head in his hands he shook the confusion from his head. He wished all this angst would disappear.

"Now, you know why I did not want to say anything until I knew all was in place. And to be sure she did not overhear one word of my plan. She and her faithful servants have been watching you and me carefully."

"Watching me? Why on earth has she been watching me?"

"Quite simple, my son. She has been waiting for you to take Louisa to your bed." Chalanor shook his head as he stared at his father. All these plots and plans seemed to be coming from a gothic novel rather than the life he had known. His mother was acting beyond what he believed her capable. But he did not doubt that all his father's plans were to protect him and the estate. Beside he would never put Louisa in such a situation. He planned to bed her but as his wife.

He gathered his thoughts. "What about Midhurst? Are you not frightened he will tell his wife and that she in turn will tell mother? After all, Lady Nell is mother's closest friend." He waited for his father's response.

"No. He has told me of the many things he has kept from his wife, including his own affairs. And I believe he will keep quiet. Your mother has no idea we know. I don't believe she will hear anything from him."

Chalanor looked at his father as the words suddenly made sense. "Oh Father, you're not telling me it is Midhurst who is mother's lover?"

"That is what the servants believe. So, he can't be the one attacking Louisa. Think about it. He did not ride with us the day of Elspeth's accident. He arrived within a minute of the urn dropping. There is no way he could have reached the accident so quickly if he had been on the roof. Especially as we know that the villain killed poor Alice before he came down."

"You are right and yes I doubt I would have believed you if you had not argued those points, which puts us back at the beginning. Who has made the attempts on Louisa's life and why?"

"That, my son, has me totally at a loss. I just do not know. I keep going over the events and the faces of all the guests and I draw a blank each time. I know of no one who is capable of such villainy."

"I need to tell you Father, I am convinced that mother is somehow involved. The look on her face when Louisa screamed after the pot fell! There was no shock, just a perverse joy. She just smiled a horrid knowing smile. She must know who is making these attempts. Perhaps Prescott is involved and mother is acting for him? But then who would have killed Alice on their behalf? It is not making much sense, is it?"

His father stood and walked to the fireplace, then he turned and faced his son.

"I, too, believe that the perpetrator is somehow linked to your mother. She wants the girl rid of so that Frances has a clear passage to your affections. The servants have indicated they believe there may be another man she is bedding. They are certain of Midhurst but know that someone else is going to her bed when he is not."

Chalanor could believe it. His mother's appetite for men was insatiable. There could be no other explanation. She was bedding another man. "I think we had better make a new list of possible culprits and determine who it might be." Chalanor and his father went over to the desk pulled up some chairs and sat on the other side of Peterson. The two men continued to discuss various people and who could possibly commit murder. This also included servants especially those who came with the guests they did not know. Eventually they came up with a short list of servants and guests they needed to keep an eye on. The fact they were able to even attach names to that list disturbed Chalanor more than he could voice to his father. Would his mother lower herself to sleep with a servant? A woman of her class and respectability? Had her hunger for men made her drop her previous standards? He shook his head. His mother had no standards. She had fallen beyond them.

*S*ir Peter and Lord Midhurst slipped into the study through the doors to the garden Ramsay had opened. Ramsay was pouring tea for all the guests. Chalanor went over to Sir Peter.

"Is Louisa safe?"

"Certainly is, my boy. I took her to Elspeth's room myself where she is now sitting with her, and Freddie. All is well." Chalanor breathed a sigh of relief.

"Your footman is also standing outside the room."

"Midhurst," his father spoke, "Thank you for helping me this morning. But now that we are in private, I ask that you say nothing of this to either your wife or mine."

"You have my word."

"That also means when you slip into my wife's bed tonight."

Midhurst stared at Lord Farraday. He was stunned as if he had been slapped in the face. He tried to say something but only vague grunts and groans came from his mouth. His skin began to pale. Sir Peter raised his eyebrows and turned to look out the window.

"Don't fret yourself, man. I am well aware of my wife's faults. I just thought you had more sense than being drawn into my wife's lies. If you have an intelligent mind, and I always have thought you did, I suggest you stop now before others find out."

"Farraday, I apologize. I had no idea. I thought…"

"No sir, I don't believe that you did think."

Midhurst went to the fireplace and sat in one of the chairs in front of it. He was paler than Chalanor had ever seen him. Chalanor went to the sideboard and poured a small brandy. He brought it over to Lord Midhurst.

"You have my word I will tell her this afternoon that it ends now." He swallowed the brandy in one go.

"Good man. Then we will say no more about it."

Chalanor's breath hitched just looking at his father's composure. What his father had put up with all these years now gave him even more respect for his long-suffering father.

The men duly witnessed the new documents. His father bid the witnesses farewell and then they slipped out, the way they had come in. His father also bid a goodbye to Mr. Peterson, who left to return to London.

Chalanor could see the witnessed documents on the desk. His father came over, went to the drawer and unlocked it. He pulled out similar documents and took them over to the empty fireplace. He lit them, stood back and watched it burn. Within moments they had turned to ash. He came back to the desk placed the new documents in the drawer and locked it.

23

The morning's events had given Chalanor a lot to think about. After luncheon he and Louisa went for an afternoon walk. On this occasion they walked toward the site of the old manor. They spoke little at first as he was going over the things which had happened earlier.

"Can I ask you if there is a problem? You seem distant, perhaps deep in thought."

"My sincere apologies Louisa, you are right, I am deep in thought." They not only could think so much alike but they were able to almost read each other's thoughts. He stopped walking and stood still looking at Louisa.

Louisa stopped, turned and looked into his eyes.

"If you have doubts..."

He didn't let her finish her sentence. He reached out and took hold of her hand. Bringing her fingers to his mouth he kissed them.

"No. I have no doubts. I promise to discuss with you my thoughts but I beg of you to distract me for a moment." He drew her hand around his back and placed his arms around her. Her other arm now held him.

"How is it that you wished to be distracted?" She asked, with a knowing grin.

"I know that I am being very forward and with your father only few feet away."

"Go right ahead, my boy. I will tell you when to stop," piped up Sir Peter. He was on top of his horse and turned to face the other way.

Louisa was laughing and the joy she gave to it was contagious. He laughed with her. "Seriously, may I be so bold as to kiss you?"

She leaned closer in response and he closed his eyes. Her lips were soft and warm and tasted of peaches. She tasted like the first peach of summer and he delighted in the sensual experience. Never before had his senses been so aware. He could hear the birds tweeting and the sun warm on his back. He could smell the scent of flowers in the air and the warmth of her body in his arms sent thrills racing through him. He opened his eyes and drew back from her mouth and could see the radiance of the woman in his arms. This is the woman he wanted, this wonderful, strong, talented, affectionate and lovely lady. Her eyes sparkled as he gazed at her. He reached for her mouth again with his. He would make this kiss last longer. He tasted her again and craved for more. Time had stood still and she was all he could think upon. Reluctantly he pulled away as he heard the voice of Sir Peter.

"Perhaps we should keep walking."

His complexion warmed as he turned and still holding her hand continued on their walk. Glancing at her he saw the pink in her cheeks. He smiled at her and she looked up into his face.

"Will you please tell me of your childhood? You are an only child, are you not?" he asked as he remembered their first kiss.

"I believe, sir, that you have obtained most of that information from my father already."

"That is true but I would dearly like to hear it from your own beautiful lips and your unique perspective."

"Then you shall. Let me see..." She raised her other hand to her mouth and touched her lips with her finger. It would seem that her thoughts were also on their first kiss.

After a moment she began.

"We have always lived in Chertsey. Well, at least since I was born. Mother loved to garden and enjoyed sharing that love with me. As you know my favourite flowers are roses but I love all flowers. You are correct, I am an only child. My parents had a boy after I was born but unfortunately and with much sadness to my mother, he died but a few days after. This affected my mother's health and she was never a strong lady after his death." She paused looking ahead but he could see that her thoughts were many miles away.

"I love to ride and my father has spent many hours teaching me. He has also taught me how to distinguish good horse flesh from bad. My father has taught me a great deal over the years even if it took me years to learn." She turned and smiled at her father and he looked lovingly at his daughter and returned the smile.

"So far we are alike. That is to say that we have similar interests." They stopped and looked at each other. He could not get enough of just looking at her. She was beautiful but also the way she spoke and showed concern for others. All of these things drew her to him. After a few moments they continued to walk, and he was delighted her hands were still in his. Louisa continued to share.

"Mother loved to make things. She could embroider and sew. She often made my clothes. She read widely and encouraged me to do so when I was older. I have looked after the household for my father since my mother's death. It has been difficult on occasion as I did not have my mother there so I could ask appropriate questions. But I believe I have managed. Have I not, Papa?"

"Most assuredly, my dear." Sir Peter trotted by them on his horse and went ahead and took the lead. "Perhaps you could tell him of your love of architecture and history." Louisa's gaze followed her father as he moved ahead. They followed him.

"I was getting to that, Papa. As I was saying...I adore the history of our country. I read as much as I can both about monarchy and the people. But I love architecture the most. I wish I had the ability to restore the ancient buildings of our country so that many in the future could enjoy the grandeur and the beauty. Similar to what you have been able to achieve on your own estate."

"You're different from many young ladies. They do not usually speak of such things."

"That is true but then I have not been in much company over the past years, so I have had a great deal of time to determine my own interests."

"From what I can see you have not wasted your time." He smiled at her and her face lit up.

"I have not wasted my time, Chalanor. And I also do not want to waste time now. Ask of me the things you wish to know. Do not stand on convention. Ask what you wish." Her eyes were fixed to his. They had again stopped in their tracks and were looking deeply into each other's eyes.

"Do you forgive my actions from that house party?"

"Yes. Do not doubt it. You need not ask again."

"Thank you." He could see it there in her expression. "I will not from this moment on, I promise. Now, let me return to my earlier thoughts. Will you allow me to be frank with you in relation to my parents?"

"Yes. I know that you were distracted earlier, but I would be happy for you to share with me. Can I be so bold as to say that I would be honoured?"

They continued to walk and he shared the events which occurred that morning. Sir Peter was aware of some of it and Chalanor hoped he listened to the rest of the information that was shared. He knew what he said to Louisa could be shared with his dear friend Sir Peter. Chalanor was happy for him to be aware of them. Louisa occasionally asked for clarification but was relaxed and free with all her comments. She listened carefully, and never once said anything to belittle or degrade either his father or the actions of his mother. This made him love her more. Yes, there was no doubt for him now. Not that he had any real doubts. He was in love.

24

That night at dinner, with all the information was now at his disposal, he looked around and felt he was in a play rather than living his normal, uncomplicated life. He was determined to take the time to examine all the players. His beautiful heroine Louisa was seated near Freddie and her father. This pleased him as he knew that she would be safe in their care. His eyes wandered to his father. He was smiling and happy. In fact, he could not remember an evening for some years when his father appeared as relaxed as he did this evening. This added to the joy he felt to be in love with the delightful Louisa.

His mother, in his eyes was the current villain of the performance, and she was not happy. She was angry. Her colour was high and she did not smile. She seemed distant to all around her. But he could see she frowned toward his father, Midhurst and Louisa. He assumed Midhurst had told her they would not continue their affair. She scowled at Midhurst for most of the evening. The rest of the company seemed relaxed, amused and unaware or not interested in what she was angry about. Many of the guests had learnt to pay little attention to her conversation. He wished she could see the damage she did to her own status and position because of her actions.

What of the other characters? He had Frances still sitting beside him trying to gain his attention. But his friend Reverend Hutton was on his left and held her in conversation, much to his relief. Bartley was also engaging Louisa in conversation. The Burgesses, Beaumonts and the Midhursts seemed happy enough. The Edwards girls were disinterested and distanced themselves from any conversations. They had announced that they would be departing in the morning. The servants were another state of affairs. He knew the household staff but did not know the servants of the visiting guests. He knew that Ramsay was monitoring them. Actually, he had no doubt Ramsay was doing just that. He was extremely loyal to his father.

That left him, the hero. The hero to Louisa's heroine. He was enjoying Louisa's company and getting to know her better. He remembered the kiss he had shared with her that afternoon. How glorious it was. A thread of dread still tinged his spine as to who the unnamed villain was, other than his mother. It couldn't be Midhurst. He was just a fool believing the flattery his mother no doubt sprouted. There is no way he would have tried to harm Louisa even if his mother had asked him too. It was definitely not part of his character. Besides he had been nothing but polite to Louisa.

So, that left one of the other gentlemen. He looked at them all, trying to imagine any of them doing the things that had already been done. Could any of them kill to get what they wanted? But to him no one seemed capable of the deeds already performed. He had to discover the true villain and then claim Louisa as his own.

*A*fter dinner Elspeth was carried down from her confinement to enjoy the company of all the members of the house party. She seemed to have a wonderful evening and he and Louisa stayed close to her side to attend to her needs.

"Let us play charades," Freddie's voice rose above the sound of the quiet conversation.

"Yes do," echoed the voice of Frances Midhurst. "Chal, come and join in the fun."

"Thank you Frances, but I would like to keep company with Elspeth at the moment."

"No need for concern, I shall come and sit with her." Chalanor could hardly believe his ears as his mother stood and came over to sit next to Elspeth, unfortunately putting her too close to Louisa.

"Now off you go my boy, and play with the others." His mother dismissed him like an errant child.

Chalanor looked at Louisa then back at his mother. Louisa stood and began to excuse herself, "Please excuse..." But she never got the chance to finish.

"Now Miss Stapleton, let's have a friendly chat."

Louisa sat back in her chair staring at Chalanor who also stood a few feet away wishing he could somehow get her out of the situation she now found herself in without causing a scene. He slowly moved away but not too far. He could tell that Elspeth sensed her friend's fear and engaged Lady Farraday in conversation, hoping to distract her. Thank you, Elspeth.

"Thank you, Lady Farraday. Your kindness in allowing me to stay since my accident, has been most generous of you."

"Do not fret yourself, my dear. Of course, we look after our friends. Now why don't you help me discover more about your friend, Miss Stapleton?"

"Ma'am?" Elspeth was taken aback, not sure what to say next. Her politeness was not what she had expected to hear.

*L*ouisa could only imagine what terrible things the lady was preparing to say. So far, she had not said one word of welcome or had opened her mouth without degrading Louisa in some way. She had no doubt that she was to experience more of the same.

"Well, she has not been part of the ton for such a long time, I wanted to know her thoughts and dare I say, her intentions." The lady turned her attention to Louisa.

Louisa's fears multiplied with that statement. The tension building in her stomach made her sick. She hoped she would not be ill in front of her.

"You don't need to worry dear." Lady Farraday placed her hand on Louisa's arm. "I'm sure you have nothing to hide and we already know of your reputation." Louisa's stomach churned but she stayed still while Elspeth came to her aid.

"Lady Farraday, please could we watch the charades? It does look so very interesting." Elspeth was doing all she could to distract Lady Farraday.

Lady Farraday ignored Elspeth's pleadings. "Now, now, dear, there are no secrets between friends. Why my dear, you look warm. Do you need to get a breath of fresh air?"

Louisa could stand it no longer. She quickly stood up. "Please excuse me Lady Farraday, but I do suddenly feel very warm." Fumbling for words she continued. "Please excuse me as I step outside."

"Take the door to the balcony my dear. You do look very warm."

Louisa turned and went to the balcony door, opened it and stepped outside and closed the door behind her. She had escaped.

*L*ouisa did not see Lady Farraday's knowing smile but Chalanor did. He could see that she was delighted Louisa had gone out to the balcony. Now Chalanor tried to determine why his mother wanted her out there. He wanted to follow but could see no reason to leave that would not draw attention to Louisa's plight. He thought it best to watch and wait to see what his mother would do next. He looked for his father but noticed he was nowhere to be seen.

25

The cool air was wonderfully refreshing. Louisa went to the balcony edge and looked over the railing. At least she could not be tormented here. She took some deep breathes but her fear would not abate. She sensed unease around her. A cold chill went up her spine and she knew someone else was close by.

"You are more beautiful now than you have ever been."

And she was right. The shivers down her spine multiplied.

Louisa closed her eyes in the hope to find she was dreaming. After having had to deal with Lady Farraday the last person she wanted to hear, let alone see was Prescott. He placed his arm around her shoulders.

She shuddered then spun around. "Get your hands off me," she declared, "Or I will call my father."

"There is no need to be like that Louisa, all I want to do is have a conversation with you. I am sure your father would like us to talk." His voice was low and sounded treacherous. Yes, it sounded treacherous, just like him.

"We have nothing to communicate. And my father would not

want me anywhere near you, sir." She tried to control her anger and speak as civilly as she could. She took another deep breath.

"Ah, but your father and I have had many conversations about you, my dear. Your father has always wanted me to be joined to you. We were to be married you seem to forget." She knew her father's mind. Her father despised this man as much as she did.

Louisa stepped away. "You have no idea what you are saying. My father would die before he would allow me to be joined with you." She would defend her father as she would defend herself. She was not the shocked and innocent girl she was the last time they had seen each other.

"That's where you are wrong. I am the only one who can clear your name. I was the one who blemished your reputation. And only I can clear it. No one will believe you, a mere daughter of a baronet. But I have no intention of clearing your name until you promise to marry me."

She laughed out loud. If he truly believed that, he was a fool. All that Chalanor had done was enough to give her hope and her reputation was already clearing. She knew that Chalanor wanted her for who she was, not for her money, as little as that may be.

"I will never marry you. You disgust me. Do you hear me? No one who knows the truth behind the lies you told would ever marry you. If Belle had not listened to your lies, she would not be dead."

"The pathetic chit died giving birth. That can hardly be my fault."

"Yes it is, as she gave birth to your child. You rejected her and the babe she carried. How can you not see your part in her death?" Louisa was shouting at him. She took some deep cool breaths to bring her emotions under control. She wanted him to see her as strong not weak. He stood there with his arms folded. He had no intention of giving up this stupid discussion.

"She slept with many men. It could have been anyone's bastard."

"Accusing her of being a harlot, are you? After she gave up everything because she was foolish enough to believe that you loved her." She was yelling at him again and found it cathartic. "You utterly disgust me. You should be ashamed of yourself, you vile man." She turned to go back into the house. She was not prepared to listen to another word but Prescott grabbed her and pulled her into his body. He held her tight not allowing her the chance to escape.

"I wanted you then and I want you now." His breath was on her neck and she shuddered. She struggled but his hold on her was too tight.

"But you did not have me then and I will die before you get this close to me ever again." She elbowed him in the stomach. He was winded but he would not let her go. She started to struggle with greater effort and a few of her curls fell from their place. She also heard something rip but continued to struggle.

The double doors were swung open from the evening room and the light fell onto Louisa being tightly held up against Prescott's body. Lady Farraday stood there looking at them. The smile on her face was sheer delight. This was exactly what Lady Farraday wanted. To catch her in a compromising position. Chalanor, Freddie and her father stood behind her ladyship looking out on to the wretched scene. What would he think of her? She knew that she was ruined all over again.

"Well, what have we here, a lover's tryst? It would appear Sir Peter, that your so-called daughter has not lost interest in the man who ravished her."

"I hate this man." Louisa cried out. She was not about to lay back or blubber like a baby. She had fought too hard to have come this far and then be pulled apart by her ladyship. "He is holding me against my will," Louisa protested to the assembled audience. The more she tried to hit him the harder he held her. She could see the other guests gather behind the man she loved. She tried to get

Prescott to let her go, fighting like a wild cat. "For God's sake, let me go." She again elbowed him in the ribs but unfortunately to little effect.

"Get your hands off her, Prescott," demanded Chalanor. He began to step toward her but his mother's arm came across his chest.

"I believe Miss Stapleton that you have been again found out. We now see you as you truly are." She turned to look at Chalanor. "Don't make a fool of yourself, you stupid boy." Then she turned back to Louisa and continued, "I believe that it is now time for you to leave my house."

Louisa was distressed as the scene unfolded. Her life was again falling apart. Life was repeating itself. She could hear Elspeth calling her name and crying but to Louisa nothing could break the picture that was before her. Chalanor's eyes were fixed on her but he said nothing. She knew now that it was as before. She would not see him lift a finger to help her. He did not love her. So, she would defend herself.

"I have done nothing," she demanded. "This man is a liar."

"How dare you call a gentleman like Prescott a liar? Be silent." Lady Farraday retaliated.

"I will not be silent. HE IS A LIAR!" Louisa was screaming at her. "Look how he holds on to me? I want nothing to do with him." She was not going to lie down and give in as she had two years ago. She held her head high with a total air of defiance. "He is the liar!"

From out of the darkness to the right of the balcony doors stepped Lord Farraday.

"Actually wife, I believe it is Prescott who will be packing his bag. He has done nothing but lie since he got here, it would seem."

"What ever can you mean, sir? We have caught them in the act of making love on our balcony. Tis the girl who lies and I want her gone."

"Well, actually that is not true. I have been here on the balcony the whole time. In fact, I followed Prescott out here because I had a feeling he was up to no good. And it would appear that I was right." Every eye was focused on his lordship. No play could have produced a more captivated audience.

He went over to Louisa, took her hand and brought her away from Prescott. "I have never trusted him and if you had even listened to our son, you too would not have invited the cur to MY home. I saw Louisa come out onto the balcony and Prescott slipped from the shadows and grabbed her. I also heard the threats he has made to her. You see, I was here and a witness. You, madam, were inside. Miss Stapleton is completely innocent. Ravishing and discrediting her was all that was on Prescott's mind. Louisa wanted to get away from him. Now, what do you have to say, wife?" Many of the guests drew in their breath at the frank declarations and challenge from Lord Farraday.

"I am sure you must be mistaken, sir. She is not a gentile lady but a girl of dubious character."

"Enough, madam." Lord Farraday handed Louisa's hand to her father. He then walked toward his wife. Standing before her he said, "I have had enough of this. It is your character that I would call into question. Prescott, if you value your life you will pack your bags and leave my house immediately. Do you understand?" He never once looked to see if Prescott had moved. He just continued to stare into his wife's eyes. She could see that Chalanor was enthralled with the actions of his father and was unable to take his eyes off the events before him. He did not move. Louisa then returned her gaze to Prescott and could see the colour rise in his complexion. He backed away but not quickly.

"Come, Prescott," Freddie came up to stand beside him. "It is time for you to leave." The whole time Lord Farraday continued to stare down his wife. Louisa was engrossed in the drama playing out in front of her.

"You're a harlot, Louisa." Prescott yelled. Before another word could be spoken, Prescott was on the floor with Chalanor standing over him. Chalanor had hit him.

"Withdraw that statement, sir, or I promise that I will beat you to within an inch of your life." Blood flowed from the side of Prescott's mouth.

"Chalanor, don't be a fool." It would appear his mother did not know when to keep her mouth shut. She had to surely see that all was at an end, that her plan had been undone. She need not have worried as Lord Farraday put her ladyship in her place much to everyone's surprise.

"Madam, not another word from you, I suggest you go to the library and wait for me there."

"I have no intention of doing as you say," she raised her voice. "You pitiful man."

"Go now or so help me... Ramsay, escort Lady Farraday to the library." From the shadows Ramsay came.

"Madam." Ramsay stood at her side.

"You will regret this. You cannot humiliate me in this manner and get away with it. How dare you? You're protecting a harlot. You saw it with your own eyes." She continued her tirade.

"No madam. I do believe that you will be the one with the regrets." He replied as she walked out of the room followed closely by Ramsay.

Freddie helped Prescott get up off the floor and also escorted him out. Chalanor made his way to Louisa and wrapped his arms around her.

"Did he hurt you, my dear? Please tell me you are well." Louisa just took hold of him, hugging him and not letting go. He still wanted her. He still loved her. For a moment she had thought she had lost him forever.

Lord Farraday then turned to address the waiting guests. "Ladies and Gentlemen, I would suggest that you all retire for the evening. I will talk with you all at breakfast. I promise that all will be explained. Let me say one thing before you retire. Miss Louisa Stapleton is innocent of all the slander that has been levelled against her. I do not want to hear another word or accusation against her. Have I made myself clear?" Louisa watched as people nodded. "Now, I would ask you to be patient and wait till I talk to you all in the morning."

"But Farraday, you can't treat your wife and my friend in such an infamous manner."

"Lady Midhurst, I suggest you do as I say or more details may emerge that may distress you." A mere look from Lord Farraday to Lord Midhurst had him taking the arm of his wife and turning her away from the current scene as quickly as he could.

"What on earth do you mean, Farraday? Tell me?" She called out to him. But Midhurst continued to escort her away from the scene they had just witnessed. Their daughters hurriedly followed them out of the room. The Burgesses, Beaumonts, Bartley and the Reverend followed them.

"Can I suggest that we come into the evening room and be seated?" Lord Farraday had taken complete control much to Louisa's delight.

"Elspeth is quite distressed. I ask that you stay with Elspeth and await my return. I wish to deal with my wife first. But I need to talk with you all before the evening finishes."

With that he left the room. Louisa sat with Elspeth who was still crying and much distressed. The two ladies held each other in their arms and continued to silently weep. Louisa was crying from relief. She had stood her ground and defended herself. Lord Farraday had then defended her, much to her surprise and delight. And Chalanor had come to her defence also. A night of incredible events.

Chalanor and Sir Peter allowed them time to gain control of their emotions. The gentlemen gathered some chairs around the chaise and sat waiting. A few minutes later Freddie returned.

"Prescott is gone. I loaded him into his curricle myself. I will have his belongings sent to London tomorrow." He then sat in one of the chairs laid out near the chaise.

"Louisa, Elspeth? Is there nothing I can do to relieve your present state?" Freddie asked in a quiet voice.

The ladies looked at each other.

"Thank you, Freddie, but I think we are just bewildered as to what has just taken place." Louisa responded.

"Louisa? I need to ask you if he hurt you. Are you damaged? I can see that part of your dress has ripped." Chalanor looked most distressed.

Louisa looked down at her sleeves and could see that it had indeed been ripped. She examined as much of her clothing as she could but found no other damage.

"I believe that the sleeve is the only damage." Her response was cautious. Chalanor got up and rang the bell. A moment later a footman entered.

"Would you please arrange for tea to be brought to us immediately, and also some brandy?" The footman left. Chalanor paced backwards and forwards obviously distressed.

"I say old boy, whatever is the matter? Prescott is gone and Louisa is safe and as for your mother, well, I dare say I would rather not be in her shoes at the moment."

"It is nothing." He stopped and stood at the fireplace and looked long and hard at Louisa but she had no idea what he was thinking. She could attempt to guess but that would do her no good. She had to wait till he was ready to talk. All she knew was that he was not happy and seemed very angry.

26

L ord Farraday closed the library door behind him. His wife
turned, ready to argue him to the floor, but he did not allow
her the opportunity. "Do not say a word. I have had enough. Your
meddling, your infidelity, and most of all you, madam." He stared at
his wife. She was still beautiful in looks but all he could see was the
ugliness of her spirit and that made her look wretched.

"What do you think you are talking about? Your mind is quite
unstable, sir." She showed no fear. She looked ready for a fight.

"Oh, is that how you plan to try and steal my estate? Accuse me
of madness?"

"What foolishness are you talking of?" The lady's face went
pink. He could see that he had hit a nerve. That must have been her
plan.

"The new will, madam. The one you wanted written up to disin-
herit our son. I was wondering how you planned to get rid of me. I
thought you would have murdered me but accusing me of
madness? Much more creative. So that's what you would have done
to use the new will against Chalanor." He came and stood directly
in front of her. "I will not stand for this disgrace. After your display

on the balcony no one in society will believe another word you utter. But I should tell you that your plan is ruined, as another 'will' has been created, making yours null and void." He watched her face as the smirk changed to a look of disbelief. "Yes madam, it is true. Your wishes are nothing to me. So, go ahead and declare me mad, if it gives you comfort. It will make no difference whatsoever. The boy is of age and does not need to answer to you."

She looked at him uncertain what to say next. Then a change overtook her features. She was not ready to declare his victory, she had other weapons.

"He is not your son." She declared as she crossed her arms.

"Well, that is just another one of your lies madam that no one will believe." He went and sat on the chair. He was determined for her to see he was not threatened and very relaxed. "Besides if it were true, I honestly don't care. He is more my son than you are my wife." He paused allowing time for that comment to take hold. She just looked at him, shocked. "For years you have declared that you provided me with an heir but that you would not provide me with a litter. Until he was born, I loved you, both in my heart and in my bed. Then you would not have me. So, your comment was very true as all your lovers will attest."

"He is not yours. He is my son but not yours."

"That madam is where you have no idea of what goes on around you. Chalanor is my son. And we both know it." He crossed his arms and his legs.

"He will listen to me. Fetch him so I can declare the truth to him."

"He will not believe you and he will not protect you. Nothing can save you as you well know. Chalanor has not listened to what you've had to say to him for some time. For example, you're thrusting Frances at him. Do you honestly believe that he could marry a misery such as her? She has no character and is far from beautiful in her features let alone her personality." He watched as she turned to sit in the chair by the fireplace. "But let me continue. I have lived with you all these years while you bedded other men. Under my own roof! Chalanor knows all about it and has known for years. But I will not be cuckold any longer. You madam, will leave my house tonight."

"Don't be so ridiculous. This is my house. I have no intention of leaving." She stood up and again crossed her arms. She seemed determined not to allow him to continue in this manner. "I will not be going anywhere."

"Well, we are at a stalemate then, madam, because I will not have you under my roof a moment longer. The dower house at the other end of the estate is ready for you. I had hoped not to use it. I was still sentimental enough to hope that you might come to your senses and give up the foolishness you have been displaying for all to see."

"You mean my revealing that slut Louisa, for what she truly is? Oh, you stupid man. Have you been felled by her foolish words?"

"No madam. While she has been here, she has not said one word against you or tried to flatter me. She has been nothing but sweetness and light revealing your vile nature under the glorious rays of her beauty. Do you understand me? I will not deny that I believed your lies about her at first but as I have come to know Miss Stapleton, for who she truly is, her beauty, her true beauty, has shone through. Even Midhurst, your current lover has come to his senses. So, madam, I have had enough." She paled at his words. "No madam, I will not put up with this stupidity any longer."

"I have no idea what you mean. Bed Midhurst, you must be joking." She tried to feign innocence but continued to pale.

"Well then, let me enlighten you. I know of many of the men you have been consorting with over the years or should I be more vulgar and say that you have been having sex with?" She continued to pale. She slowly lowered herself into the chair.

"I will gladly provide you with a list. Drummond, Stephens, that twerp Thompson. Let us not forget poor Burgess. But for me Midhurst was the last straw. He is as rich as I and is as old as I, yet you would play with him instead of your husband? No madam, you just don't care who you hurt, humiliate or embarrass. Your belongings are being packed at this very moment. They and you will leave within the hour."

She sat there with her mouth open as if unable to comprehend what he had said. He had never spoken to her, defended himself or argued with her like this. She was allowed to think her word was law. But he could see from her expression she was not going to let him win.

"Delia was not your daughter either…"

"I am aware of that. But I will always love her. She will be my daughter forever. When your cousin revealed the poor girl's real father to her she fled rather than stay and have you as her mother."

"She did not flee far. She is dead." She was wringing her hands and growing paler by the minute.

"Well, more lies from your mouth. Why am I not at all surprised by that?"

"She is dead. I saw her body. I buried her."

"What lies are you prepared to give to try and save yourself? Truly madam, I have had enough!" He stood and walked over to ring the bell.

"I do not lie, listen, please. She had met someone out at the crofter's cottage in the woods. I knew she went there to be on her own. She often spoke to me that she went there to think of her brother Chalanor. Except the last few weeks before she died, I knew she was meeting someone. I don't know who. So, I went there to look for her. Well, that last time she was not alone and someone had her and then killed her. I could not bear to see her fussed over so I buried her myself and allowed you all to think she had run away."

"Madam, these lies will not change my plans for you. It will not save you." Lord Farraday shook his head stunned, at the lengths she was prepared to go to.

"They are not lies, I swear. You must believe me. She is buried under the oak next to the cottage."

"Not another word. I will not listen to another lie. Your lies will not save you. You are banished from this house. I will not listen to another word. I do not want to see your face again." He did listen and would check to see if this revelation was true. He hoped beyond hope that they were not. He did not want to believe any more of her lies. She was trying to save herself but this might be true. It would explain why Delia could never be found. But in his heart, he knew she was alive and well.

"The dower house has been locked up for years. I can't live in that mess."

"True. But I have had a team of estate workers cleaning the rooms and the garden in case I needed to act. So, it would seem that my actions will benefit you, madam."

Then as the truth dawned on the lady, she fell from her chair, dropped to her knees and wept.

"Your tears, madam, will not make me change my mind. You will wait in this room until you are taken to the dower house. Tomorrow I will meet you there and I will tell you how things will be from this moment on."

He turned to leave the room as Ramsay opened the door and entered. "Do not let her leave this room." He said to the footman as they closed the door on her. "Ramsay, is another footman at the door that leads to the garden?"

"Yes, my lord."

All he could hear as he returned to the evening room was her sobbing. He was not heartbroken. He was relieved.

27

L ouisa watched as Lord Farraday entered the evening sitting room and closed the door. She and Elspeth were holding each other while seated on the chaise. Freddie, Sir Peter and Chalanor were seated on chairs around them. Chalanor got to his feet as his father entered, fetched another chair and brought it to where the others were assembled. He came over and sat down.

"I want to thank you Freddie, for your actions tonight in ridding me of Prescott," he started.

"That is certainly my pleasure, sir. I was happy to escort him off the premises."

"Now as to what I have arranged." He paused as if to catch his breath. Chalanor got to his feet and went to the sideboard and poured his father a brandy. He brought it to his father and handed it to him. Lord Farraday thanked his son and took a sip. "Lady Farraday will shortly be escorted to the Dower House. She will not be able to hurt or speak to anyone here again."

She could not believe what she was hearing. How could this be? Chalanor seemed just as doubtful as she.

"Father, are you sure she will do as you say?"

"Yes. I will broker no excuse. Freddie, can I suggest that you take your sister to her room and allow her to rest? It has been a difficult evening for her and I promise to fill you both in on the details in the morning. You may ask as many questions tomorrow as you wish. But there are things that I must discuss with my son privately."

Freddie got up and bowed to his lordship. He then picked his sister up in his arms and carried her from the room. Louisa stood to follow.

"Please my girl, would you mind sitting with us for a moment longer. I would like to discuss with you and your father some decisions I have made."

"You have been so kind sir, but I really can't see what it has to do with me. I appreciate your coming to my defence as you did." She lowered her head. Her father stood and drew her into his arms.

"Please sit down, my dearest," he whispered. "Sit down. I am sure that Lord Farraday would not ask you to stay unless he felt it was necessary."

She lifted her head and while silent tears still ran down her face she sat back down on the chaise.

Lord Farraday moved his chair in front of Louisa. He sat and then took her hand and held it in his. His hand was warm but hers were cold.

"My poor girl you must be cold." He looked at Chalanor who immediately got up and rang the bell.

Ramsay entered the room. Chalanor instructed him to bring a rug for Louisa. As he left the housekeeper and a footman brought in the tea. Chalanor dismissed them, poured tea and brought a cup to her. Louisa accepted it without saying a word nor looking at him. Lord Farraday continued.

"I must first apologize for the ordeal that you had to go through tonight, my dear. I had no idea what my wife had planned with that scoundrel Prescott. If I had I would have put a stop to it. But I am glad that it has now happened. For a number of reasons that I think even you will see as fortuitous. Those who witnessed it will be sure to tell the rest of the ton of the event and your name will be finally cleared. Prescott will not be able to talk his way out of this, not with so many important witnesses and that it happened in my house. In turn I have finally put my wife in her place."

Louisa kept her head bowed. She was more distressed than she had expected. But then her heart was broken. She had waited for Chalanor to come to her, calm her, show her he was concerned for her. But he had not. Love had gone. She was convinced.

"I thank you Lord Farraday, and I am sure that you are right. But this is an evening that will not warm my memory. If you don't mind..." She placed the cup on the table next to the chaise and again stood up. This time Chalanor stood and took her into his arms.

"I wanted to kill him for even laying a hand on you. Please tell me that you are well? Did he hurt you?" She stood there stiff as a post.

What? What was he saying? Now? Why didn't he step up then?

"He hurt my pride, sir. My pride is wounded. Thank you for your concern."

"Louisa, you are not yourself. I understand that but why will you not look at me?"

She looked at his lordship and not at Chalanor. "Please sir, allow me to go to my room. I will not embarrass you any longer. Please let me go."

Chalanor placed his finger under her chin and lifted her face so she could look into his eyes. She tried to resist. "Louisa? I will never let you go. You must know now, more than ever, that I love you and want you to be my wife?"

"But...you said nothing. I assumed you wanted nothing more to do with me. That I was an embarrassment."

Chalanor moved his head to rest his forehead on hers. "I was horrified at what he had nearly done to you. I remained silent because I was afraid. I wanted to kill him. I knocked him down but I wanted to rip his arms off. He threatened you. I knew that I could not control myself. It took all my concentration to resist. Can you understand? I am angry at him not you. I have no doubts about you. I want you to be mine. Please be mine."

"I would say that was a proposal, my girl." Lord Farraday stood and placed his hand on Louisa arm. "What do you say?"

She looked at Lord Farraday, then at her father and finally back into the eyes of his son.

"Can you ask me again tomorrow after you have thought about it?" was her quiet response.

"There is no need to think any more about it. I have thought of nothing else for the last week. Please know that I ask for your hand, for you to freely give it and for no other reason. The events of tonight have only made me more determined to have you as my wife. You fought like a wild cat to protect yourself from Prescott. You gained the respect of every person who witnessed his tawdry behaviour. I was so proud of you."

"But it was the truth your father declared that saved me. Not my own defence."

"I beg to disagree." Lord Farraday intruded. "All saw how you bravely fought for your reputation. I just acknowledged and confirmed it. Wait to see how you are received by the guests tomorrow and you will see that I am right." She lowered her head again.

Chalanor continued. "Nothing gave me greater pleasure than to hit him. I am not a violent man but I was delighted to see him on the floor. Don't hide behind your courage. Be proud of your fighting spirit. I am. I wish I could have saved you but I realise now that you needed to save yourself and you have."

She had imagined that she had lost everything. Her reputation, her courage and her Chalanor. Yet here he was declaring his love and everyone around them were smiling and encouraging her to believe what she was hearing. "Look at me, the man who loves you. If I was silent it is because I wanted to tear Prescott to pieces. He made me so angry. I do not want you to think anger was levelled at you. I love you."

She was still in doubt and Chalanor tried again.

"You have always been truthful with me. You have let me into your life despite your concerns. I know your strengths. I know who you are. I know the real Louisa not the Prescott version."

It was then than the truth was revealed to her and she knew what she had heard was true. He believed in her.

"Yes, you do." She smiled at her father then at Lord Farraday. Then she looked in to Chalanor's eyes and said, "I am Louisa Stapleton and I say yes."

"*M*y valet told me where Farraday had sent you. The servants have been speaking of nothing else but your banishment. They are crowing about it. I could not believe he would do that to you?"

"Well, he has. I will probably have to spend the rest of my life in this small insignificant house." The lady lay in his arms, no longer shaking or cold.

He nuzzled her neck and kissed her ear lobe. He too was no longer cold. He had watched from outside of the dower house to see a light in her window. He knew she would point out her room, so that he could find her. Then he slipped into the house and into her bed.

"I will always love you if you will have me?" He did not mean it but thought she might relax more if she heard his lie. After all, lies were what she was so good at. He was good at lying too, for that matter. His erection pushed up against her bottom.

"He didn't mention your name."

"What do you mean, my love?"

"My husband listed the names of other men I have had relationships with over the years." In the dark he could not see her face clearly but could see that she had turned her head toward him.

"Well that is good, isn't it?" He could imagine that list. How many hundreds had she had? He didn't care because he didn't care for her. He was just using her body to satisfy his lusts as she had used others. It was good news for him because he could have his lady and now that she was removed from the manor, he could have free rein to get his hands on Louisa without his lady watching. His lust for the trollop had not diminished. Her fighting behaviour tonight only made his lust grow. How he longed to rape her so he could squash that spirit. If Farraday did not know that he had bedded his wife then he could still move freely in the manor.

"Will you come to me every night? And not leave me alone?"

"You know that I need your body to satisfy me. Shall I take you again and prove it?" With a quick and simple movement he placed his member between her legs.

"That feels good."

He altered his position slightly and slid inside her tight moist hole then pinned himself to her. "Now shall I have you?"

"Yes, and quickly."

So, he took her till she screamed in release.

28

True to his word Lord Farraday addressed all the guests at breakfast. He assured everyone that despite the events of the previous evening he wanted the guests to stay for another week at least.

"I am sorry that you had to witness my wife's terrible attempt at blackening the name of a lady who is innocent. It only leaves me to say that Lady Farraday has other issues that she and I have discussed at length and I have insisted that she will now be residing at the Dower house."

Lady Midhurst stood. "Well, I have no intention of staying in this house while you treat my friend with such disrespect."

"Sit down, madam." Lord Midhurst intruded. "The girls and I are staying and I suggest you do the same." The Midhurst girls looked with shocked faces at their father. But they did not move nor say anything to contradict him.

Lady Midhurst slowly lowered herself back into her seat. She had been shocked into silence. It would seem the courage he had last night had rubbed off on Lord Midhurst. After some further discussion, Reverend Hutton, the Ismays, the Burgesses, the

Edwards, Bartley, the Beaumonts and Louisa and her father also agreed to stay.

Lord Farraday continued, "So despite the events, I wish to carry on with the plans I have made. In three days from now the estate fete is to be held. This has usually been held at the end of our summer house party. But I would like you to stay another week after this event. I want this fete to be bigger and better than it has ever been before. We have not had one on the estate for some time, what with the war and all. But some weeks ago, before your arrival, Ramsay and I determined to renew the tradition."

"It is strange sir, that you have your servants making such decisions and not your wife." Lady Midhurst chucked and looked away. However, her comments were ignored by all as the conversation continued.

"What would you have us do?" asked Chalanor.

"Enjoy yourselves. My staff and the villagers from Loose have arranged to do everything. There will be stalls of all kinds; food, archery, crafts, dancing, music, cheeses and other produce, tug of war, other games and much more. As my guests I want only for you to find enjoyment in all that is on offer. So, from today you will see various areas around the gardens being set up with what will be needed for the fete."

Lady Midhurst again added her comment. "And, may I ask, your wife? Where does she appear in these plans?"

"She does not, Lady Midhurst. She is my wife in name only. She will be spending the remainder of her life at the Dower House and that is all."

"You cannot treat her like this, sir. It is insupportable."

"I beg your pardon, madam. But her actions have been beyond the pale. She must now suffer the consequences of those actions." He looked directly at her, stood and placed his hands firmly on the table in front of him. He leaned forward toward her ever so slowly.

"I will not be cuckold in my own home any longer."

Everyone heard her draw in her breath. "Your language sir, please cease."

"Madam, she is gone. She still remains under my protection but she is gone. There is nothing more to say." Lord Farraday gave a brief bow and headed for the door. He stood still for a moment, turned back towards the gathered guests.

"No one and I repeat no one will visit Lady Farraday. Do I make myself clear? I will let you know when I will allow it and not before."

He slowly turned and left the room.

*C*halanor escorted Louisa into the library where his father waited for them. Sir Peter had arrived before them.

"Come and sit down, my dear," Louisa's father stood and pulled out a chair for her.

"What was it you wished to discuss, Father?" Chalanor asked as he sat on a chair next to hers.

"I am about to go and see your mother to discuss our ongoing arrangements. I have in mind what I would like to do but as you will one day inherit, I want your opinion on the matter. I will write to Petersen and I am sure that considering the changes, he won't mind coming from London again to see that all is in place."

"I am sure that your decisions will be fine, sir." He was so proud of his father and what he had already achieved in relation to his mother.

"That might be so but I will be happier to know that you approve." Chalanor nodded at his father.

"But sir," Louisa intruded. "You do not need to discuss this with my father and myself." She stood. "We will be happy to wait in the foyer for you to finish your discussion."

His father laughed but not at her. "My darling girl, you heard

Chal's declaration last evening. You are soon to be wed to my boy. I could not be more delighted. As you will need to deal with this eventually, when you are mistress of this house, I would prefer that you were here. I would value your thoughts." Chalanor took her hand and drew her gently back into her chair. He did not let go of her hand but brought her fingers to his lips and kissed them.

"Then sir, I will happily give you my thoughts."

"This is what I suggest. Lady Farraday will be given the use of the Dower house until her death. It will always remain part of the estate however. I will give her a small income but no more. She will not be allowed access to this house or our house in London and our staff will be instructed to remove her should she attempt to gain access to either. She may have a maid and cook only. She will have no driver or any horses or carriages. She needs to be cut off from doing any further damage to you, Louisa, or interfere in anyone else's life. It is also my suggestion that you do not allow her access to your own estate, my boy. This will limit her influence. Word will travel to London quickly enough that she has fallen from grace. I think she will find her sphere of influence will decrease substantially in the coming months. That will, I hope, give her food for thought."

"These arrangements seem sensible to me." Chalanor responded. "Surly she will see that you are being more than fair considering her actions over many years." His father stood and walked to his desk and then back to the chair.

"In your mother's mind she may see things very differently. But after I have died, she may very well be still alive and you will need to deal with her. Are these arrangements acceptable to you?" his father continued.

"Yes sir. As far as I am concerned I would have her as far a distance as I could from my Louisa." Louisa looked into his face and he hoped she could see that he had every intention of never allowing his mother anywhere near her again.

"That settles it. All the appropriate documents will be arranged and I will make sure that your mother agrees to them. I will ride over to the Dower house this morning and deliver our proposal to her."

"Chalanor and your Lordship, I do have a suggestion?" Louisa began.

"And what is that, my love?" Chalanor asked.

Louisa looked from one man to the other. "I think it might help to strengthen your father's position if you accompany him to visit your mother. If she hears that you are both determined that she face a different life, then, you may convince her of your plan for her. Perhaps then she will avoid trying to divide the two of you."

"That's a very good idea, my love. But I am reluctant to leave you alone."

"That is simple enough." Louisa added. "I will spend the morning with Elspeth while you both go to the Dower house."

"What do you say, Father?" Chalanor asked.

"Louisa my dear, I knew you would lend a hand with your suggestions. I think you have it aright. If her ladyship sees our united determination she will perhaps be less of a problem."

Chalanor stood. "Then it is settled. I shall take Louisa upstairs and leave her with Elspeth."

"Unfortunately, we have another problem." His father continued. Chalanor resumed his seat. "I had your mother's maid remove the family jewels from your mother's belongings before they were sent to the Dower house. While going through them she came across these." He pulled out Louisa's pearls from his pocket.

"My pearls!" She took them into her hands and hugged them to her chest. "I swear I never thought I would see them again." Her father placed his arm around her shoulders and gave her a little hug.

Lord Farraday continued, "Her maid did not recognize them but your missing pearls immediately came to her mind. This would confirm that your mother may have had something to do with Alice's murder or it could be a coincidence of timing, perhaps stealing them from Louisa to torment her. I would rather accept the latter explanation than the former. But we will need to confront her with this evidence."

With that Lord Farraday rose. He walked over to Louisa and took her into his arms. "Thank you for your well thought out suggestion. And I am glad you have your pearls back." He turned to look at Chal. "I'll meet you at the stables." He left the room.

Louisa looked at Chalanor. "Would you put them on for me before you go?"

"Definitely." He took them from her hand and placed them around her neck. "Now let me escort you upstairs."

"Don't worry, my boy," Sir Peter interrupted. "I'll take her up. By the way when you get back, we have a wedding to discuss." Chalanor grinned, gave a little bow and went to the stables to meet his father.

"*W*hat do you want?" Lady Farraday sat back down on the chaise in her new sparsely furnished parlour.

"I suggest madam, that you keep a civil tongue in your head." He sat in the chair opposite the chaise. "I hope the accommodation is acceptable?"

"Of course it is not. I want to go back to the manor." She folded her arms and pouted.

"Madam, this will be your home for the rest of your life." She opened her mouth to speak but he lifted his finger and she paused. He continued. "I have discussed this with Chalanor who has agreed to continue my plans after my death, to ensure that you have a roof over your head."

"I want to see my son. I cannot believe that he would allow me to stay in these conditions let alone agree with you, you weak minded man."

At that moment Chalanor walked into the room. He had suggested he come in a few moments after his father. He had stood out in the hall waiting for what was the correct moment.

"Good morning, Mother. Please be careful what names you call my father."

She arose from her chair.

"My darling Chal. I am so glad you have come. Your father is determined to reduce me to poverty."

"As always Mother, you exaggerate. And before you go on, I happen to agree with father. I think you had best get used to your new surroundings. And father has come to his senses as far as I am concerned." He looked at his father and smiled. She slowly sat down again.

"How could you possibly allow me to stay like this?"

"Quite easily ma'am, your actions give us little choice. Besides there would be many who would not protest to such surroundings."

"My actions, are you mad also? I am trying to protect you from that harlot Louisa…"

"That wonderful young lady, madam, will be my wife so I would encourage you greatly to mind your tongue."

"You cannot be serious? Do you really think that I will allow you to do this? That girl will never take my place in the manor."

This time it was Lord Farraday who defended Louisa's honour. "I would rather ten such ladies like Louisa over one of you to reside in my house. Now keep your mouth closed a while as I lay down some rules which you will be expected to observe." She sat there open-mouthed, no doubt shocked that he would stand up to her after all these years.

"You will not be allowed visitors until I believe you will behave in a suitable manner. Visitors will be strictly monitored for the time being at least."

"You cannot be serious? Am I to be your prisoner now?" She stared at him.

"You might call it that. I would say that you are receiving your just reward. If you treat people with contempt, the likelihood is that is how you will end up being treated." He crossed his leg and continued. Chalanor got another chair, and sat down.

Lady Farraday just looked at the two men in front of her and recognised immediately that she would not be able to change their minds with mere discussion.

"Chal, did your father tell you about your sister?"

Lord Farraday interjected immediately. "No more madam. Your lies will not be repeated."

"Then I suggest," she went on "that you reconsider because I am convinced that the same person who killed her also killed Alice and has his sights on Louisa."

"Very well Mother. Father and I will discuss it and if I should believe your theory, I will return so that you can tell me who it is." Chalanor stood and walked to the door. "Shall we leave, Father?"

"Most definitely, by the way my lady, how did you obtain Louisa's pearls?"

"Ah. So, you took them from my jewels. I am sure you would like to know. It would appear that we have some negotiations yet to perform."

Lord Farraday stood and walked to the door. "Madam, we will return with Peterson once the papers have been prepared."

"I will not sign them. Do you hear me?"

"Then madam, I suggest that you write to one of your lovers and see if they will house you for I have no intention of keeping a roof over your head unless you obey." With that he walked out of the room and the house with Chalanor.

"What was the woman talking about? What does she think she knows about Delia?" Chalanor did not look happy.

"As far as I am concerned, she is again telling lies to save herself.

She said she found Delia at the cottage in the woods and that she was dead. She said that she buried her under the oak tree. But I don't believe it. I know that she does terrible things but to bury her own daughter and not tell anyone? Even for her that seems beyond the bounds of belief. Can you imagine her even knowing how to dig a hole? Besides, what she does not know is that I have had news of her whereabouts. It is from a good source. I am having it checked out."

They mounted their horses and began the ride back to the manor. After a few moments Chalanor continued.

"Thank you, Father. That gives me relief. I believe that you're right. Mother is trying to save her own neck. I hope your news will give us all relief."

The moonlight filled the room with strange shadows, distorted but gave enough light for him to see her face.

"I am glad you have come. My husband has no intention of allowing me the opportunity of returning to the manor. Which now places me in a difficult position. I do not want to stay in this small rabbit warren."

He moved to sit next to her on the bed. "What will you do then?"

"Well I thought, we could run off together and I could live with you?"

"That is out of the question, my dear." He nuzzled up to her neck as he undid the buttons of his shirt.

"Why is that?" She gave him a gentle push away from her so that she could see his face as he answered.

"The scandal of course, I will not allow the scandal."

"What of the scandal if they find out you killed that poor maid?"

"That is easy enough madam. I will tell them you demanded that

I do it. So, if they take me then they will take you. But we will not go down that path, will we?" He laid her down on the bed and straddled her body. She lay there stiff as a post.

"And why won't we?"

"Because my darling, we both have too much to lose. I want you and you know that. So, stay here in the Dower house and I will always be here for you." He kissed her and she softened beneath him.

"Do you promise? To always be here for me?"

"Always." He lied of course. He had no intention of spending much more time with her. Now he had to be concerned that she might change her mind and reveal his identity to Farraday especially if it suited her purpose. He could never trust her again. He will watch her and listen for now but he would not let her remain alive. Not now that she dared threaten to expose him. That was her biggest mistake.

He made love to her long and hard, leaving her asleep in her bed, for now. But only for now.

29

"I'm so pleased that we can walk around the garden again without worrying about what mother will say and do." He took Louisa's hand in his and gave it a squeeze. It had been hectic in the days leading up to the fete. The servants were getting all in readiness. The guests were excited about the upcoming event and the general mood of happiness invaded the house.

"I agree, my dear. But it makes me sad that she will not see the errors that she has made and try to make amends." Chalanor stopped walking and took Louisa into his arms.

"That is your nature, my dear. You want to think what the best could be even when those around you don't want to. It's her decision, my love. She must live with it."

They continued their walk.

"I know but I guess that I would like all to be as happy as I am. I am excited that we are announcing our engagement at the fete. It just may put to rest all that has happened. And perhaps who wants to hurt me may give up."

"I hope that your theory is accurate. That would be the best for all concerned. The formal announcement would be in the papers in London on the same day. Peterson had sent word that he will arrive the night before the fete and stay to enjoy the pleasures of it and then complete the necessary paperwork for mother at the same time. I hope that you are happy with the arrangements?"

"How could I not be?" she whispered.

He took her into his arms again and this time kissed her. It was light but with a hint of passion. He longed to have her in his arms for ever. And with the announcement soon to be made that dream seemed a reality.

---

*L*ouisa looked around the room at the guests who quietly talked among themselves. She had in just three short weeks been brought back into society, not completely but well on the way. She had fallen in love with a man she had once hated and looked forward to a future that would be the envy of many a debutante.

Chalanor leaned over to whisper in her ear. "I don't believe anyone is yet aware of what we will announce tomorrow."

"Perhaps, but they know that you have intentions for me."

"What makes you say that, my love?"

"You follow me everywhere. You hold my hand every chance you get. And since your mother left, I now sit next to you at every meal." She moved in a little closer.

"That is true. But you are forgetting one important thing. Neither of us can stop from looking at each other. It is not just I."

"Again, you are correct." She gave a little chuckle. She then whispered to him, "I want to speak with you before we announce our engagement. May we go somewhere and speak in private?"

Chalanor looked deep into her chocolate eyes. "My love, you are not having second thoughts, are you?"

"No, on the contrary. There are things I wish to discuss with you and there is one thing in particular I would like to establish."

"Very well."

She looked into the magic of his eyes and knew that he would do anything for her if it meant they could spend the rest of their days looking into each other's eyes.

"I will escort you to the stairs. Go to your room. Wait for me there and I will come to get you."

"To go where?" she asked.

"I will take you to my father's library. But I will not have you go there alone."

"Very good. I will head to bed now then." Louisa went to her father and bid him good night. She bid the other guests a good evening including Mr. Petersen who had arrived just before dinner.

"Early night, Miss Louisa?" asked Reverend Hudson as he stood with Freddie and Bartley.

"Yes sir, such a big day tomorrow with the fete I felt it would be best to retire early."

"I most heartily agree," replied Freddie. "The fete will be a wonderful event. I look forward to hearing all about it tomorrow evening."

"Do you not plan to be here?" Louisa asked.

"I do but I am interested in what you think of it." He bowed, "Until tomorrow." With that Freddie picked up her hand and kissed her fingers.

"I also look forward to that discussion," intruded Reverend Hutton. He gently took her other hand and kissed the fingers of that hand.

"If I may," added Bartley, as he took Louisa's hand from Freddie and also kissed her hand.

"Now, gentlemen," Chalanor interrupted. "The lady needs her rest." He bowed and then taking Louisa's hand, resting it on his sleeve, he escorted her to the bottom of the stairs. A footman followed a few feet behind. When they reached the bottom of the stairs the footman passed them and went up the stairs and waited at the top.

"I will go back for a while so as to cause no tongues to wag. I believe all will settle shortly and I will come and get you."

She turned and went up the stairs.

"*I* hope that Louisa is well, old man?" Freddie asked, with concern in his voice.

"She is well, just a little tired." Chalanor replied looking at the clock on the mantle.

"Perhaps we should play charades," suggested Frances who was now standing with Freddie, Bartley and the Reverend.

"Thank you, but no. I plan to finish my tea and head to bed also. It will be a big day tomorrow with the fete, a busy and tiring one I am hoping." He turned and went back to the chaise and sat down. His father and Sir Peter came and joined him.

"I will be off to bed shortly. Is Louisa well?" Sir Peter asked.

"She is fine." He chuckled that everyone had noted her departure. He was glad that he had decided to return for a while before retiring. He did not want to reveal that they planned to have a private get together.

"I am looking forward to announcing your betrothal tomorrow, my boy." His father whispered. "By the way, the special license arrived this afternoon. Do you still plan to marry a week from tomorrow?"

"I do sir. The sooner, the better it will be for me, I can assure you. I do not believe the threat to Louisa is yet gone. We have silenced mother but not I believe the person whom she was working with. Prescott was involved but as a minor player. Of that

I'm sure. There is someone else, who still wants to hurt her. I know it." The men looked at him in surprise.

"Do you truly believe that someòne else is involved?" Lord Farraday questioned.

"I do. Mother was with me when that urn fell. Remember?"

"Yes, you are right," concluded Sir Peter.

"She would have had someone do the deed and then murder Alice to stop the girl from telling what she had seen, namely the man who came off the roof. This is far from over. As for the wedding date, I will confirm it with Louisa but I am sure she will agree. The sooner Louisa remains permanently, in my arms the happier I will be, if you will excuse me?" Chalanor stood and the other two gentlemen also stood. They wandered the room bidding all a goodnight and then all three men retired for the evening. The remaining guests soon followed.

*C*halanor made his way down the corridor to Louisa's room. All the guests had gone to bed early and he wanted to be sure that the night was quiet before he came to her. He had hoped that she would not be too anxious, being later than he thought he would be. He did not want her to think he was not coming. He quietly opened the door and slipped silently into her room. Louisa sat in the chair in front of the fire. She was a vision of splendour. Her golden hair was loose and flowed down, to rest on her shoulders. Her clothing was the finest lace that he could imagine. But then he really didn't care because every item of clothing looked beautiful on Louisa. She lifted her head from the book she was looking at. He was not surprised. It would appear that her ears were attuned to the door awaiting his arrival. Her glorious brown eyes sparkled with joy and excitement as he walked to where she was seated and knelt before her.

"Now my dearest, shall we go to the library?" Chalanor asked.

"I'm happy to talk here."

"Very well. But I am concerned that no one knows I am here. I still wish to protect your reputation. What is it you wish to discuss?"

"It is quite simple, I love you. I have no doubts. I think I have loved you in my heart even when my head wanted to hate you. But even more than that, is you love me. I know the difference between infatuation and real love. You have proven to me time and again that I am more important to you than anything or anyone else."

He took her hand and squeezed it.

"I am delighted to hear you say this, my love. And I am the first to say it is you I love. The person you truly are."

"Then I have a favour to ask."

"Of course, please make your request."

"I know that tradition dictates what little wealth I have will go to you on our marriage."

He looked at her quizzically and waited for her to continue. She continued.

"My mother handed down to me a sum that was to be for my benefit. I would like to keep that under my control when we marry."

"Is that what you are concerned about? My darling Louisa, I am not marrying you for your money. Of course, you can do with it what you wish. Do you have something specific in mind?"

She reached over and hugged him. "Yes, I do but I will share that with you after we are married if I may."

"Is that all that concerns you?"

"That was the major concern of which I did not need to be concerned it would seem."

He stood up and brought her into his arms. He held her close. Could he get any closer? He wanted her closer than she was. His arms tightened around her.

"Do you really believe that this villain will not cease tormenting me?"

She had read his mind again.

"Simply, yes."

"Then it seems simple that we must marry as soon as we can."

Chalanor took Louisa by the hand. He sat in the chair and drew her on to his lap. "I have longed for those words to be spoken. I want for nothing else but to be with you, always. So, the sooner we marry is what I also desire."

He looked into her dark eyes. "I would have you here and now my love but I don't want your disrespect. I want to show the world that I love you by taking you as my wife. I respect you more than just taking you to my bed. Do you understand?" He leaned down and kissed her, tasting her mouth and wanting to taste her whole body. With an effort, he slowed his kisses.

"Then my future husband I think you should leave."

Reluctant but he knew he had to, Chalanor stood up and went to the bedroom door. "You will be marrying me sooner than you think. Sleep well my dear, tomorrow the world will know of my commitment to you."

He opened the door and silently slipped from the room.

---

*H*e stood in the shadows watching Chalanor slip from Louisa's room. If that stupid footman was not there, he would have gone to her and slapped her around for daring to take Chalanor to her bed. The slut was going to regret this night.

30

I n the Dower house he moved to get up out of bed and return to the manor. He had come in later last night than he intended after spying on Louisa and Chalanor. He needed to get back before the servants began wandering around the house.

"There is no need for you to leave. I have told my servants not to wake me or disturb me and to go to the fete. I thought we could just enjoy being with each other for the morning. You won't be found out as no one comes to see me except you."

He lay back next to her and took the lady into his arms. She snuggled into him. He had waited for this moment, the chance to rid himself of her and concentrate on Louisa. He never imagined that it would come so quickly, and on the very day he planned to take the whore. He did not trust his lady to keep her mouth shut about the murder of Alice. He had enjoyed taking Alice. She looked so much like Louisa, her blond hair and plump breasts. He shuddered reliving the moment that he had taken Alice's life, not from disgust but from the pure pleasure he had gotten from her murder.

"Are you cold?"

"No, I'm just thinking of how we can enjoy this morning."

"Mmmm, yes please."

But the lady in his arms would talk if it suited her purposes. She was after all a wonderful liar. When she would discover he had taken Louisa she would talk. She would be jealous. She would want to hurt him. So, it was time to act. Knowing her servants would not be coming to her in the morning was perfect. She would lay here in her bed dead, until after he had taken Louisa. He could not believe his luck. But he could enjoy her first.

He got out of bed and went to her chest draws. He reached into the top drawer and took out a handful of her stockings. He came back to the bed and opened the curtain behind it. The soft morning light drifted into the room casting a little light on his lady's face. This was good, he would be able to have a good view of what he was going to do to her.

"What are you doing?" she asked, turning on her side to look at him. She flashed her mischievous grin at him. He would miss the sex, that was certain but he would not miss her.

"I thought we would have some fun as we will be alone for a while." He took her left hand and tied one stocking around her wrist. "I want to tie you to the bed and make mad passionate love to you. By tying your hands, I make you my prisoner, my love prisoner. That way you cannot stop me making love to you the way I want to. And it will be more intense for you."

She lay back down. "That sounds wonderful. Go right ahead." If only she knew the pleasure would be all his and little for her. She would enjoy the beginning, until she realized what he was going to do to her. Then he would feed on her fear and relish it. He got so excited on the fear. He finished tying her other wrist on the other side of the bed, then the feet to the posts at the end of the bed. She waited patiently for the fun to begin.

He stood at the end of the bed and looked at her. He was naked and she could not get her eyes off any part of him. Her lustful looks added to his lust for her. His member grew large and harder with each movement of her eyes. "Please be quiet, my love," he said, "The servants do not leave for a while. I do not want them to think you are in pain."

He walked to his coat pocket and pulled out his kerchief. He went back to the bed and sat beside her.

"My darling, why would they think I was in pain? They have no doubt heard me moaning as we have made love before and not come to disturb us. Why would they now?"

"Open your mouth, my love." She did. She was so trusting of him. Fool. He opened his kerchief and gave it a shake then screwed it up and placed it in her mouth. She looked at him and laughed. It was muffled by the kerchief. He smiled at her. "I am going to make love to you in ways that no one has done before and kill you as I do it." She looked at him and then realized what he had said.

She laughed again as he touched her cheek with his fingers, then he slapped her. The stunned look on her face began the fear she would soon discover he could produce in her. He closed his eyes breathing in deeply and could smell the fear. She pulled at the stockings to see if they would give. They did not. She screamed but the kerchief was doing its job of muffling the sound. He hit her face again. She began to weep.

"Now you know why I have to kill you, don't you?" She shook her head and muttered something unintelligible.

"You will save your own skin to get back into the manor. I know you. Yes, and in more ways than one." He ran his hand across her stomach. "I will miss the sex. We have been good together. I have so enjoyed it." He sat astride her to prevent her making unnecessary movements. "But I cannot trust you. I do not trust you. You will tell whoever you want about me and what I did to Alice. So now I will love you, my darling, for the last time and you will die at my hands. Do not move. It will be easier on you if you don't." He leaned down and suckled at her breast. The fear in her eyes was very evident. She was weeping so he hit her a few more times to quieten her. "I will enjoy your pain and your blood. Then he bit her right breast hard and the blood flowed. He liked it, the warm red blood. She was screaming so he slapped her again. "Shut up, whore. By the way, I plan to take Louisa into my bed today. She will be so wonderful to fill with my seed." He breathed out and smiled at her.

"You know I might let her live so she can produce me a child. Something you couldn't do, old lady." He placed his mouth over the weeping wound letting her blood moisten his lips and then kissed her mouth. She continued to cry and scream through the kerchief but to no affect. Her own blood was on her lips and face.

He did unspeakable things to create pain in her body. He enjoyed her body in ways only he could, terrifying her. Finally, he climbed atop her and thrust his aroused member deep inside her. As his ecstasy grew his hands reached around her neck. He went harder and harder. He was sailing higher and higher in his ecstasy and all because he was killing her. At last he reached his peak and she died on cue as he climaxed. He lay atop her still form for a few moments then he stood and walked to the window. This had to be the best he had ever had. And he still had Louisa to come. He stood there for a while enjoying the morning light and the early birds singing their waking songs. After some time, he saw the maid and cook, her only servants, leave the house to walk to the manor to attend the fete.

He looked down at his dead mistress, smiled and took his pleasure in her one last time. Then he took the scissors from her table and took a cutting of her glorious black hair. He took a ribbon from her drawer and tied it around the clipping. He would take a piece of Louisa's hair too. That way he could remember the dark of his lady and the light of the whore that was Louisa. He then washed and dressed and left the room, leaving the door closed behind him.

*H*e was lucky the servants were so occupied with the fete that they did not notice him as he slipped into Maidstone Manor. He rang for his valet and dressed for the day. He was sure his plans for Louisa would work beautifully. He discussed his plan again with his valet, as he was an integral part of it and both were convinced it would all go on without a hitch.

He went downstairs to breakfast. He had a big appetite today. This was the best day of his life.

31

Breakfast was a festive time. Many of the guests discussed the various stalls and games that the fete would hold for their enjoyment. What a beautiful way to start a new life with the person you loved more than any other in the world. Louisa looked and spoke with all the smiling guests at the table.

She leaned over and whispered into Chalanor's ear, "I will always love you."

"And I you, my love," He looked into her eyes and smiled. He handed her a rose. "I took it from the garden when I had an early morning walk. You will have one every morning from this day on." She gazed into his eyes, amazed at his thoughtful and romantic gesture.

Lord Farraday stood up to address his guests. "I want to thank you all for sharing this day with us and for staying to enjoy it. Elspeth my dear, I am even more overjoyed that you are down here this morning to share in the joy. Sir Peter, will you join me?" Sir Peter stood and came to stand next to Lord Farraday.

"We want for you all to join in our mutual joy. Chalanor has asked Louisa to become his wife and she has accepted. Will you please congratulate the happy couple?"

Chalanor stood and brought Louisa to her feet with a touch of his hand. He was so proud of her. She looked radiant. She looked so beautiful. She was dazzling in her yellow muslin with her mother's pearls again around her neck. There was much noise as some of the guests stood to cheer and come to their sides to congratulate the happy couple. So moved by the congratulations and involved in their love they did not notice the faces of those who did not share their joy.

Lord Farraday continued. "The couple will be married here in a week. You are all most welcome to stay and join us for that wonderful day."

Chalanor watched as Louisa went to Elspeth and hugged her friend. Oh, if only Elspeth could find the love that he felt for Louisa. Both ladies were crying with joy and he knew Elspeth would be glad they had found each other.

"The fete will begin in a few moments. The villagers and friends of the manor are gathering at the front of the building for me to open the fete. I will also announce the engagement of my son and Miss Stapleton. Let us ready ourselves, my friends."

---

*A*s the majority of the guests gathered around the happy couple, Frances came to stand beside Freddie. "You don't seem happy for them?" she asked.

"On the contrary, I am delighted," Freddie looked down at the girl and smiled, "delighted beyond words." He crossed his arms and grinned at the happy couple.

"Well I'm not. He was supposed to be for me." She crossed her arms and shook her head.

"Remember what they say. You don't always get what you want." He walked away from the sulking girl.

*T*he announcement was made, the villagers and all the visitors to the manor were excited that the fete brought the added joy of an engagement. Louisa and Chalanor walked around the grounds and were greeted by many of the visitors.

He was watching them, waiting for when the right moment would come. His valet was in the woods also watching and hoping that he was able to get the chance they were looking for.

Louisa and Chalanor made their way to the edge of the woods where the archery stall was set up. It was nearly time for luncheon and Lord Farraday was to hand out a prize for the best shot of the morning.

"*F*ather is so excited about today. After all the unhappiness he has experienced with my mother it gives me great joy to see him enjoying himself so much. Also that mother has not embarrassed us by showing up uninvited."

"I knew he had not been happy from all you had told me. But I am delighted to think that his years from this moment on will have more joy than pain in them. Well, this is what I hope."

"And I also," he leaned in and whispered in her ear. "You give him joy."

"Do you really think so? Do you believe that he does not harbour any doubt about my reputation?"

Chalanor stopped walking and turned her toward him to look into her face. "I know that he does not."

She looked at the depth of his blue eyes and marvelled at the thought of what they would soon do together. He honoured her by waiting. Trusting that she was both a maiden and the love of his life. She would love him all her life, however long that would be. He leant down and kissed her, a brief gentle kiss. A kiss that promised so much more than what he could display here.

They walked on toward the archery.

Lord Farraday was standing on the back of a cart ready to announce the morning's winner. As the crowd began to gather a whishing noise could be heard and suddenly Lord Farraday fell from the cart to the ground. Chalanor ran to his father's side and Louisa was not far behind him. His father was moaning and struggling to get to his feet. Chalanor stopped him from getting off the ground. There in his right arm was an arrow. It had gone right through.

"Father please, stay still." He did not want to take the arrow out of the arm in case he added to the damage already done. He threw off his coat, and then started to undo his cravat. Once off he tied the cravat around his father's arm to try to stop the bleeding. Louisa had rolled up Chalanor's coat and placed it under Lord Farraday's head.

People were coming from everywhere. Ramsay appeared and Chalanor said to him, "Try to keep his lordship awake. Keep him talking. I'll run to the house and see if the doctor is at the fete or if he needs to be sent for." He looked at Louisa, "Do not leave his side I beg you." He turned and ran toward the house.

Louisa looked at her future father in law and hoped and prayed that he would be all right. Who would do this, his wife? Did she even know how to shoot a bow and arrow? She stood and tried to get the crowd to move on and give his lordship some room. Some of the servants who were nearby came to her aid and helped to keep the crowd that was slowly growing at bay. Then Freddie came to stand beside her.

"Chalanor is searching for the doctor. They believe he is near the lake. He's asked me to come and get you and bring you to the house."

"But he told me to stay here with his father. He didn't want me to move."

"I guess he changed his mind. Probably thinks this is another trap to hurt you, a possible distraction. Come with me, my dear. We only want what is best for you."

It made sense that Chalanor would want her out of harm's way but she was reluctant to leave his lordship. She leaned down to one of the maids who was next to his lordship and told her she was going with Freddie.

"Don't leave, Louisa," His lordship begged her.

"I don't want to be a target sir, it is best that I go. The servants will stay with you until the doctor arrives." She stood and looked at Freddie.

"Very well," she said and they turned to walk toward the house.

"I think we might go via the edge of the wood. It provides you with cover should anyone be searching for you. We don't want to give them a good target with any further arrows."

"I do hope that he will be alright." Louisa walked on with Freddie but her thoughts were for Lord Farraday. She could hear him calling her name. "Perhaps I should stay with him."

"I am sure that he will be fine. Now come with me." He led her further into the woods.

"But this is getting further away from the house? Shouldn't we be heading more that way?" she pointed toward the house.

"Don't worry. I just want to be sure no one sees you." He gently took her by the hand and she followed. But deep inside her heart there was a growing uneasiness. Her heart was beating harder. Freddie wanted to protect her, didn't he?

*C*halanor made his way up the steps to where Elspeth sat on a chaise that had been brought out onto the balcony so she could be part of the day's activities. She looked upset.

"Is your father alright? One of the servants just brought the news that he was shot by an arrow." She looked troubled.

"He was when I left him with Louisa. I am just going back to him now so that I can bring him and Louisa into the safety of the house. Will you keep an eye on Louisa for me and make sure she stays with you?"

"But Louisa is already with my brother."

"Freddie? What is Freddie doing with her?"

"I have been watching the crowd of people gather near where your father was hurt. I saw Freddie take Louisa by the hand and lead her into the woods. I am sure it was her. Her beautiful yellow dress can easily be spotted in this crowd. I thought it was strange but then thought you had asked him to protect her. It was but a moment ago."

"I did not. Oh my God. It can't be Freddie." Chalanor stood there for a moment and all the pieces fell into place. He had been on the ride, he was overly upset about his sister's accident knowing he had hurt the wrong person. He knew nothing of horse flesh by his own admission. He had been nowhere in sight when the urn had fallen. He must have killed Alice.

Was he having an affair with my mother?

He did not delay. He called the footman who was watching over Elspeth.

"What is the matter, Chal?" Elspeth asked with growing concern.

Chalanor addressed the footman. "Find my mother's maid. Tell her she is to bring my mother to the library as quickly as possible." Then pointing to another footman walking by, "You man, get me my horse, quickly." He saw one of the maids and called her to him. "Stay with Miss Elspeth and send any message if she sees her brother or Miss Louisa." He looked down at Elspeth. "If you see Freddie or Louisa, send word to my father and Sir Richard."

"But what is it, Chal?"

"Trust me I will explain later. I have no time."

Chalanor then ran to his father with every ounce of energy he had. A moment later he reached him. "Father?"

"Son, go to the woods, now, I think to the crofter's cottage. I saw Ismay taking Louisa that way. I tried to stop them but the crowd got in the way."

Chalanor shuddered.

"Father, the men here will take you to the house. Please tell some of the gentlemen, Midhurst, Beaumont and alike, to gather and come toward the cottage being careful to pay attention to what is happening. They must come up quietly, please stress that they must come quietly. I will go after Louisa." He did not wait for an answer but ran toward his horse coming at speed toward him with a stableman riding it. The horse pulled up just a few feet away from him. The stableman leaped off and he got on. He turned and rode north. He would come around from the rear, hoping to arrive at the cottage before them. If Freddie got her in the building, he doubted Louisa would get out alive.

32

F reddie was sure he had succeeded. There was no sign of his valet which meant all was clear and no one was coming after them. He had to get her to the cottage. But she seemed to be deliberately dragging her feet. He had hold of her hand and was pulling her up the path.

"Oh Freddie, can't we stop. I am sure we are safe here." She leant up against the nearest tree. She lifted her foot and rubbed her ankle with her other hand.

"No, we are still out in the open and I am sure Chal won't like that." His eyes drifted to her ankle and his lust rose.

"Well, I don't really care. I think I would prefer to be near him at the moment. The archer might be here in the woods for all we know." She tried to pull her hand from his but he would not let her go. From his pocket he pulled a knife. He slowly raised it to her face and pointed it at her.

"Well, that is a pity but you see I want you near me. Do you understand? I want you, with me."

"Freddie?" She looked at the knife with disbelief. Fear crossed her face. He smiled. He had her now. She won't take him for granted any more.

---

*S*he then looked into his eyes. They had changed. This man was not the joking, happy go lucky man she had known all of her life. He looked wild, dishevelled and angry. She had never seen him like this. A chill went through her. She was suspicious of why he was leading her into the woods, so she walked slowly. But now it was obvious to her. That smile was not happiness. It was sinister. Her skin tingled as sweat formed on it.

"You killed Alice, didn't you?" not expecting an answer. She knew she had to keep him talking so that Chalanor could find her. Or she might get the chance to get away herself. She would have to try as it was her only hope. She had no idea how long it would take Chalanor to realize she was even gone.

"Why are you doing this?" She found it hard to believe her friend was her attacker.

"You spoilt everything. You know that, don't you?" His look was menacing.

"Freddie? What is it I have done? What have I spoilt?" The hair on her arms rose at the truth of the situation. But she needed to know.

"You have ruined Elspeth's chances of marrying Chalanor. You know that? She could have been happy and wealthy. I would do anything for her to have that kind of happiness. I have lost all my wealth. I have no dowry for her. I had to protect her and Chalanor was my solution."

She had to keep him talking but his revelations disturbed her. "What do you mean? Elspeth doesn't love Chalanor." She knew that Freddie was not himself but she needed to remind him Elspeth had her own opinion on marriage. It was not for him to decide. Elspeth would never allow it.

He raised his voice, "Of course not. How could she even stand a chance with you in the room? He only has eyes for you. The stupid man is besotted."

"No, that's not what I mean," she interrupted. She looked hard at him. "Elspeth has never loved him. We talked about it and she says she sees him as a brother." She hoped her comments would make him see reason, but as her stomach churned, she had her doubts.

"She saw that you loved him so she stood aside for you. That's the kind of person she is. She would sacrifice her own happiness for someone else."

He was getting angrier so she knew she had to change the topic.

He pushed her against the tree. "I couldn't get her to change her mind since she believed the lies you told her." He lifted his knifeless hand and fondled her breast. She shuddered and he smiled. "Are you afraid?" He laughed.

She lifted his hand and removed it from her breast. His lip curled. His touching her in such an intimate way filled her with even greater fear. If she reacted to his touch he could lash out and hurt her. She needed to distract him. She didn't want to look at him.

"I'm sorry, Freddie," she stuttered, "but can you tell me why you want her to marry Chalanor? I thought you didn't like marriage. And Elspeth says she doesn't want to marry either. She prefers to be on her own," She closed her eyes trying but not succeeding in erasing the feel of his hand on her breast.

He took her hand in his again.

"I don't want marriage for me. Why would I? My mother only married my father for his money. They argued and screamed at each other all the time. It was a wonder to me they even had Elspeth and me. But it doesn't matter. Now, they are both gone and so is the money. Elspeth has no choice, she must marry."

She seemed to be doing enough to distract him. But she was wrong. Suddenly, he turned around to look through the woods they had already been through. All was still. Nothing moved. There were no sounds, not even birds singing. Perhaps that is why he was on the alert. She had to continue to distract him and get him to talk. She needed to know more. She still could not believe the change in him. Playing dumb and not understanding was what she would do to delay him. She only hoped it would work.

"How did your parents die?"

Distract him, distract him.

"You know. Don't pretend to be the fool. It does not suit you. I know that you know all the details." He laughed. "You and my sister talked about it all the time. A storm hit the area near our home and the carriage ended up in a ditch and they were both killed. But it was I who made sure the accident would happen. Does that make you feel better? See, I can put it so simply?"

"I'm sorry Freddie. I know how hard it was for you and Elspeth. I am sorry." She had angered him more. But he had revealed the truth. He had rid his parents so he could inherit.

Take it slowly.

"I don't care about that. I wanted Elspeth to marry for money. So that she would be protected. Now that will not happen. And we are bankrupt."

He let go of her hand and began to pace back and forth in front of her. She looked around but the grass was too long and there seemed no where she could run to get away from him.

If someone came however…

"I will have to sell the estate to pay off the creditors. My stupid father had huge gambling debts a mile high and I added to them. That's why I killed him. To stop his madness. But Elspeth won't marry him now, will she, because you will marry Chalanor. You have ruined all my plans. Now keep moving."

She stood there looking at him in shock at his revelation. He had killed his parents and now wanted his sister to marry money. Money, he could get his hands on? He had been the one to hurt her. But she could not believe that he would do it all for Elspeth. Would he truly kill for her as he had killed Alice? But he admitted to killing his parents.

All of this she was finding difficult to believe. Elspeth obviously had no idea what her brother had been planning. She would have said something. Elspeth would never marry for the sake of marriage nor allow him to do what he had been doing.

"Now move, bitch." He pointed the knife at the trail to her left, further away from the house.

Again, her thoughts went to diverting his attention and delaying him as much as possible. Then she could try to get away or hope that someone would come after her. Deep down she did not want to know the real reason he wanted her. She believed, no felt, that revelation would disgust her. She was in shock of both his behaviour to her and his revelations. Had Chalanor noticed yet that she was missing?

"I said move." He grabbed her by the arm and began to pull her along the path again.

"Very well, just a moment. I have a pebble in my shoe. Let me rid myself of it." She went over to another tree and lent on it. She took off her shoe and pretended to shake it out. Then she slipped it back on her foot. He grabbed her by the arm and bodily pushed her ahead of him.

Distract him, talk about something, anything.

"Can I ask you why you have been so kind to me if you hate me so much?"

"I only hate that you are in love with Chal and not me." He grabbed her and turned her around. "You have money and we could have been happy. I would have married you despite your reputation. But you want Chalanor and now it's all gone wrong. But once I have you, trust me, you will realize what a mistake you have made. Then you will marry me or die. I have every intention of having you."

She doubted love existed anywhere in Freddie's heart. Now her fear was peaking. She could see the lust in his eyes and the way he grabbed her and touched her. So, he wanted her body, which only added to her fear. She could not stop him from touching her though she wanted too. She feared he would kill her on the spot if she objected.

Let him think I am a whore if it stops him from hurting me. Distract him, distract him.

"What about the money? You said there is no more money."

He pushed her and she fell backwards to the ground. "Would you like me to take you here?" Louisa was sweating and shaking. But she did not want to show her fear and knew she had to distract him. She had to keep trying. She slid backwards on the grass away from him. He moved forward and stood above her, looking down. She would not get away with her bottom on the ground.

"Freddie, help me up? Please?" She put out her hand. He took it and helped her to her feet. He pulled her into his embrace. The arm with the knife in the hand held her tight and still. He took her hand with his other hand and placed it on his engorged member.

"I need you. Don't you see? Feel my lust for you? I have been wanting you for so long, to be inside you. Now I have you, you can't deny me. I won't let you." He nibbled at her neck breathing hard and then bit her. Not too hard but hard enough for her to know that he had every intention of doing what he intended to do.

She shuddered at the touch. She did not want this.

Distract him. Distract him.

He turned her around and pushed her forward.

"Hurry up or I will have you right now."

"I am just trying to understand what you have been doing and why. It makes no sense to me?"

"Why should it make sense to you? I do what I want. I answer to no woman." His features were full of lust for her. She was but an object. Nothing more. It was plain to see on his face.

She could see the cottage ahead and her trembles increased. Fear was filling her soul and she tried to push it away. She had to live to survive. They were closer to the building than she thought. This was where she imagined he was taking her. She had a good knowledge of the estate from all her after-luncheon walks with Chalanor. If he got her into that building, she would die but only after he had taken her. She knew that with every fibre of her being. She needed to keep them out in the open. She looked at him and could see his determination, his lust.

Distract him again.

"I know that you don't need to tell me anything but we have known each other for a long time. Why did you not tell me you cared for me?"

He grabbed her arm and swung her around, again pulling her into his embrace. He began to kiss her neck and nibble at her ear lobes. She shuddered and then he laughed out loud. She looked into his cold grey blue eyes. They were nothing like Chalanor's glorious blue. Why would they be? She wondered if she would ever see her love again.

He held the knife to her throat and licked away a tear that had come from her eyes. She had not even realized she was crying.

Stop crying, you fool. He must not see your weakness.

"I don't care for you," he said. He reached up with the knife still in his hand and took a hand full of her hair into his grip. He yanked her head back and licked her throat. "I just want to have sex with you. I desire you. You say you want the truth, I will tell you. It will be the best sex I have ever had. I know it. You will wonder at how marvellous it can be especially between you and me." With his other hand he grabbed her bottom and forced her into his erection. He groaned. "You pretend to be so innocent when the entire ton knows that you are one of the great harlots. Many other men of note have raved about your prowess. You have been the talk of all sexual game for years."

He pushed her again and she fell to the ground. She looked desperately from side to side for something that would help her escape. Before she could move he was on his knees over her. He grabbed her and turned her over pushing her face into the dirt. He lay on top of her and rubbed his engorged member against her bottom. Despite the clothing she could feel it as if it were his naked flesh on hers. She shuddered again. She wanted to be loved by Chalanor not him. She could remain quiet no longer.

"Get your body off me." She tried to get up but he pushed her down flat on the ground again and turned her over. He hovered above her and held the knife in front of her face. He laid down on top of her pressing his member into the space between her legs.

"Stop struggling. We both want this. It is me that you truly love. I will have you. Trust me. But not here. I don't want to be disturbed when I take you." He got up. Pulling her to her feet he propelled her forward. She took very small steps. Her heart was thumping against her chest. She was sure he could hear it. "I can do a lot of damage with this little tool. Leave marks on you that won't kill you but will certainly hurt you." She had no doubt he told her the truth. He took her hand and drew blood from the back of her hand and sucked it into his mouth. "Now you will walk into that cottage or I will kill you here and now."

In the distance they could hear horse's footfalls. "They can't be searching for you already? My man would have warned us." He listened for them again but the sound seemed to have gone. He turned this way and that looking for the object of the sound. All was quiet.

Louisa had heard them and it gave her hope. She looked around but could not see anyone near. She would say anything now to keep from going into that cottage.

"Perhaps they have caught your man and they are leading him

here to catch you." He placed the knife in his left hand and slapped her across the face with his right. She lost heart. Delay him again. If someone is near, they might hear him.

You must delay Freddie.

It took what little courage she had left.

"Freddie. I understand you want my body not me. I understand also that you wanted Elspeth to marry Chal for his money. Now can you tell me before I die why you killed Alice?"

He closed his eyes. Louisa could imagine what was going through his mind and it gave her no hope. He opened his eyes, looked at her and took her hand. "I loved you once but then you gave yourself to Prescott. Then I just wanted to hurt you. So, I killed the maid."

"But I honestly never did go with Prescott." She needed to voice her innocence even if he did not believe her.

"We will soon see, when I take your maiden head, like I took Alice's. She was so sweet and pure just like you pretended to be. But I was Alice's first. She was very lovely, and she loved me making love to her. I would have liked to have kept her for a while. But she had seen me come down from the roof. She would have told you and then you in turn, would have told Chalanor. She would have given me away. They all do. They promise they will love you forever but they don't. They just want my title and my money. I could not have that so I had to kill her. I loved her body. It was fresh and untouched. Not old and used like my Lady Farraday."

He pulled Louisa into his body and again she could feel that he was fully aroused. He whispered into her ear, "I won't kill you yet, not till I have been deep inside you. If you are innocent as you say then I will be your first and last. All the other men mean nothing. I am all that matters." He could feel the shudder that went through her body and he smiled. "I love your fear."

Her trembling could not be controlled. She was now shaking and was twisting her hands to try and prevent it. But she could not let him take her into that cottage. She struggled to find out what more she could say. She turned to face him. They were directly under the oak tree next to the cottage. "So, you were having an affair with Lady Farraday? We thought it was Midhurst. In fact he admitted it."

That made him angry. He pushed her from his body but kept a hold of her hand. "That bitch, that harlot. She was doing him at the same time she was doing me? She deserved to die. I wish I had known that while I was killing her. I would have made her suffer more." He grabbed her by the shoulders and pushed her to the ground hard.

"God, I will have you now..."

She heard a thump and lifted her head to see the body of a man on top of Freddie. She recognized the hair of her love Chalanor.

He had found her. Thank God.

Chalanor got off Freddie and tried to pull him up by the shoulders. Freddie rolled over and looked with disgust at Chalanor. He still had the knife in his hand and she could see that Chalanor was unarmed.

"Come to save the harlot with your bare hands, have you?" He got to his knees. "You are crazy if you would risk your life for that harlot." He gripped the knife tighter and pointed it at Chalanor. "Now I will wound you enough to incapacitate you. Then you can watch as I fill your woman with my seed." He was about to get up but turned his head when he heard a twig break.

Chalanor seized the moment and kicked the hand that held the knife, making it fly through the air. Freddie fell backwards. "Get up scum. Tell me now what you planned to do to my Louisa? And I will kill you slowly."

Freddie quickly stood. "She is mine, fool. She will always be mine." He replied as he dove to the place where the knife had landed. He rolled picked it up and stood. He saw a number of the men of the house party and the men of the estate making their way toward him.

"You will not escape." Chalanor stood in front of Louisa, determined to die protecting her from this attacker.

"You cannot stop me. None of you can. I will not be judged by you or any man. I will not let you. I am above you all." He looked at Louisa then raised the knife to his heart and rammed it home. Louisa screamed. Freddie sank to the ground on his knees. His eyes lifted to look at her again, "I would have been so much better than him," he said as he fell to the ground.

Chalanor turned and took Louisa into his arms then lowered her to the ground. It was over.

"You came for me. Thank you. Thank you. Poor, poor, Freddie."

Chalanor held her and hugged her. "You had a part in that, keeping him talking and delaying him. I heard you from my branch in the tree. I am so proud of you."

Louisa pulled away and looked into his blue eyes and asked "Is that where you came from?"

Taking her by the hand he led her away toward the path leading back to the manor. Finding a green patch of grass about twenty feet away from Freddie's body he sat her down. The men began to search the area to see if there were any other persons involved. Some of them made their way to where Freddie lay.

Chalanor sat down next to her. "First, tell me did he hurt you?" He took her into his arms and brought her close to his chest. She shuddered and he held her closer.

"Only some scratches and bruises, I think. Poor Freddie." She wept and he dabbed at the tears streaking down her cheeks. He held her. He took her hand and kissed her fingers. He could see the cut that Freddie had made on the back of her hand. It was still bleeding though slowly. He took his kerchief from his pocket and gently tied it around the wound.

After a time, she continued, "Now tell me how you got up into the tree."

"I rode a horse around the back of the woods as close to the cottage as I could and hoped I would get there before you did. I knew if you got to the cottage before me, he would have locked you and himself in there, killing you and then himself." He felt her shudder.

Louisa took his hand. "But how did you know he would come to the cottage?"

"Elspeth saw you being taken in this direction. It is the only place he could hide you. So I came. I know my father's land." He put his hand on her hair, taking a strand and rubbing it through his fingers.

She needed to talk. "I knew the hut was here, from our walks, and I also knew that if he got me in there I would die." She turned to look at the cottage. "But I was looking at the cottage and did not see you come from that direction?"

"That is because I came from above."

She looked above the cottage and could see that the oak tree's branches reached out over Freddie's body.

"You came from the tree. From above." she stated simply.

"I did. I hid behind its trunk and could see you slowly coming toward the cottage. I climbed the tree and went out on the strongest branch in a hope that you would walk underneath. You did, so I jumped down on top of him. I had no idea he was armed. I just thought once I had him on the ground, I could fight him till he was knocked out." He reached up and moved one of the curls that had displaced itself. Then he ran his finger down the side of her cheek. She shuddered but not in disgust. Feeling his hand on her skin renewed her faith in love. True love.

"He pulled the knife on me on our way here. I was trying to delay him by talking to him and tripping and taking stones from my shoes. I just knew I would be dead if I enter that cottage. I thought if I delayed him enough you might get to me in time. Or I might get the chance to run away. And you did find me."

He pulled Louisa over to him and placed her in his lap, holding her in his arms. They just held each other. Bartley, Hutton, Burgess, Beaumont and Midhurst came to see how they were. They had been with the other men from the estate and village. All gathered round the two lovers and Louisa told them what had happened, how she had delayed Freddie and what he had revealed. She surprised herself by remaining calm. Watching the men taking control calmed her. They had come for her and she was relieved.

Midhurst went over to Freddie's body for a few moments. Then came back and confirmed that he was dead. They removed the knife and wrapped it in one of the men's kerchiefs and placed it in Freddie's pocket. They then draped his body over Chalanor's horse.

Chalanor offered to carry Louisa but she insisted she was fine and just wanted his arms about her. The group headed out of the woods and back to the manor.

33

On their return to the manor all was in uproar. As soon as they came to the rear of the mansion they were surrounded by the villagers and staff. Chalanor took immediate control.

"Everyone please go on with the fete. This afternoon I will reveal to you all the events and what you need to know." People quietly dispersed and the gentlemen and Louisa entered the house and went to the sitting room. There Chalanor found all the remaining guests and his father, who refused to go to his room or be examined by the doctor until he knew Louisa was safe.

"My girl, tell me you are unharmed. I wouldn't let them touch me till I knew you were alive and safe." Tears were streaming down his cheeks. He looked pale and exhausted.

Louisa let go of Chal's hand and ran to him. Gingerly she knelt at his feet. Placing her hand on his she looked up into his face. "I am fine but you, sir, are not. You have lost a lot of blood and need the doctor to now take care of you. I will not be far away and I promise to sit with you later. But please let the doctor see to your injuries."

Relief washed over his face. He squeezed her hand. "I am so pleased you are alive and well my dear. And I will do as you say.

Please Louisa please, stay by Chalanor's side and I will be content." He looked to his son. "Marry her tonight. You have the special licence. Marry her tonight. You have my blessing."

"I will, sir. We promise to come and sit with you after all is mended." She looked exhausted but her only concern was for his father. Her love for his father and concern only made him love her more. He took heed to what his father had said. They would marry tonight if he had his way.

The doctor, Midhurst and Beaumont helped carry him upstairs to his room so that the arrow could be removed from his arm. He protested at being carried but relented and allowed them to do so.

Chalanor rang the bell for Ramsey.

Louisa remained on the ground, placed her face in her hands and silently wept.

He came over to her, lifted her up and placed her on the chaise. Her father then came and sat with her. He held her in his arms as her body shook as she wept.

Ramsay entered the room and bowed before Chalanor. "What is it that I can do for you, sir?" He asked.

"Please have Elspeth brought to us. And have tea and a light luncheon brought to us here."

"Yes sir. If I might also intrude, I need also inform you sir, the maid from the Dower House is awaiting to see you. She says that it is urgent."

Chalanor was concerned because he believed he already knew what the maid would say after overhearing Freddie ranting.

"Have her brought in." Ramsay turned and left. "I fear that Freddie has killed my mother." He was looking at Sir Peter. The shock on his face was exactly what he expected and what he knew he would see on many faces as he revealed what had happened. "I think that is what he said just before I jumped on him."

Louisa's head shot up. "Yes, he said that, I am sorry. I should have said something earlier. Yes, he said that. He did. I am so sorry."

Louisa was upset and that is not what he wanted her to be. She had already been through so much. She had shown so much courage only now allowing all that had happened to sink in.

They looked at each other and Louisa was weeping. "I should have said something but it all happened quickly. Please forgive me. He never said why he killed her. I know your mother has been unpleasant but she did not deserve to die at his hands nor anyone else's."

Her father stood and began to pace the floor. Chalanor sat next to her and placed his arm around her drawing her into his embrace. He thanked God that he had found a woman who was concerned for others even those who treated her badly. He held her close. This was a woman of immense courage and he was glad she was safe.

The maid entered a moment later and it was obvious she had been crying and was upset. Quietly, she explained how on his earlier instructions she went and knocked on her mistress's door to fetch her to the mansion. When she had received no response, she had entered the room and found her ladyship dead and tied to the bed.

"I took the sheet, your lordship, and covered her. I touched nothing else but locked the bedroom door and came back here to wait to see you." She handed Chalanor the key.

"I am sorry Betsy that you had to find your mistress in that way. Go to the kitchen and have a cup of tea. Then please get your belongings from the Dower House and return to the manor. Tell cook to do the same. We need to take care of you both."

She curtsied and left the room.

Louisa had stopped crying and took Chalanor's hands, she said. "My dearest. I am so sorry. She did not deserve to be treated like that."

"Perhaps, but my mother played with fire. This time she went that little bit too far and was burnt. I am sorry for what she has missed out on in the past and what she will miss out on in the future." He took Louisa into his arms again and the two silently wept. Chalanor had not cried in many a year but the shock of what could have happened to Louisa and what had easily happened to his mother had taken its toll on him also. He had lost his mother long ago and now he lost her again. He nearly lost his future bride and his father but deep down rejoiced that he had not. The two emotions clashed against his heart. Tragedy and ecstasy.

They were still locked in their embrace as Elspeth was carried into the room. Chalanor did not really want to tell her what her brother had done. But he had no choice. They revealed to her the things that Freddie had said, and what he had planned, and had murdered Alice and Lady Farraday. She was shocked but at the moment in control of her emotions. Tears slowly swam from her eyes. She looked utterly devastated at the news they had revealed.

"I do not doubt you but I am shocked. I never thought my brother capable of such horrendous actions. And where is Freddie now? How do you plan to deal with him? I love my brother but this cannot go unchecked. He must face his actions."

"Elspeth, I am so sorry," Louisa began.

"He is dead?" Elspeth asked, already knowing the answer.

"I jumped from the tree on top of him to protect Louisa. I was unaware that he had a knife in his hand. He tried to threaten me but I kicked it from his hand. He went after it and then stabbed himself when he realised he was surrounded by many men. Can you forgive me?"

"My brother has killed an innocent girl and was about to kill my dearest friend and may have killed you as well. Can you forgive my brother and me?' Tears were now flowing freely down her face.

"Elspeth, I do not need to forgive you. You have done nothing wrong, in fact it is clear you knew nothing of your brother's actions. Freddie, I do believe, was unstable in his mind, and he made some terrible decisions. Unfortunately, he has paid the ultimate price for his folly." He gave her a moment to absorb that information.

"I'm sorry my dear friend but there is more you need to know and it is not good." Louisa added. "He admitted that your estate is penniless." Louisa went on to explain what Freddie had told her.

Elspeth explained she had no idea that the estate was in such bad condition. She cried for her brother. A brother lost to insanity and depravity. She cried for a lost estate, a family legacy gone forever. Louisa and Chalanor sat quietly as she cried. After a moment Louisa went and hugged her friend and silently cried with her.

The two gentlemen gave them time to absorb all the information. Luncheon arrived and Chalanor dismissed the servants. He and Sir Peter poured a cup of tea each for the two distressed ladies.

After a time, Elspeth pulled herself together and looked at Chalanor. "Can I suggest that you talk to his valet, he may know more? I have seen them talking at great length, at unusual times of the day, today. In fact, their relationship has been questionable in my mind for some time. But I never talked about it with Freddie. I now wish I had. It would seem there was more going on than I had imagined." She paused and he could see the look of concern on her face and the faces around her. "If you do not mind, can I return to my room please? And can we keep quiet the information about the estate for the time being? I will need to find out just how bad it is."

"Of course my friend, do not fret. No one will hear it from us. My lawyer can help you gauge the true state of affairs of your estate. If it will help, I will have him available for you. Perhaps you could talk with him tomorrow?"

"Thank you Chal. Yes, that would be suitable. Perhaps tomorrow." She repeated.

"Of course Elspeth." Chalanor went to her side and hugged his friend. It disturbed him that she was placed in such a terrible situation. He went and rang the bell. The footman came and she was carried back to her room. Chalanor arranged for whatever she needed to be supplied to her immediately. Sir Peter went with her to ensure that she was settled and that her maid remained with her so that her needs could be provided for. There was no need to have the footman on guard any more but Chalanor wanted her to be with someone. Louisa promised to see her after they had both rested.

$\mathcal{T}$he remainder of the afternoon they sat in relative silence as they awaited news of Lord Farraday. To lose one parent was bad enough but to lose both on the same day was something Chalanor did not want to think about. He understood the damage the loss of Freddie's parents had done to him. Chalanor had ink, pen and paper sent in and occasionally he would go to the mantle and write something down on the paper he placed there.

At last the doctor came down and sat with them.

"Your father has lost a lot of blood but your actions," he looked at Chalanor, "tying on your cravat around his arm, above the wound, probably saved his life. The arrow has been removed and I had to perform some minor surgery. He will be weak for some time but I believe he will survive." Chalanor heard Louisa breathe a sigh of relief. "I must emphasize I cannot guarantee it. If he gets an infection from the wound, I cannot promise his survival." He looked at them as that information sank in. "One more thing, I will not be sure how much use of his arm he will have. It is difficult to say exactly how much damage was done. We will need to wait and see."

Chalanor stood, "Thank you doctor for all you have done. It is greatly appreciated." He bowed to him. The doctor stood and Chalanor walked him to the door, whispering to him, handing him something before he left.

Louisa asked him, "Is there something I can do for you? Would you like me to ring for more tea?"

"No my love, I was just making arrangements with the doctor to confirm how mother died. He is going over there now. He will return tomorrow to let me know. Let us know." Chalanor corrected. He had no intention of keeping anything from her. He noted her gentle manner earlier, when trying to find out what was going on. So very different from his mother.

Louisa stood and walked to him and wrapped her arms around him. "I hope you understand that I am very pleased you came to rescue me." She looked into his eyes.

Such pain and torment she had just faced but there she was standing straight and tall by his side. "I heard you speak with him. Had I not come you may have found your own escape."

"Perhaps but you came and helped save me. Thank you."

"You are most definitely welcome. Now my love, I would like to suggest you take a bath and rest for the remainder of the afternoon. Would you do that for me, please?" Chalanor held her closely hoping she would see and feel his concern for her. Not that he wished to get rid of her. He most certainly did not.

"I will bathe and change but I would prefer that we talk about the events of the day together. I do not wish to be alone at the moment. You are sad and I understand that but I am frightened that these events will alter your feelings for me. I can understand that they might. I wish to assure you of my love."

Chalanor kissed the top of her head. "That will never happen. Go and bathe. Then my love, return to me in the library. We will then address the crowd and we can spend the time together before dinner."

He leaned down and gently kissed her lips. The taste was tantalizing. He wanted this woman and nothing was ever going to change his feelings. After all they had been through today, his love for her was even deeper and stronger than it was before.

*S*he looked at her body in the mirror. She had some minor scratches and bruises but on the whole her body was intact. Her mind however was another matter. She saw Freddie's face as he stabbed himself and died. It played over and over in her mind. She slowly slipped into the bath water and let the water's warmth wrapped around her. All she could only think of was his dead body. How would she ever forget this day? In fact, would she ever be able to forget? Freddie was a friend and his death and the events that lead to it were more tragic than anything she could have imagined.

Thank God Chalanor found her.

What would have happened if he had not come? What Freddie had done to Chalanor's mother and to Alice only heightened her anxiety. She got out of the bath and towelled herself dry being careful not to rub the areas of her skin that were bruised and battered. She knew that Chalanor loved her and she hoped those feelings would remain. She wanted to think about a future and how much she wished to spend the rest of her life within his arms. She hoped and prayed what he had said about his unchanging feelings for her was true. She wanted more than anything they would spend the rest of their lives together.

After dressing, she went down to the library. He was there waiting for her. Tall, strong. He too had bathed and changed. In his dark blue jacket and neatly folded cravat he was high born distinction and grace. She came over and stood beside him just happy to be near him. He took her by the hand.

"I need to address the crowd and I want you to stand with me, if you feel strong enough? I know you have been through so much. You are my future wife after all, if you will still have me?"

She placed her arms around him and hugged him close. He

returned the embrace. "Of course I will. I love you and wish to be by your side. To do all I can to help you."

"I love you beyond measure, my Louisa. The sooner we are wed the happier I will be." He took her by the hand and went to the door that led to the garden, where a gathered crowd waited to be addressed.

---

*T*ogether they told the gathered guests, villagers and estate workers of the death of Lady Farraday, and also about the abduction. Not in great detail but enough to keep them from adding details that did not exist. They also made sure they mentioned the villain had died and no one had anything to worry about. The threat that had existed was gone. The gathered crowd seemed content with that. Some said their goodbyes to them both and others just quietly drifted away.

Louisa and Chalanor went to the library to be alone. They sat together in the quiet and Chalanor wanted nothing else but this. He did not want to wait for Louisa to become his wife. He had no intention of facing a future that did not include her.

"I want us to marry as soon as we can."

"I understand that Chal. It is what I want with all my heart." She took hold of his hand. "But we have to wait. Your father will need time to recover. He will want to see his only son wed. Just as my father will want to see me, his only daughter, marry the man I love."

"I know but I want to insist that we sleep together from here on. I want you by my side permanently and every minute of the day. I cannot bear the thought of you being alone ever again."

Before she could answer, Ramsay came in through the door and announced Sir Peter. He came over to the seats near the fireplace and sat down.

"I did not want to disturb you. I just finished telling everyone you needed to be alone. But I felt the need to see you are both in reasonable spirits. I would say from the looks on your faces that some words of wisdom may be needed. Can I offer any of those words or would you prefer that I leave?"

"Papa, we are trying to determine when to marry. So much has happened and we have so many bad memories to deal with. Let alone awaiting the healing of Lord Farraday."

"I know you will think it shocking sir, for me to suggest this," he looked at Sir Peter, "but I do not want Louisa anywhere else but with me, regardless of the marriage. I wish her to be by my side both day and night." He looked hard at his friend. Then he softened his gaze as he had to remember that he was Louisa's father.

Sir Peter gave him a knowing look. "Ah. I have been in love before. I do understand, I have been thinking along similar lines and I think I have a solution. Can I suggest, that as you already have a special license, you marry immediately? Then when things settle down and we know that Lord Farraday is well, we'll do the full ceremony in the parish church as planned. I'm sure your father will understand."

Louisa looked at Chalanor. "Can it be done?" asked Louisa.

"I'm unsure." Chalanor went to the bell pull and called for Ramsay. "I'll have Hutton called for and we can ask him." Ramsay came and Hutton was sent for.

"While we wait, I want to tell you both how delighted I am that you will soon be together. I have been certain for some time Chalanor that it was more love than concern for Louisa's wellbeing that you wished to involve her in this house party."

"Sir, you have me at a disadvantage, because I myself was unaware of those feelings." He looked at Louisa "I really did not know until you were here, then I began to suspect I was in love with you. I am glad however that it was my heart ruling my head."

Louisa laughed. "I had no idea and my shutters were firmly in place so I doubt I would have noticed anything." She laughed. "Love is not why I came but I am glad that I found it where I least expected it."

"For me I could not be more delighted. You have both faced some terrible events over the past years and of course most recently but your love for each other will bring you through I believe." Sir Peter placed a hand on each of their shoulders. He looked into his daughter's eyes, "Your mother would be delighted beyond words. Be happy, the both of you. Love is the most important thing that you share. It will get you through all life's good and bad times."

Louisa hugged her father. "Thank you, Papa. I know you and mother loved each other deeply. I love you both. And I miss mother too. Thank you..." They were interrupted as Reverend Hutton arrived.

Chalanor wasted no time but immediately told Hutton what was pressing on his mind. "We wish to marry immediately but also would like to have a delayed church service, for when father has recovered. Can this be done?"

"You will need a special license." Hutton responded.

"We have that." Chalanor added.

"Am I correct that at a later date you would like to do the ceremony in front of guests and your father when he has recovered?"

"That is it exactly." Louisa contributed.

"Under the circumstances I cannot see why we cannot go ahead. I would be delighted to perform both ceremonies for you. May I add that I have watched your love bloom and can see that you need and want each other?" Ennis moved over to stand in front of Louisa. He put his hands on her shoulders. "My dearest friend I do want you to be happy." He then looked at Chalanor. "You were meant to be together. Your engagement was announced before all this happened and you have the special license. Yes, I think we can arrange this."

"Then my dear," Chalanor took Louisa into his arms "it takes but one question to be answered. Will you marry me as soon as possible?"

"Let's." she replied.

---

*A*t dinner Louisa and Chalanor entered the room together. Chalanor had a hold of her hand and had no intention of letting it go. "It would appear that everyone is here. Please sit down where you would like. I do not wish to have any formality this evening. We all need to relax somewhat." Chalanor noted that all eyes were fixed on him, awaiting all the news he promised to share with them.

"Firstly, I would like to say that Elspeth will not be joining us this evening. As what I will reveal to you has been a terrible shock for her. She has asked that she be excused."

The first course was being served as Chalanor revealed what he now knew of Freddie's unusual life. He attempted to answer any questions or divert them if he could. He did not reveal the state of the Ismay estate of Broadbank, preferring to concentrate mainly on the events they were already aware of. Such as the horse accident, the urn falling, the murder of Alice. Finally, he confirmed to them the death of Lady Farraday, by Freddie's hand. He also told them that Freddie's valet had disappeared and it appeared he may have been aware of Lord Ismay's actions. His belongings were gone so it was assumed he had run off.

They discussed the plans for the burial of his mother at the Parish church in Loose, for tomorrow afternoon. He also confirmed that Lord Farraday was unaware, at the moment, of her death. He was also to have no visitors until he had been told. As soon as his father was well enough he personally would reveal the news to him. He went on to discuss the condition of his father and the importance of the next few days for him.

"The doctor has given him a draught allowing him to sleep solidly. This will enable my father to recover more quickly we hope and speed his healing. Infection is the only concern at the moment. I will let you know when he will be allowed to have visitors. But for the time being Louisa and myself will be his only visitors."

The conversations were relaxed and Chalanor did his best to answer all their questions. But he was tired and drained and wished to go to bed. He especially wished to lie in the arms of his love. So that left one final act for the evening. Chalanor looked over to Sir Peter and nodded.

Sir Peter stood and addressed the guests. "We have heard of all that has occurred and as you can imagine the day has been a hard one for Louisa and Chalanor. But they wish to end the day with a memory that they will long remember. So, with the help of a special license and Reverend Hutton I ask that you step into the ball room to witness the marriage of Miss Louisa Stapleton to Chalanor Farraday, Viscount of Lightfoot."

<hr />

"*Y*ou looked radiant tonight. That golden evening gown really gave you the air of an angel. It was perfect as your wedding gown." Chalanor held her just a little bit tighter.

"My husband has a tendency to exaggerate I think." Louisa laughed out loud.

"My husband. Mm, I like the way you say that." He was grinning like a cat that had stolen the cream from the kitchen.

"Besides, I was too tired to be radiant." Louisa corrected.

"Never. You will always be my radiant bride. Are you too tired to make love with me?"

"Never," she chuckled. "Today more than ever I want to show

you how much I both love and want you. You came and saved me. No other man would have done that for me."

"On the contrary your father would have. As would have my father and a number of other gentlemen were not far behind me if you remember. I just got there quicker, that was all." It was his turn to laugh a little. "I will always love you. Now let me show you."

---

*L*ouisa had dreamed of this moment. The fire was lit but that was the only light in the room. Being summer it was not too cold in the evenings but it made the room feel cosy. Holding her hand, he brought her to the chaise he had obviously placed before the fire ready for their love making. Louisa saw the curtains were closed and the bed was turned down on both sides. He helped her out of her dressing gown. She sat on the seat and Chalanor sat next to her.

"Is there anything else you would like to say? Trust me once I lay my hands on you, my mind will be focused only on your beautiful body and the pleasure I mean to give you."

He was waiting patiently to hear what she may want to say.

"It is because I love you and the love you have for me. You told me you loved me for who I am, Louisa."

She raised her fingers to touch his lips as she was sure he was about to say something. "Say nothing. I want you and I want you to make love to me."

"I love you. You know that I will be the luckiest man in the world if you want me. You see, I love only you. In my heart I believe you have saved me. Not the other way around."

"Then no more discussion."

Chalanor leaned in and without touching her with his hands, he kissed her. Finally, he drew her into his arms and began to caress her, exploring her back and her bottom.

"I want to undress you," she added, "so that I know exactly what you look like as I take each piece of clothing off." He stood. She stood and began to take some of his clothing off.

She had succeeded in taking off his coat, while placing kisses all over his face and head. Slowly she removed his cravat. It did not take her long to get that off. Finally, his shirt was on the floor but not until she had tasted his neck and chest.

---

*H*e had tried to deal with her ministrations by slowing his breathing and resisting the urge to throw her over his shoulder and carry her off to his bed. His resistance was flagging. Again, he slowed his breathing. Unfortunately, it did nothing to quench his desire. He could wait no longer. "Come to my bed, my Louisa."

"But I have not finished."

"That is true dearest but I will be finished completely if I cannot get my hands on you. Let me make you weak at the knees, and then you will know what I mean."

She chuckled as he took her hand and guided her to his bed. He sat her on the edge as he took off his boots. She could see his impatience so waited till he was ready. Then he took her into his arms and lifted her from her feet and laid her on his bed. Then he slowly began to open the buttons on the lace bodice that finally allowed him to feast on the glory of her breasts. He touched her left nipple with his fingers rubbing it ever so lightly. Then she drew in her breath as his mouth descended on to her right nipple. He caressed and kissed them both, loving the feel of her. She was exploring his back with her hands. It seemed then she could no longer wait and began to undo the buttons holding his trousers in place.

He jumped off the bed and removed his trousers. He stood there but a moment as she absorbed the view of his erection.

"Can you stand there for a moment so I can look? The only man I have seen naked, I never want to see again. I would like to have the view of your body etched in my memory instead."

He knew she spoke of Prescott and that terrible night. He wanted to give her what she wanted, a night she could hold in her memory, replacing all those bad feelings she had once held and all the bad feeling she had faced today. He stood there and said, "I will give you my body now and always. I am yours." And he meant every word.

The smile that filled her face was aglow with light. "I give you my body to have and hold. Love me and love no other."

"I adore you and do not want anyone but you." He returned to the bed and lay next to his bride. "I love you." He took her into his arms and kissed her. Moving his hand to the moist area between her legs he began to fondle and caress her. He let his finger find the opening and gently placed his finger inside.

She moaned with pure pleasure as she felt his finger slide inside. He could feel her barrier and he gently pushed against it. "They say that your first time is painful. I do not want that for you. I want to make it the most beautiful experience of your life." He lowered his head and again caressed her nipple with his mouth. He then kissed her lower on her tummy. Finally, he descended to the junction between her legs. His mouth and tongue danced among the private and special places of her body and she revelled in it.

His control was great but he gently softened and stretched the area where he soon would enter. He kissed it many times and tasted her inner being. He had made love to other women but never like this. He was consumed in giving all pleasure to her. He knew that when he finally filled her it would be the most joyous experience of his life, and that they would reach the heights of pleasure together.

She moaned and stretched beneath his body and finally she took his member in her hands and all his thoughts fled. He felt her only, her against his skin. Then she directed his swollen pleasure to her opening and ever so slowly and gently he pushed in. They both felt her barrier give way but he stopped and allowed the area to fathom the volume of his erection within it. Then slowly he rocked back and forth, deeper and deeper. Her desires and moans increased as did his movements. Her legs wrapped around him and she moaned louder. This was heaven and she was his angel. Both of them moaned at the glory. Higher and higher their pleasure raised. On the final push she shattered beneath him her muscles grabbing and pulsating as he spilt his seed into her body. He lowered himself slowly and kissed her mouth and whispered, "I love you."

34

The happy couple slept late and had their breakfast served in their room. The morning saw the first rain arrive for the whole time of the house party. It seemed appropriate as his mother was quietly laid to rest in the afternoon. The rain persisted all day. Chalanor was sad that she had made bad decisions that ended her life sooner than it should have. He would mourn her as his mother and all that she would now miss out on. The pleasure he hoped she would have had if he had presented her with a grandchild. But that fact wouldn't have made her excited. He knew it would only have made her feel old. She would have hated Louisa and made her life unbearable. Yes, he would grieve his mother but that was all. Any dreams needed to be put away. What if's were of no use to any of them.

The doctor reported to Chalanor that morning that Lady Farraday had definitely been murdered. He confirmed that the likely culprit was Ismay as a kerchief found in her mouth had the initial FI embroidered on them. It fitted with what details Freddie had surrendered to Louisa before he killed himself. It helped him to understand what had driven his mother and also the madness that had taken hold of Freddie. Though it didn't make it any easier. He also found the locks of hair of what appeared to be five different ladies inside a pocket of Freddie's jacket. This shocked Chalanor and Louisa both. They were able to recognize what they thought was his mother's hair. Also, one for Alice's hair. The other three were a mystery. The madness that had claimed Freddie may have damaged other ladies.

Only a few of the guests attended the funeral and some of the servants. A brief notice was placed in the London papers stating only that she died suddenly at Maidstone Manor Estate. Chalanor had requested of the guests not to allow his mother's reputation to be sullied any more than it already had but to let her rest in peace. They had all agreed that enough had been said and done and to allow all further details to rest with her in her grave. He knew most of London would know that she had been murdered but would speak only of it in private. Lady Myra Farraday would soon pass from the ton's memory. He felt that was the best he could do for her.

He stood in the rain with Louisa, as his mother was lowered into the grave. Hutton conducted a brief and respectful service, most of which Chalanor ignored. He was only thinking of the love that he held for the woman who stood by his side and for his father who was still ill in his bed at the manor. Being married was what he wanted but the sadness hanging over everyone was not. He looked forward to many years of joy with his Louisa and prayed and wished for it to come sooner than later.

Hutton escorted them to the carriage that would take them back to the manor. He took Louisa's hand in his and kissed her fingers. "I hope that you both will seek some rest. I know the cost to your emotions the past few days have taken on you. If I am needed send for me." The unspoken meaning that Lord Farraday might not yet make it through his illness was heavy in the air.

"We appreciate all that you have done, Ennis. Thank you so

much for marrying us yesterday. I would not have wanted anyone else to do the honours." Louisa reached up and kissed him on the cheek. Chalanor watched as the colour rose to his face.

"I wish you both joy and a long and happy life together." He bowed and left them to their thoughts.

Chalanor helped Louisa into the covered carriage and out of the rain. They had a few more moment of quiet together. Sir Peter had stayed with Lord Farraday so that he was not alone. Chalanor took Louisa into his arms. "Thank you for being with me."

"There is no need to thank me, Chalanor. Even if we had not been married, I would have been with you as your friend."

It seemed to Chalanor that would be very true. Only Lord and Lady Midhurst had come to the funeral along with Bartley and Hutton. Bartley had briefly told him that he had no idea of what his friend Freddie had been doing. He had no idea of the affair with Lady Farraday or little else. It was easy to believe. Freddie had deceived even him and they had known each other for so many years. The carriage gently rocked as it made its way down the long drive to the manor.

"When do you wish to go to our own home?" Chalanor asked. He longed to take her to the tower. He wanted so much for her to enjoy her new history instead of being a bystander to it.

"Our home. Seems strange to even think of Stone Maiden Tower as our home and not just your estate." She looked into his tired and unsmiling face. He was tired and there was little to smile about at this moment in time. But he wanted to reassure her. He smiled.

"I do hope you know that it is our home. And I mean our home." He returned the gaze, looking into the deep chocolate of her eyes.

"Of course. It just feels strange. But for the time being, you are needed here at Maidstone to help your father and also to help Elspeth with all that she needs assistance with. Let us wait till the second wedding. Then when all is right, we can start our new life together afresh and in a place we both love. Our future awaits us there."

Of course, she was right and Chalanor hugged her closer. How often he had marvelled at her wisdom. The truth was that they were treading water as they waited for the turbulent waters around them to subside. Louisa, though a young lady, had given great advice and wisdom and he was so proud that he could call her his wife.

---

*T*hree days later his father was deemed to be out of danger. But now that he was well enough Chalanor began to tell him of the events since he had been shot by the arrow. He was downtrodden to hear about the fate of his wife.

"Perhaps I should not have banished her?" His voice was full of regret.

But the last thing Chalanor wanted was his father's newly found strength and assurance to disappear. "Father, you cannot blame yourself. She had made those decisions leading you to make yours. I am in fact proud that you stood up to her and still allowed her so much. You could have divorced her. No, this is a terrible act but she played with fire. It is unfortunate but not your fault."

The room was dimly lit but Chalanor could still see the tears rolling down his father's cheek. Though love had gone, for his father at least, it had run very deep. Not for the last time Chalanor regretted the death of his mother and how it had affected all of them. But he was being realistic too. As Louisa had stated there was nothing anyone could have done, as no one knew who the villain had been.

"I know that the events have placed a great deal of pressure on you both but I assume you still have every intention of marrying Louisa?"

"I do hope you understand, Father, that I had no intention of letting Louisa out of my sight. I know that the danger had passed but the thoughts of nearly losing her pushed me to my limits. So, Sir Peter came up with the idea of using the special license that we already had and marrying immediately." His father seemed disappointed. "But we spoke to Hutton who agreed that we could marry and then have a special ceremony, after you are well enough, in front of the church and all our family and friends."

"Just so long as you are together. I am glad and relieved. In fact, I am delighted. I must talk to Sir Peter. The delayed ceremony is a stroke of genius."

He seemed to be tiring. "Father, let me leave you to have a rest."

"Not yet. I want you to know that I understand why you wanted to marry Louisa so quickly and I do approve your choice." He sighed deeply but continued. "I am sure that I will be well enough in a few weeks. Please talk with the doctor and determine when and set the date."

Chalanor was glad that his father understood his need to have Louisa at his side from then on. After he spoke with the doctor and he agreed his father was out of danger, they worked out a time line for full recovery at three weeks. So that was when the ceremony was planned. In three weeks they could marry again, in front of his father, Elspeth and all their friends.

EPILOGUE

The morning of the wedding saw the sun shining and the last of the summer roses blooming to perfection. Elspeth was able to stand and attend Louisa on her special day. Though she still limped a little no one would notice unless they knew she had broken her leg. They had shared many tears together over the previous weeks but now it was a day of joy. Both ladies had dresses of ivory lace that looked superb on them. Louisa wore her hair down under the veil, which was unusual for the fashion. But she wanted it that way because Chalanor loved to see her hair down. She looked like a medieval maiden with her blonde mantle under the fine lace, for all to see. Elspeth had hers curled and beautifully pinned, interlaced with small forget-me-nots on the crown of her head.

The ladies had spent the morning enjoying each other's company and remembering the wonderful things they had shared together over the years. Louisa wore her mother's pearls around her neck. For her it was important that her mother was also with her today. Chalanor had given her a matching bracelet and her wedding ring would have three small pearls set in gold. The pearls will always be a reminder of her mother's love and the new and glorious love that she now shared with Chalanor.

Chalanor arrived at the parish church in Loose, in a carriage before Louisa. He had waved to all the villagers who had come to see him marry. His father was with him. He was excited at the prospect of seeing his son renew the marriage that had taken place just three short weeks ago. The church was packed with many friends and relations. He longed for his sister to be there.

Father had traced her to Scotland and a distant relative. His mother's lies again revealed. His sister had promised to come down to Kent soon. And he hoped she would. For now, he and his father made their way up the isle to await Louisa's arrival. Other than his sister coming home, nothing could make him happier.

---

*L*ouisa got into her carriage. She could see the carriage of Chalanor and Lord Farraday heading down the drive. She had watched from the top of the stairs waiting for them to leave through the front door. She wanted to be as close behind Chalanor as she could. This was a happy day even though it was for the benefit of others. The fact that she was already married added to the excitement that was before them. In their bed the previous night they had shared their excitement of returning to Stone Maiden after the celebrations this evening. She thought about how her father had gone back to Chertsey and her old home to have her belongings packed and brought to Stone Maiden Tower. That was her new home and she relished its coming. Soon what little she kept from her old life would be gracing the rooms of her new one.

She made her way into the carriage that awaited her, ready to leave for the church and all that was to come. Elspeth tucked the train of Louisa's veil into her lap, and then went to the other side of the carriage where Sir Peter helped Elspeth into her seat and then entered the carriage himself. Elspeth rode in the seat opposite the bride and her father.

As the carriage made its way to Loose, Elspeth took the quiet moment to speak with her friend

"You know that I am truly delighted you and Chalanor have found each other." She took Louisa's hand and gave it a little squeeze. "Tomorrow I will return to Broadbank. Then when all has been settled on the estate I will be going to my mother's brother on the Isle of Skye."

"So far?" Louisa intervened.

"I need to be away from society. What my brother has done is insupportable and you know what that feels like." She looked at her friend and smiled. "I have been tarnished by his brush. Time away will do me good. My uncle would like me to be the Chatelaine for his small estate on the Isle. It is a modest estate compared to the grandeur of Maidstone, Stone Maiden or even Broadbank. But it will be home for me. I feel that under the circumstances it is the best I can do or even expect. My uncle has been extremely kind and I do greatly appreciate that he has not deserted me. Many other family members have." Louisa could see the pain of rejection and lost love etched on her face.

"I am sorry that you should suffer in this way. I wish you would accept the money we offered you." Louisa was distressed that her friend found herself in this position.

"No money my friend, but I thank you for the offer. Louisa, look at what you have suffered over the years and now your dreams of returning to society and finding the love you never thought you would have, are yours. Perhaps one day my dreams will also come true." A small tear trickled down Louisa's cheek. "No, my friend, no tears, this is a joyously happy day. A day we share together." She held her friend's hand and gave it a little squeeze.

"I am also so proud of you. Using your own money to create a school for children of the estate. Alice's School. It is a great tribute to her and to you." Heat rose in Louisa's face. But she was grateful for her friend's comments.

"Promise me that we will write." Louisa pleaded. She took a kerchief from her reticule and dabbed her eyes.

"Of course, we will and perhaps one day you both will come to visit me?"

Louisa nodded. "Yes, we will. Chalanor has already suggested that we would visit you wherever you went to live. Nothing would give me more pleasure."

Sir Peter took his daughter's hand, and with his other hand picked up Elspeth's. "We wish you love and happiness, my dear. You have been the best of friends. Enjoy your new adventure. I am sure you will flourish."

The carriage drove on and finally came to a stop at the church. Many of the villagers and the servants of the manor had packed the church inside and out awaiting her arrival. They had grown to admire her in the short time she had been in the manor. Their smiles and well wishes as she got out of the carriage gave her great joy. With her father on the right and Elspeth on her left they made their way to the doors of the church.

Her father kissed her on the cheek and said. "I want you to be as happy as your mother and I were. For then you will be truly happy indeed."

"Thank you, Papa, my dearest Papa. I am." She smiled, thinking about the rose that Chalanor brought her every morning. Just as he promised.

The organ began to play and Louisa was led up the isle by the father she loved, to the man she adored and who loved her for who she was. As she got to the front of the church she looked into his blue eyes.

I am Louisa and he is mine.

ABOUT THE AUTHOR

Joanne loves to write and she loves to travel. She is married to Andrew and lives in Central New South Wales Australia with him and their two cats Arthur and Oscar. (Meet them on Joanne's webpage) She has two grown sons and four beautiful granddaughters. Her imagination loves to take her on various trips but mainly in the area of the regency romance.

She also loves meeting new people so do drop a line to her on:

www.JoanneAustenBrown.com

ACKNOWLEDGMENTS

Many thanks to my editor, Nas, who has assisted me in fine tuning my story.

To my critique group who have been there every month to offer advice and ideas. Thank you, Rosemary, Winsome, Sue and Kerry.

To my RWA Australian mates who have educated, encouraged and supported my journey to publication.

To the many English local historical groups who have answered my questioning emails.

To Draft2Digital and Self-Publishing Lab for helping me achieve my goal.

I thank you.

COMING SOON

Always Elspeth ~ Always Series Book Two

We find out how Elspeth has survived her trials. And can love find her, even on the Isle of Skye?

New Series ~ Come with Me

Book One – Rachael's Jaunt

Lightning Source UK Ltd.
Milton Keynes UK
UKHW041240090223
416605UK00008B/265